SCRUB-A-DUB DEAD

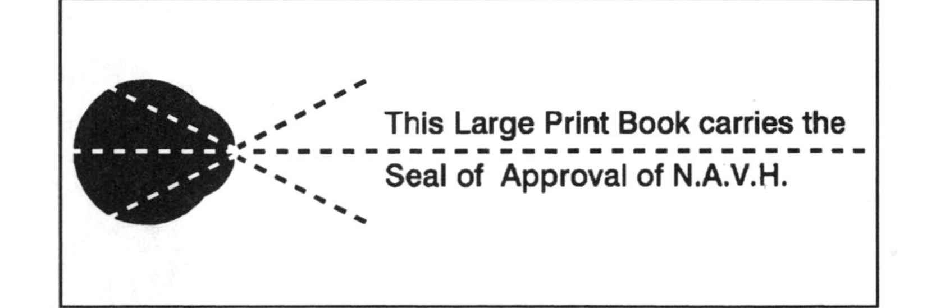
This Large Print Book carries the
Seal of Approval of N.A.V.H.

A CHARLOTTE LARUE MYSTERY

SCRUB-A-DUB DEAD

BARBARA COLLEY

WHEELER PUBLISHING
An imprint of Thomson Gale, a part of The Thomson Corporation

Detroit • New York • San Francisco • New Haven, Conn. • Waterville, Maine • London

Wheeler Publishing Large Print Cozy Mystery.
The text of this Large Print edition is unabridged.
Other aspects of the book may vary from the original edition.
Set in 16 pt. Plantin.

LIBRARY OF CONGRESS CATALOGING-IN-PUBLICATION DATA

Colley, Barbara.
Scrub-a-dub dead : a Charlotte LaRue mystery / by Barbara Colley.
p. cm. — (Wheeler Publishing large print cozy mystery)
ISBN-13: 978-1-59722-475-8 (softcover : alk. paper)
ISBN-10: 1-59722-475-8 (softcover : alk. paper)
1. LaRue, Charlotte (Fictitious character) — Fiction. 2. Women cleaning personnel — Fiction. 3. New Orleans (La.) — Fiction. 4. Large type books.
I. Title.
PS3603.O44S37 2007
813'.6—dc22 2006100409

Published in 2007 by arrangement with Kensington Books, an imprint of Kensington Publishing Corp.

Printed in the United States of America on permanent paper
10 9 8 7 6 5 4 3 2 1

To New Orleans, a city that refuses to
die in spite of a catastrophic hurricane.

ACKNOWLEDGMENTS

I would like to express my sincere appreciation to all who so generously gave me advice and information while I was writing this book: Molly Bolden, bookseller extraordinaire of Bent Pages in Houma, Louisiana; Nicholas A. Genovese, Jr.; authors Rexanne Becnel, Jessica Ferguson, Marie Goodwin, and Karen Young.

I also want to thank Evan Marshall and John Scognamiglio. Their support and advice is invaluable.

Any mistakes made or liberties taken in the name of fiction are solely my own.

Chapter 1

The water was rising. It was in her house, already waist high and still inching higher.

Trapped.

She was trapped like a rat on a sinking ship. She should have left like the others. Shoulda, woulda, coulda. Too late now. She'd waited too long.

Get higher.

The attic. Get up in the attic. Surely the water won't get as high as the attic . . .

With a gasp, Charlotte LaRue sat straight up in bed, her heart pounding like a jackhammer. In spite of the air-conditioner running on high to counter the outside heat and humidity, her pajama top was damp with sweat.

A nightmare. Calm down, it was just a nightmare. You're safe. You're high and dry.

Charlotte sighed and glanced at the bedside clock. Six a.m. Almost time to get up anyway. With a shake of her head, she reached over and shut off the alarm that she'd set for six-thirty, then climbed out of bed and headed for the bathroom.

It had been a while since she'd had the nightmare, but with the one-year anniversary of Hurricanes Katrina and Rita fast approaching, everyone in New Orleans was on edge wondering what the odds were that yet another catastrophic storm could hit.

Strange. The whole nightmare thing was strange, especially since she hadn't even been in the city when the levees broke. Unlike so many others who had chosen to stay or couldn't get out during Katrina, she and most of her family had left well in advance. She shuddered. How horrible it must have been for those who had no transportation, who had no way of leaving.

But the fact remained that she had left. So why would *she* be having the nightmare at all?

Second-hand trauma, they called it. "And TV," she muttered as she squeezed toothpaste onto her toothbrush. She had sat glued to the television almost 24/7 and watched the horrors of the aftermath of the storm . . . the levees breaking . . . the water rising . . . people wading through armpit-high water . . . people trapped on their roofs for days without food or water . . . the daring helicopter rescues . . .

With a shudder, Charlotte recapped the toothpaste. No time to dwell on it now. If she didn't get a move on, she was going to be late. And one thing she didn't want was to be late for this particular job.

Charlotte brushed her teeth then rinsed her mouth and toothbrush. Cleaning hotel rooms was not her favorite type of work. Years ago when she'd started Maid-for-a-Day, she'd made the decision that her cleaning service would be strictly domestic. But her old friend Carrie Rogers had called in a favor and asked for Charlotte's help.

Unlike Charlotte, Carrie ran a commercial cleaning service, and Carrie was shorthanded. In spite of Charlotte's own hectic schedule, there was no way she could refuse, especially after Carrie had so generously offered Charlotte and her family the use of her country home during the Katrina evacuation. If not for Carrie's generosity, they would have ended up in a shelter, or worse, camping out and sleeping in their cars.

After turning on the shower, Charlotte took off her pajamas and slipped a shower cap over her hair. Though Carrie's country home had been small, it was a soothing oasis in a world gone crazy. Nestled in the midst of a forest of pine trees and located a mere twenty miles from the small town of Minden in the northwest corner of Louisiana, the old house had served her family well for the three weeks they'd stayed there.

Charlotte sighed, her thoughts returning to the two-week commitment that she'd made to Carrie as she stepped into the warm spray of water and soaped up her washcloth.

The Jazzy Hotel was just one of Carrie's many commercial clients. But like with so many other businesses in the city, many of Carrie's employees had never returned after Katrina, and had, in fact, decided to settle in the towns to which they had evacuated. Out of the three women that Carrie had working at the Jazzy, one could only work half-days, one had to have surgery, and the third one had been caught stealing and had to be fired.

Working at the Jazzy would make for a tight schedule since most of Charlotte's regular clients had returned to their homes in the Garden District. But with Dale's help, she felt sure that she would be able to manage the hotel work for the two weeks Carrie needed her. That the hotel was located nearby on St. Charles Avenue, less than ten minutes from her house, was also a plus.

Thinking about Dale, Charlotte smiled. What a gem he'd turned out to be. He was dependable, efficient, worked hard, and surprisingly, her clients had wholly accepted the idea of a male maid, especially Bitsy Duhe. Just yesterday, the old lady had called her, raving about Dale. According to Bitsy, Dale had made several suggestions on reorganizing the multitude of kitchen gadgets she'd collected over the years, then dug right in and did it for her without her even asking him.

As Charlotte drove beneath the green canopy of oaks down St. Charles, she couldn't help remembering how the avenue had looked during the cleanup after the hurricanes. All of the broken branches covered with dying leaves had been stacked along the avenue on either side like huge walls. Driving through the walls was like driving through a dying forest. Even so, the Garden District, along with the French Quarter, had been fortunate considering the complete devastation of other parts of the city.

Charlotte shuddered. In other neighborhoods, the streets had been littered with appliances, Sheetrock, carpet, roof shingles, and various pieces of furniture, all water-soaked and moldy. Then, there were the neighborhoods where nothing but the foundations were left. It had taken months, and the majority of the mess in the Quarter and Garden District had been cleaned up, but like a sore that just wouldn't heal, the memories still lingered.

Charlotte flicked on the turn signal, slowed the van, and turned into the driveway of the hotel. Though New Orleans would never be the same as it was before Hurricane Katrina, she still couldn't imagine living anywhere else. It was home, a place like no other with a unique culture all its own.

Charlotte parked the van, climbed out, and locked it. As she approached the house, she wondered what it looked like inside now that it had been renovated into a hotel. Even before renovations it had been one of the largest of the old Greek Revival style mansions that fronted St. Charles Avenue. With the add-on of extra rooms to the back of the house, now it was huge.

In spite of its present size, Charlotte still had her doubts about it qualifying as a real hotel. Without the extra rooms added on, in her opinion it would have made a much better bed and breakfast. On the other hand, she supposed that it was just good business sense to opt for more rooms. More rooms equaled more income.

Charlotte had been instructed to report to the front desk when she arrived. Glancing around the wide central hallway that had been turned into the hotel lobby, she was pleasantly surprised by what she saw. The owners had kept the original ambiance of the old home. A long mahogany counter topped with marble was trimmed with the same embellished moldings that edged the high ceiling. A turn-of-the century settee, a pier mirror, a rosewood plantation secretary, and several old portraits, along with a misty-looking Drysdale landscape added to the elegance of the space. She wondered if the owners had carried through the same old-world ambiance in the rooms as well.

"May I help you?"

Charlotte approached the counter and smiled at the young red-haired woman standing behind it. "I'm Charlotte LaRue. Carrie Rogers sent me."

"Oh, hi, Ms. LaRue. I'm Claire Reynolds, the manager. I can't tell you how much we appreciate your being able to help out on such short notice."

After a brief rundown of the hotel operations, Claire led the way to the supply room where she showed Charlotte how to fold the washcloths, hand towels, and towels, and demonstrated how to adorn the extra rolls of toilet paper with the decorative bands that carried the hotel logo. After showing her which products she should leave in the bathrooms, she handed Charlotte a list of her assigned rooms.

When Charlotte entered the first room, an odd twinge of disappointment rippled through her. Except for the high ceilings, there was little to distinguish the renovated room from any other modern hotel room. Even the furniture was contemporary, not at all in keeping with the period of the old house.

"Too bad," she murmured. And just one of the many reasons that she preferred cleaning homes. Individual homes had character and history, whereas hotel rooms were, for the most part, all the same.

Charlotte timed herself on the first two rooms, and after doing a quick mental calculation, she decided that she needed to work faster to be finished by four-thirty. Yet another reason she preferred to clean homes instead, she thought as she entered the third room.

When she'd made the decision that her cleaning service would be domestic, it had been at the urging of a college professor who had known that Charlotte had no choice but to quit school and go to work after her parents' death. As a single mother, Charlotte had been faced with making a living for herself and her infant son. Her college professor had suggested that cleaning homes, especially those in the exclusive Garden District, could net quite a bit of money, and she could almost pick and choose her hours to accommodate her little son's schedule.

By ten-thirty, she had finished cleaning six of the first-floor rooms. On the second floor, she approached room 201. Noting that there was no DO NOT DISTURB sign hanging on the doorknob, she knocked. "Housekeeping," she called out. Waiting a couple of minutes, she knocked again. "Housekeeping."

Since there was no response, she used the master key she'd been given, and opened the door. Inside, the bedroom didn't look all that dirty, so she figured it shouldn't take long to clean.

A smile pulled at her lips when she picked up a polyester red scarf from the floor near the dresser. As she folded it neatly and placed it back on top of the dresser alongside two other identical scarves, she recalled the conversation she'd had the previous day when Carrie had filled her in on the group staying at the hotel.

"Most of them will check in either late Thursday or early Friday," Carrie had told her. "We're ready for the Thursday bunch, so I need you to start on Friday morning. I think the majority of the group are booked for a week, then a different group is due to arrive the following week."

Carrie had gone on to tell her that the first group was from Shreveport and called themselves the Red Scarf Sorority.

Thinking that Carrie had made a mistake, Charlotte had laughed. "Don't you mean the Red Hat Society?" she'd asked.

"Oh, no," Carrie had replied. "That's a completely different group. Though the two organizations have the same basic concept, the Sorority group is a bit younger — mostly in their forties — and considers themselves to be more socially elite than the Society group."

A flicker of gold caught Charlotte's eye and she examined the scarf more closely. Embroidered with a fine gold thread in the corner were the tiny initials TM. "Well, now that's different," she murmured as she checked each of the other two scarves for the gold initials.

Suddenly the door burst open. Charlotte

jumped and whirled to face the intruder.

"What are you doing in my room?" the woman yelled. "Get out! Get out now!"

For a moment Charlotte was stunned speechless. For one thing, she wasn't used to being screamed at by a client, but even more disconcerting, the woman was almost a dead ringer for the comedian Joan Rivers. Couldn't be Joan Rivers though. The voice was all wrong and this woman was probably in her mid-to-late forties. "Ah — ma'am, I was just —"

"I said to get out!"

"I'm the maid," Charlotte said evenly.

"I don't care who you are. I put out the DO NOT DISTURB sign. And that means keep out!"

Charlotte's gaze slid to the doorknob. Clear as day, the DO NOT DISTURB sign was hanging on the inside of the door, not on the outside. Temptation to point out that the sign was on the wrong side of the door was strong, but Charlotte resisted.

The customer is always right, her voice of reason argued.

Even when they're obviously rude or crazy or downright wrong? she argued back. But Charlotte already knew the answer. Biting her tongue, she quickly gathered her cleaning supplies. And though the words almost choked her, through clenched teeth she said, "Sorry, ma'am," as she marched out of the room and firmly closed the door behind her.

To Charlotte's surprise several women had gathered in the hallway by the cleaning supply cart. It was obvious from the distressed expressions on their faces that they had heard the woman's outburst. It was also obvious that the small group were members of the Red Scarf Sorority since each woman wore a bright red scarf tied loosely around her neck.

One of the women stepped forward. Her face was flushed and she was wringing her hands. "Sorry about that." She tilted her head toward the room. "But please don't take offense. Tessa — that's the woman inside — well, she's just upset right now."

Upset? In Charlotte's opinion, *rude* was a more apt description, but she summoned a smile and simply nodded.

"If you'll wait a moment," the woman continued, "I'll persuade her to let you finish cleaning the room."

Before Charlotte could object, the woman walked past her, knocked lightly on the door, then opened it.

"Tessa, it's Mary Lou." Without waiting to be invited inside, Mary Lou motioned for the other women to follow her.

Since the last woman who entered didn't bother closing the door, Charlotte had a full view of the room and its occupants and watched with curiosity as the women formed a tight circle around Tessa.

"Now, honey, we know you're hurting," Mary Lou told Tessa. "But remember our creed. We're here now, and your pain is our pain."

"Your pain is our pain," all of the women chanted softly in unison. "We're here for you," they continued. "And you're here for us, and together, we can face anything."

Each woman took a turn hugging Tessa, and before the last one took her turn, tears welled in Tessa's eyes and she began to sob. Within seconds, all of the women were crying and muttering words of sympathy.

"Just let it out, honey," one of the women encouraged.

"Yeah, let it out," another one chimed in.

"Oh, you guys are-are too-too much," Tessa cried.

Charlotte simply stared at the group. Oh, brother, she thought, what a crock. Lending sympathy was one thing, but the creed chanting part reminded her of the sister witches on the TV show *Charmed* chanting one of their spells.

"It-it's just th-that I saw Lisa," Tessa sobbed, "and-and we had words."

"Now just what did that husband-stealing hussy say to you, darling?" Mary Lou asked. "You just give the word and we'll go pull her hair out by its bleached-blond roots."

Tessa's lower lip quivered and fresh tears filled her eyes. "She-she said th-that Frank has asked her to-to marry him."

"Nooo," the women objected in unison, shaking their collective heads in disgust.

"No way," Mary Lou reiterated. "That's just so totally uncouth. For one thing, he's old enough to be her father, and for another, he's still married to you."

"But, sh-she had a ring and everything," Tessa cried.

"Oh, phooey," Mary Lou retorted. "Ring, fling, doesn't mean a thing."

Clearly still upset, Tessa shook her head. "I should have stayed in Shreveport. I should never have come to New Orleans in the first place. But-but when I found out that Frank was coming down here on business, I-I hoped that by coming, Frank would see how much I still love him, and now . . ." Her voice trailed away, and she shrugged.

"That hussy was probably lying through her teeth," one of the women retorted. "Did you see the ring?"

Tessa frowned thoughtfully, then slowly shook her head. "No, I didn't, come to think of it."

"Well, there you go," the same woman said triumphantly. "Yes sir — lying through her pearly whites."

Mary Lou placed her arm around Tessa's waist. "You just hang in there, honey. Frank Morgan might be running the show right now — down here wheeling and dealing and playing the big business man and all — but you just remember that you're the one who still holds the purse strings. And since you haven't signed the divorce papers yet, he doesn't have a leg to stand on. Once he realizes that, then he'll come running with his tail tucked between his legs and beg you to take him back."

Tessa shrugged. "Maybe, but —" She bit her bottom lip and stared at the floor.

Out in the hallway Charlotte frowned. She'd always been a private person, the type who wouldn't think of airing her personal problems to anyone but possibly her sister Madeline. Even then, she'd think twice. But these women seemed to know a lot of really personal stuff about Tessa. Was it possible that telling all to the whole group was a prerequisite for joining the Red Scarf Sorority? She shuddered. If so, they'd never have to worry about her applying for membership.

Inside the room, Mary Lou reacted to Tessa's "but" by narrowing her eyes suspiciously. "But what?" She questioned.

Tessa shook her head. "Nothing."

"Aw, come on now, there's got to be something else."

Again Tessa shook her head. "I can't talk about it. Not now. Not yet," she whispered.

"Hey, I've got an idea," one of the women said. "We could always make this Lisa person disappear. Permanently," she added with a giggle. "We could do it and no one would be the wiser."

Several of the women snickered.

"I have an even better idea," another offered. "Let's make Frank disappear permanently instead."

"No, no, that's too easy," another woman argued. "Besides, Tessa still loves him. What about if we cut his thing off though. Then see how Miss Lisa likes him."

When the other women howled with laughter, Charlotte decided that she'd heard enough. As far as she was concerned, they were all crazy, but a fun kind of crazy, and though she certainly didn't agree with their little joke or the invasion of privacy, she found that she was just a wee bit envious of the sisterly camaraderie they seemed to share.

Figuring that no one was going to miss her if she left and also figuring that she'd come back to clean Tessa's room after lunch, Charlotte grabbed the supply cart.

"Ah, excuse me. Wait a minute."

Out of the corner of her eye she saw Tessa wave at her. Swallowing her impatience, she paused.

"Don't leave," Tessa pleaded.

Suddenly conscious that every eye in the room was staring at her, Charlotte waited as Tessa hurried to the doorway.

"What's you name?" Tessa asked.

Uh-oh, now what? Maybe she's going to report you.

Yeah, yeah, I'm shaking in my tennis shoes. Big hairy deal. "My name is Charlotte LaRue," she said evenly.

"Well, Charlotte, I owe you an apology. I'm really sorry for my earlier outburst. Please come back inside and clean."

An apology was the last thing that Charlotte had expected, and when the women inside the room abruptly burst into cheers and applause, she felt her face grow warm with shame and embarrassment. Being the center of attention left her little choice but to accept the apology as gracefully as possible, so she nodded. "Everyone has good days and bad days."

"Oh, that's so generous of you," Tessa said as the women dispersed and filed out of the room. "And please don't be embarrassed." She motioned toward the group. "That was just their way of confirming that I've worked through my crisis."

Well, whoop-de-do, good for you. The instant the sarcastic thought popped into her head, Charlotte's conscience whispered, *Shame on you.* And she was ashamed. After all, who was she to criticize another person's way of handling a crisis? *Judge not, lest ye be judged . . . different strokes for different folks.*

Forcing a smile, Charlotte said, "I'll get to work, then," and she headed for the bathroom.

Once in the bathroom, all she could do was stare. Every available surface in the small room was covered with beauty products or jewelry. She'd cleaned a lot of homes over the years and had worked for many women who were obsessed with youth and beauty, but she'd never seen such a collection in one place before, enough to fill a whole suitcase. Why anyone would want to haul all of that stuff around was beyond

Charlotte's comprehension.

"Sorry about all of that," Tessa said, entering the bathroom. "Here — why don't I just get some of it out of your way." She walked to the sink countertop, picked up a velvet jewelry bag, and began gathering up the jewelry. "I know it's silly, but I just can't bear to go anywhere without all of my things. My daughter calls it my bling-bling." She laughed. "I call it my security blanket."

Whatever floats your boat. Charlotte winced the instant the flip words popped into her head. What on earth was wrong with her today? She'd always believed in "be ye kind, one to another," and all she could do was think ugly thoughts. With a sigh and a silent prayer for a better attitude, she picked up a lone earring that Tessa had missed.

"You missed this one," she said. Staring at it, she paused to admire it before handing it to Tessa. Normally she preferred stud earrings to dangling ones. The stud earrings were much more practical for her line of work. But the earring was gorgeous. Light as a feather and made of hammered gold, it was shaped into a triangle that dangled from a post that was faced with a much smaller identical version of the triangle. The pyramid shape of the earring reminded her of the type of jewelry displayed in the King Tut exhibit when it had visited the New Orleans Museum of Arts years ago.

"This is just beautiful," she murmured, picturing in her mind how it might look on herself. "It's so simply elegant," she said, handing it to Tessa. "Not too large or gaudy, but not so small as to be insignificant."

"Yes, it is elegant, isn't it? That particular pair is my favorite — an anniversary gift from my husband last year." She blinked several times as if to hold back tears, then said, "I had hoped to wear them to our banquet tonight." Tessa frowned, then sighed. "Problem is, I can't find but one of them. At first I thought it might have been stolen by that maid that they fired, but since nothing else was missing I decided that I must have either accidentally left it at home or, Lord forbid, I lost it. Anyway, I've looked everywhere." She waved her hand to include the bathroom and bedroom. "Like I told the other maid who cleaned yesterday, if you happen to find it, I'd be ever so grateful."

"I'll keep an eye out for it," Charlotte assured her.

"Thanks," Tessa replied.

When Tessa left the room, Charlotte sprayed window cleaner on the mirror behind the sink. But her thoughts drifted back to what Carrie had told her about having to fire one of the maids for stealing. Maybe the maid who was fired *had* stolen Tessa's earring. But no, stealing just one earring didn't make any sense.

With a shrug, Charlotte exchanged the window cleaner for an all-purpose cleaner, and sprayed the counter top and sink.

Several minutes later, Charlotte was just finishing up the bathtub-shower combination when Tessa stuck her head in the doorway.

"Ah — excuse me, Charlotte."

Charlotte gave the edge of the tub a final swipe, then turned to face Tessa.

Tessa had changed blouses and was holding the one that she'd changed out of.

"Two things. I hope you don't mind, but I've changed my mind. I feel a migraine coming on, and the only way to get rid of it is to take my meds and sleep it off. Would it be too much trouble for you to come back a little later? A couple of hours or so should do the trick."

Charlotte's gut reaction was that the woman was lying through her teeth. Though she'd never experienced migraines herself, she knew they could be painfully debilitating, and nothing about the way Tessa looked even hinted that she was in pain. Why lie though?

Gathering every ounce of control she could muster to keep her irritation in check, she simply nodded. "I'll be back later then, and I hope your headache gets better."

"And the second thing —" Tessa held up the blouse she'd changed out of. "Could you please see that this gets cleaned?"

"Sure," Charlotte answered, taking the blouse.

"The dye in the new scarves I just bought bled through," Tessa explained. "I ordered more — silk this time — before I left home, but I had to leave before they were ready. A friend of mine is supposed to bring them, but —" She shrugged. "I don't have them yet."

Charlotte glanced down at the blouse. Just as Tessa had said, there was a faint red tint beneath the collar where the scarf had bled through.

"Thank you," Tessa murmured.

Once Charlotte had gathered her cleaning supplies, she left the room. In the hallway she checked her watch. If she hurried, she'd have time to clean one more room before lunch time.

The room next to Tessa's clearly had a DO NOT DISTURB sign hanging on the outside doorknob, so Charlotte went to the next room and knocked. "Housekeeping," she called out. After waiting a moment and getting no response, she pulled out her entry key. Just as she was about to insert it into the lock the door swung open.

The dark-haired woman standing in the doorway was probably in her late thirties or early forties, and was dressed in slacks and a silk blouse. "May I help you?" she asked.

"I'm the maid, and I've come to clean your room."

The woman nodded. "Good. Come on in. I can use some clean towels and washcloths, and some extra packets of decaf coffee for the coffeemaker. Will it bother you if I continue working?" She motioned toward a desk that contained a laptop and several stacks of file folders.

Charlotte shook her head. "Oh, no, ma'am, not at all."

Once Charlotte had gathered the necessary supplies from the cart, she headed for the bathroom. She had just finished wiping down the mirror, sink, and countertop when she heard the phone ring in the other room.

The woman immediately answered the call. "This is Margaret." A moment passed then she said, "Oh, hi, Tessa. It's good to hear from you."

Normally Charlotte preferred minding her own business, and though many times she'd been put in the position of eaves dropping, she usually tried to ignore it. But hearing Tessa's name gave her pause. After all, what were the odds that the caller was yet another woman named Tessa in the same small hotel? Of course it was possible that the call had originated from outside the hotel. Even so she figured the chances of the caller being yet another woman named Tessa were slim. With a shrug she poured disinfectant into the toilet.

"Now, now, Tessa, just calm down," Margaret told her. "Are you sure she overheard you? Okay, okay, don't cry. I'm coming. Just give me a second to shut off the laptop. And if it makes you feel any better, I was able to pick up that package for you before I left. But I'll need the ones you have for the exchange. Bye, now."

Charlotte rolled her eyes. It was hard to imagine that tell-all-Tessa could be upset about anyone overhearing her about anything.

A minute or so later Margaret appeared at the doorway. In her hand was a small paper sack. The bright purple logo of several triangles and a tulip on the white sack caught Charlotte's eye. Beneath the logo was the name of a store she'd never heard of before.

"I've got to leave for a while," Margaret said. "Please, don't bother anything on the desk, and don't forget to leave me an extra pack of decaf."

Charlotte nodded and a moment later she heard the outer door open and shut.

Though Charlotte tried to concentrate on her cleaning and tried to ignore the one-sided phone conversation she'd overheard, she couldn't help wondering who the "she" was that Tessa had mentioned. And what was it that "she" had overheard? But even more curious, why was Tessa seemingly so upset by it?

As Charlotte reached down and flushed the toilet, parts of the conversation between Tessa and her Red Scarf sisters played through her mind. She frowned. What was it that Mary Lou had said to Tessa?

Aw, come on now, there's got to be something else.

And Tessa had answered, *I can't talk about it. Not now. Not yet.*

Was it possible that whatever Tessa couldn't talk about to Mary Lou had something to do with the phone call she'd made to Margaret?

Charlotte groaned and shook her head.

"Oh, for Pete's sake, just mind your own business."

Chapter 2

The double parlor of the old house-hotel had been converted into a restaurant. The moment Charlotte stepped inside the room a thin, pale woman who looked to be in her thirties approached her. "Hi, my name is Simone, and I'm your hostess today. May I help you?" She asked, her gaze raking over Charlotte's uniform.

Charlotte returned the gaze, noting that in addition to having below-the-shoulder-length black hair, the woman also wore a black, flowing, dress that was mid-calf length. Though Charlotte was sure the woman was striving for an elegant, sophisticated look, in her opinion she looked like a leftover cast member from *Interview with a Vampire.*

"I'd like a table for one, please," Charlotte told her. "I'm one of the temporary maids. My name is Charlotte."

"Nice to meet you, Charlotte. All of our

tables inside are occupied at the moment, but if you don't mind eating on the patio, I believe there's a table available out there."

Charlotte glanced around the room. Sure enough, all of the tables were occupied, mostly by women wearing red scarves.

"The patio is fine," Charlotte told her.

The woman nodded. "Just follow me."

Charlotte followed her through a side door onto the porch that had been extended into a covered deck area.

The woman stopped at an empty table. "Your waitress will be right with you."

"Thank you," Charlotte murmured, seating herself at the table. Though not as cool as the air-conditioned restaurant, the striped awning blocked the high-noon sun and the ceiling fans stirred the humid air, making the outside part of the restaurant comfortable.

Within minutes, a waitress appeared and handed Charlotte a menu. "What can I get you to drink, ma'am?"

Charlotte smiled up at the perky young woman. "Un-sweetened tea, please."

"And what about an appetizer?"

Charlotte shook her head. "No, thanks. By the way, my name is Charlotte LaRue. I'm the temporary maid, and I was told that meals in the restaurant were one of the benefits of working here."

The waitress nodded. "That's correct. You can choose anything on the menu up to ten dollars."

With a concentrated frown, Charlotte stared at the menu. She didn't recall anyone mentioning a limit.

"Tea, coffee, and soft drinks are free to the staff," the waitress added. "Why don't you go ahead and look over the menu and I'll be right back with your tea."

"I'll go ahead and order," Charlotte told her. "I want the shrimp po-boy."

"Dressed or undressed?"

"Just the shrimp, lettuce, and tomatoes," Charlotte replied. "No mayo or onions." Lately, every time she'd eaten anything with onions she'd ended up with indigestion, and she didn't need the extra fat or calories from the mayonnaise. "And please add extra lettuce and tomatoes."

"Okay, be back in a jiffy with your tea."

While she waited, Charlotte glanced around at the other tables. Most of the guests on the patio were women. Though their choice of clothes varied from slacks to dresses, the majority of them, like the ones seated inside the restaurant, wore a red scarf tied in a variety of ways around their necks. As far as Charlotte could tell, there were only two tables where the occupants weren't wearing the signature scarves: three men in suits occupied a table near the doorway, and two scantily dressed young women were seated at the table next to hers.

Both of the women wore short-shorts and halter tops and looked to be in their early-to-mid-twenties. One was blond, small, and petite, while the other had reddish brown hair, and though not exactly fat, she wasn't exactly petite either.

Pleasantly plump, Charlotte decided, her eyes narrowing. She couldn't remember ever meeting the young woman, but there was a vaguely familiar look about her. And from the hostile glares passing back and forth between the two, neither woman was very happy about whatever they were discussing.

Probably the heat, Charlotte decided. For those who weren't used to the humid August heat, it sometimes played havoc with their emotions and tempers grew short.

At that moment, Charlotte's waitress reappeared, a tall glass of iced tea in hand. "Here you go," she said, setting the glass in front of Charlotte. "Be back in a jiffy with your po-boy."

"Thanks," Charlotte said.

True to the waitress's word, within minutes, she reappeared with Charlotte's sandwich.

"Enjoy," the waitress quipped as she placed the plate in front of Charlotte.

Charlotte smiled, her mouth watering at the sight and smell of the small loaf of French bread stuffed full of fried shrimp, lettuce, and tomatoes. "I intend to do just that," she said.

Savoring every delicious bite of the sandwich, Charlotte took her time eating. In between bites, she found her gaze returning to the two young women. Both seemed oblivious to their surroundings and the half-eaten sandwiches on their plates. Though Charlotte was unable to hear them very well, she figured that the blond one must have been winning the argument from the smug look on her face.

Just as Charlotte finished the last bite of her sandwich, a young man approached her table.

"I don't mean to be rude or interrupt your meal, ma'am, but I noticed that you had finished eating. Since this place is so crowded and all, I was wondering if you'd mind if I claim your table? But only if you're finished," he hastened to add.

Though Charlotte thought the request was indeed a bit rude, she nodded, took a last sip of her tea, blotted her mouth with her napkin, and then stood. "Be my guest," she told him with a forced smile. "I have to get back to work anyway."

"Thanks." Suddenly his gaze shifted to her left and Charlotte turned in time to see the young blonde who had been arguing with the other woman from the next table approach.

"Christopher, what are you doing here?" she cried, clearly upset by his appearance. "How dare you follow me!"

With a frown, Charlotte slowly backed away from the table.

"Aw, Lisa, don't be like that. Of course I'm going to follow you. I love you."

Lisa! Charlotte's steps slowed even more. Was it possible? Could this young woman be the same husband-stealing hussy Lisa that Tessa and her Red Scarf sisters had been talking about earlier?

"I told you it's over," Lisa snapped. "I'm engaged now." She waved her left hand in front of his face. On her third finger was a diamond big enough to choke a horse. "This is stalking, and if you keep following me, I tell Frank, and he'll have you arrested."

Oh, brother! Charlotte sighed, and with a shake of her head she turned and walked away. For some reason, she couldn't seem to get away from these people and their problems.

Later that afternoon Charlotte once again approached Tessa's door. Wanting to give the woman plenty of time to get rid of her so-called migraine, she'd saved finishing up Tessa's room for last.

Charlotte glanced down at the doorknob just to make sure there wasn't a DO NOT DISTURB sign. There wasn't one, so she knocked and waited. Then, just to be on the safe side, she knocked again louder and said, "Housekeeping." When there was no response, she opened the door with her master key and entered the room. One glance reassured her that the room was empty and also reassured her that it looked much the same as she'd left it. Since she'd already cleaned the bathroom earlier, she began by stripping the sheets off the beds.

Minutes later, she'd just finished putting clean sheets on the second bed when she heard the key mechanism in the door click and the door swung open.

Charlotte immediately recognized the swimsuit-clad young woman. She was the same one who had been arguing with Lisa in the restaurant.

The young woman dropped her tote bag on the floor. "Hi, I'm Belinda," she said. "This is my mom's room."

Charlotte smiled. No wonder she'd looked familiar. She resembled a younger, plumper Joan Rivers with dark hair. "And I'm Charlotte, the maid."

Belinda tilted her head and narrowed her eyes. "Haven't I seen you somewhere before?"

"I believe you were eating lunch in the restaurant at the table next to mine."

"Oh, yeah, that's it," Belinda replied.

"Is it going to bother you for me to clean?" And though she had to force herself to say it, she added, "I can come back later."

Belinda shook her head. "Nope. Won't bother me." She laughed, and headed for the bathroom. "I'll be in the shower," she called over her shoulder. "Besides, now is probably a good time to clean while my mom is out. She's down at the spa getting a facial and a massage."

While Belinda showered Charlotte worked on cleaning the bedroom. By the time Belinda emerged in a hotel robe, Charlotte had made up both beds with clean sheets and dusted.

"Are you from around here?" Belinda asked as she towel-dried her hair. "You know, like, have you lived here long?"

"I've lived here all of my life," Charlotte answered as she gathered up the dirty sheets.

"So, which restaurants would you recommend?"

Charlotte paused. "Depends on what price range you're looking for and what kind of food you're interested in."

"Price is no object, and as my mother would say, I like anything as long as it's seafood. I see food, I eat it, and it goes straight to my hips." She slapped her hip and laughed. "Get it?"

Charlotte got it and forced a smile to be polite. Belinda's laugh was a pathetic sound without humor, and Charlotte felt sorry for the girl. Personally, she thought that Belinda's size was just fine. In her opinion too many young women were obsessed with being rail-thin, thanks to the super-models, movie stars, and television.

"Mother is always after me to lose weight," Belinda continued, "but I figured that since this is a vacation, I should at least sample some of the local food. After all, that's what New Orleans is most noted for, isn't it — that and Mardi Gras, and of course now, Hurricane Katrina?"

Charlotte gave a slight shrug. "I suppose.

In that case, most any restaurant in the French Quarter is good. And if you want something closer to the hotel, I highly recommend Commander's Palace. But you might want to check ahead and see if you need reservations."

Belinda nodded. "Thanks, I will. So, what about places I should see?"

Charlotte felt a jolt to her heart and her arms tightened around the sheets she'd picked up. Sadly, thanks to the devastation of Hurricane Katrina, many historic sites had been damaged. "It would probably be best if you checked at the concierge desk about that," she said. "I'm sure they would be able to arrange a tour for you."

Again Belinda nodded. Fluffing her still damp hair with her fingers, she said, "Thanks again. Just one more thing, if you don't mind. I'm a collector of sorts. I collect old movies, records, and books — stuff like that. So each time we take a trip, I like to add to my collection. Is there anywhere specific that I could find stuff like that?"

Charlotte nodded. "Your best bet would be the French Market, especially on Saturday and Sunday. That's located down on Decatur, not far from Jax Brewery and Café du Monde."

Belinda grinned. "Oh, cool. I'll check it

out, but guess for now I'd better get my hair dried."

With the sound of the hairdryer whirring, Charlotte finished cleaning the bedroom. By the time she'd vacuumed, Belinda had dried her hair and applied makeup. When Belinda came out of the bathroom, she frowned. "Are you leaving?"

Charlotte nodded.

"But you haven't cleaned the bathroom yet."

"I cleaned it earlier this morning," Charlotte explained. "But your mother was here and said she had a migraine and asked me to come back and clean the bedroom later."

With a panicky look on her face, Belinda's gaze shifted from the bedroom to the bathroom, then back to Charlotte. "Could you please, please clean the bathroom again? I kind of made a mess in there. I thought you were going to clean it, so I wasn't as neat as I could have been. If mother sees that mess, she'll be on my case big time."

Charlotte's knee-jerk reaction was one of indignation. Just because Belinda had thought that the maid was going to clean it was no excuse to be sloppy. On the other hand, having experienced Tessa's wrath herself and ever mindful that whatever she did or didn't do would reflect on Carrie,

Charlotte took pity on the girl and nodded, earning her a huge smile of relief from Belinda.

"Oh, thank you, thank you," Belinda gushed.

Out in the hallway Charlotte gathered the necessary supplies from the cleaning cart. Since she'd already given the bathroom a thorough cleaning earlier, she figured it wouldn't take long to go over it again. Then she could finally go home.

As she wiped down the mirror, countertop, and sink, she thought about Belinda and her relationship with her mother. From the little Belinda had told her, it seemed to Charlotte that Tessa still treated her like a teenager. Then again, it was always possible that earlier, down in the restaurant, she had miscalculated Belinda's age to begin with. Girls looked so much more mature than they really were nowadays that it was sometimes hard to tell their age.

Charlotte sprayed cleaner on the tile surrounding the bathtub and was wiping it off when she heard a loud knock at the outer door. Then she heard Belinda ask, "Who's there?" Though she couldn't hear the muffled reply, she did hear Belinda's greeting to the visitor. "Hey, Granddaddy."

"Hey, baby girl," a gruff voice responded.

"Is the coast clear?"

In the bathroom Charlotte paused. She'd heard that voice before, but where?

"Yeah, the coast is clear," Belinda said. "Come on in. Mother is down at the spa."

The moment that the door clicked closed the man asked, "Did you talk to Lisa?"

"Yeah, for all the good that did. I tried to make her see reason, Granddaddy. Honestly, I tried," she reiterated. "But she wouldn't even listen to me."

"Wonderful, just wonderful," her grandfather drawled, sarcasm dripping with each word. "If she goes through with it and calls in the cops I'll be ruined. But there's no way I can do what she wants. No way," he repeated.

Charlotte's nerves tensed and her mind raced. What in the world was going on with these people? First Tessa, then Belinda, and now Belinda's grandfather, and in the middle of it all was this woman named Lisa. Charlotte figured that she could be wrong, but it sounded suspiciously like this Lisa person was the puppet master pulling everyone's strings. In fact, the whole thing smelled of . . . blackmail.

You do not want to hear this. Mind your own business. Charlotte reached across and flushed the toilet to drown out the conversation in the next room.

But even above the sound of the rushing water she still heard the man ask, "I thought you said that your mother wasn't here."

"I did — I mean she's not," Belinda reassured him. "It's just the hotel maid cleaning the bathroom. She's a really nice lady. But back to Lisa, I don't think she'll actually go through with it. I know her, Granddaddy, and she's just blowing smoke. I thought I'd give her a little time to cool off, then talk to her again. One way or another, I'll persuade her to change her mind. I promise. And if I have to, I'll talk to Daddy myself. Why, without you, the company would have been bankrupt a long time ago."

"Uh-uh," the man protested. "You've done enough, honey. I don't want to put you in the middle between your father and me. I shouldn't have involved you in the first place. I just thought that with you and Lisa being old friends she might listen to reason if you talked to her."

I'm not listening . . . I'm not listening . . . mind your own business . . . mind your own business. . . . But even as Charlotte silently chanted the litany, she strongly suspected that they were indeed talking about blackmail, and she couldn't help wondering what kind of threat Lisa could be holding over the man's head, nor could she help wondering what Lisa wanted him to do.

Charlotte quickly glanced around then gathered all of her cleaning supplies. The bathroom was clean enough, and it was past time for her to leave. For one, she didn't want to hear any more talk about blackmail, and for two, she still couldn't shake the feeling that she knew the man in the other room. Maybe if she saw him, face-to-face . . .

When Charlotte stepped out of the bathroom into the bedroom the man glanced her way, their eyes met and held, and she froze. Decades had passed since she'd last seen him, and like her, he was older. But there was no mistaking the identity of the man Belinda had been talking to.

"Charlotte? Is that you?" He shook his head in disbelief.

"Mack?" Charlotte murmured in disbelief. "Mack Sutton?"

"Hey, you two know each other?" Belinda asked.

Charlotte set down the cleaning supplies, and neither she nor Mack answered Belinda as Mack rushed across the room and grabbed Charlotte up in a bear hug.

"Dear Lord in heaven," Mack cried when he finally released her. Placing his hands on her shoulders, he held her at arm's length, and stared down at her. “Talk about a blast from the past,” he murmured, shaking his head.

“To say the least,” Charlotte whispered, her mind racing back over the past forty years. No wonder his voice had sounded so familiar. Because of Mack she’d met her beloved Hank, the man she was supposed to have married.

During her short time as a student at Tulane University she had dated Mack, until he’d introduced her to Hank, his best friend and college roommate. Once she’d met Hank, it had been love at first sight, and Mack, along with all other men, paled in comparison after that. But Hank and Mack had gone to Vietnam, and Hank had been killed shortly after arriving there. Sadly, he’d never known that before he’d left, their one night together had resulted in a son.

Over the years she’d often wondered what had happened to Mack. Since she’d never heard from him again, she’d even wondered if he, too, might have died there.

“It’s so good to see you, Mack,” she exclaimed, truly happy to know that he was alive and well. “You look great.” In his younger days Mack had been a very handsome man with coal-black hair and equally dark eyes. He still stood at least a head taller than her own five-foot-three frame but now his hair had more gray in it than black.

"And you look as beautiful as ever," he told her, the compliment making her blush like a schoolgirl. "Like I always said, if Sally Field had been blond and blue-eyed, you could have been her twin."

Charlotte laughed. "And you were always full of baloney."

"Ah, excuse me," Belinda interrupted.

Mack released Charlotte, and they turned their heads toward her.

"I take it that the answer to my question is yes."

Mack frowned. "What question, honey?"

Belinda rolled her eyes toward the ceiling. "I asked if you two know each other, but it's obvious that you do."

Mack grinned. "Yeah, we do. Charlotte and I are old friends." He laughed. "And I do mean old."

"Hey, you, watch it," Charlotte warned good naturedly.

"Charlotte, this is my lovely granddaughter, Belinda. And I want you to meet my daughter, Tessa, too."

"Belinda and I have already met," Charlotte responded. "And I met Tessa earlier this morning. Of course at the time I didn't know that she was your daughter."

Mack grinned. "Good, that's good." He tilted his head. "So what about you? Did you ever marry, have kids — I mean, after Hank — you know?"

"Yes, I know," she said, fully understanding his meaning. Since she'd never heard from Mack, besides wondering about his fate, she'd also wondered if he'd known about Hank's death. And now she knew that he had. Even so, she wasn't comfortable discussing something so private as her relationship with Hank before he'd left for Vietnam or the fact that she'd never found a man worthy enough to fill Hank's shoes. "I have a son," she answered, purposely avoiding the topic of a husband and careful not to mention her son's name. Mentioning that her son's name was also Hank would require explaining things that she wasn't yet comfortable explaining, especially not in front of Belinda.

"That's great." Mack paused and his eyes narrowed. "And your husband? Do you think he'd mind if you had dinner with an old friend tonight?"

Charlotte smiled, and once again avoiding the subject of a husband, she said, "I think dinner would be just fine." There would be plenty of time later to talk about Hank Senior and Hank Junior. "How about I meet you back here at the hotel restaurant, say around six-thirty," she said as she knelt down and picked up the supplies that she'd set on the floor earlier.

Mack nodded. "Six-thirty sounds great. See you then." He opened the door for her. As he closed it behind her, she heard him tell Belinda, "Just in case we don't talk again, the other reason I came by was to let you know that your father expects you to join him and the rest of the staff for dinner tomorrow evening."

Before the door clicked closed, Charlotte caught sight of Belinda's resentful expression. Though the girl's response was muffled, it was clear from the look on her face that she wasn't happy about the command invitation to dinner.

Chapter 3

Buoyant over seeing Mack again, and looking forward to catching up on their lives over dinner that evening, Charlotte turned down Milan Street.

For most of her life Charlotte had lived on Milan in an old Victorian shotgun double, just blocks away from the exclusive historic Garden District. After her parents' untimely deaths, she and her sister Madeline had inherited the hundred-year-old house. Once Madeline had married, she'd sold her half of the property to Charlotte, and off and on over the years, Charlotte had rented out Madeline's half of the house to supplement her own income.

To Charlotte, the old Victorian was more than just the home in which she'd grown up and raised her son. The location was perfect for her thriving, sometimes hectic cleaning service, since all of her clients lived in the Garden District. After Hurricane

Katrina, each time she thought about her home, she offered up a prayer of thanksgiving that it, unlike so many other houses, had been spared. The wind damage had been minimal: just a few shingles blown off and some broken limbs out of her tree. But she was most thankful that the floodwaters resulting from the levee breaks hadn't reached as far as her neighborhood.

As Charlotte approached her driveway and spied her latest tenant, Louis Thibodeaux, pacing the length of her front porch, her spirits sagged. Though she was unable to see the expression on his face, she'd known him long enough to tell that something was wrong from just his stiff and unyielding body language.

Before he'd retired, Louis had been a New Orleans Police homicide detective, and had, in fact, been her niece Judith's former partner. Once he'd retired Louis began renting from her, and now he worked for Lagniappe Security, a company that provided bodyguards. Besides their on-again, off-again relationship of sorts, she and Louis had locked horns on several occasions, mostly due to his penchant for being a dyed-in-the-wool chauvinist, which clashed with her independent, self-sufficient attitude.

Too bad their differences, nor the fact that he wasn't exactly available, hadn't lessened her attraction to him though. For a man his age, he wasn't half bad on the eyes. Stocky with military-short gray hair and a receding hairline, he was actually handsome in a rugged sort of way. And unlike a lot of men his age, his stomach was still nice and flat instead of hanging over his belt.

The moment Louis spotted her van, he abruptly stopped pacing. Crossing his arms, he firmly planted his feet near the top of the steps and stared at her, his face grim and determined.

Knowing what a jerk he could be at times, Charlotte braced herself to face him as she pulled into her driveway. Then, suddenly, like a blast of cold water, it hit her.

Joyce. Had something happened to Joyce?

Icy dread twisted Charlotte's heart. Louis' ex-wife Joyce had cirrhosis of the liver — too many years of a poor diet and drinking herself into oblivion after she'd abandoned Louis and their son, Stephen, who had been a troubled teenager at the time. After over a decade of not knowing where she'd disappeared to, Louis had finally located her in California. At the urging of Stephen, Louis had paid her a visit, mostly to inform her that she had a granddaughter. When

Louis learned of Joyce's medical condition, the thought of her dying among strangers had been more than he could bear, so he'd persuaded her to come back with him to New Orleans, and he'd been taking care of her ever since.

Charlotte quickly scooted out of the van, locked it, and hurried toward the steps. "What's wrong?" she asked as she climbed the steps to the porch.

Louis stepped to the side to allow her to pass, and instead of answering her question, he said, "Can we talk?"

Patience had never been a virtue that Charlotte laid claim to, and for a moment she felt like stomping her foot and demanding to know what was wrong right then and there. Restraining the urge and reminding herself that Louis would eventually reveal all, but only when he was ready, she nodded and unlocked the front door.

"Come on in," she told him, "and I'll make a pot of coffee."

The moment Charlotte stepped inside the living room, her little parakeet Sweety Boy began his usual routine of chirping and preening for attention.

"Squawk, missed you, missed you," he chirped.

"Missed you too, Boy," she said, and then

promptly ignored him as she toed off her tennis shoes and stepped into the soft moccasins she kept by the door. She'd make it up to him later, she silently vowed.

She also ignored the bird's squawks of terror when Louis stepped inside, closed the front door, and passed by the cage. For reasons she'd never been able to figure out, Sweety Boy didn't like Louis, nor did he like her sister, Madeline. Each time one of them entered the living room, the bird went wild, squawking and thrashing about in his cage.

For once, Louis refrained from his usual ritual of purposely aggravating the little bird, and he followed Charlotte straight back to the kitchen.

While Charlotte prepared the coffee to brew, Louis seated himself at the kitchen table, and with his arms resting on the table, he stared out the window.

Waiting for the coffee to brew and growing more fidgety with each silent passing moment, Charlotte unloaded the dish washer. By the time she'd finished, the coffee was ready.

She poured them each a cup, set the cups on the table, and then seated herself across from Louis. Her patience at an end, she sighed. "Okay, out with it. What's happened?"

The look on his face was a mixture of misery and anger. "I caught her drinking again."

Without asking, Charlotte knew that the "her" was Joyce, and concern and relief warred within, relief because Joyce hadn't actually died, but concern because Joyce *knew* that drinking again could hasten her death.

Death.

Charlotte frowned. Joyce's doctor had warned her that another drinking binge could finish her off. Her frown deepened. On more than one occasion, Joyce had indicated to Charlotte in confidence that she hated being a burden to her family. Was it possible that Joyce was drinking on purpose?

Choosing her words very carefully, Charlotte said, "You do realize that even though she's very grateful for everything you've done, it really bothers her that she's such a burden on you and Stephen. Especially considering the circumstances of your past relationship," she gently added.

Anger flashed in his eyes, but before he could reply, Charlotte threw up her hand, palm out. "Just hear me out before you say anything. I know what you're thinking, but it's not true. You're thinking that if she was so grateful, then why keep drinking? Why do the very thing that made her sick in the first place, the thing that could kill her?"

Charlotte reached out and covered Louis' hand with her own. "Have you even stopped to consider that it's possible that she could be trying to speed things up, that she's so tired of being a burden on everyone that —"

"No!" Louis jerked his hand from beneath hers and shook his head.

Charlotte narrowed her eyes. "Think about it, Louis! What if — God forbid — the situation were reversed? Put yourself in her shoes just for a moment. What would *you* do?"

Charlotte held her breath as Louis stared at her, a myriad of conflicting emotions chasing across his face. Then, without a word or even a sip of his coffee he abruptly stood, turned his back to her, and stalked out of the kitchen. A moment later, Charlotte heard the front door open and close with a decisive click.

A pain squeezed her heart as she sat in the lonely silence staring at the steam rising from Louis's untouched coffee. Though her emotions demanded that she go after him and try to comfort him in some way, her common sense kept her seated at the table. She'd already said enough, evidently more than Louis wanted to hear.

"Que será será," she whispered with a sigh. Then she bowed her head and prayed, first for strength and mercy for Joyce, then for strength, peace, and grace for Louis, his son, and his granddaughter.

By six Charlotte had showered, applied fresh makeup, and fixed her hair. After trying on three different dresses, she finally settled for the one she'd tried on first, her old reliable, little black dress. Instead of the string of pearls she usually wore with the dress, she opted for a simple gold chain and a pair of small gold hoop earrings. While fastening the hoops, a mental image of Tessa Morgan's lone earring came to mind. It really was a shame that Tessa had lost the other one.

That's what she gets for hauling all of that stuff around.

"Not nice, Charlotte," she murmured as she checked out her image in the full-length mirror. Besides, what Tessa did was none of her business.

Giving her hair one last pat, she headed for the kitchen to check her blood-sugar level. Ever since the scary episode she'd experienced just months ago during Mardi Gras when the level had plummeted, she'd tried to be more vigilant about taking care of herself. Being a borderline diabetic was troublesome enough, but it was a whole lot better and less trouble than being a full-fledged one.

As she went through the daily ritual of pricking her finger, squeezing a drop of blood out onto the test strip, and waiting for the results from the small monitor, a sudden tremor of uncertainty seized her. It had been a long time since she'd gone on a real, honest-to-goodness date with a man. Too long, she decided, especially if just the thought of it made her insides so jittery.

The machine beeped and Charlotte glanced down at the small readout display on the monitor. "Right on the money," she murmured as she jotted down the resulting numbers. Taking her time, she packed up the machine and put it away in the drawer.

Glancing at the clock on the microwave, she sighed. "Still too early to leave," she complained.

Just as she closed the drawer, the phone rang. Again she checked the time. Wondering who on earth could be calling her, she hurried to the living room.

Though she didn't immediately recognize

the caller ID number, her curiosity got the best of her, and she picked up the receiver anyway. "Maid-for-a-Day, Charlotte speaking."

"Charlotte, this is Mack."

"Hey, Mack, I was just about to walk out the door."

"Glad I caught you then. I'm so sorry to do this to you — last minute and all — but I'm going to have to cancel our dinner date. We've had somewhat of a family crisis," he explained, "and I need to take care of things."

Though a part of her was disappointed, another part of her was relieved. "No problem," she told him, but even as she said the words, she couldn't help wondering what kind of family emergency had come up, especially after having met his daughter and granddaughter earlier. "Is there anything I can do to help?"

"No, nothing, but thanks."

Itching with curiosity, she waited a moment for Mack to elaborate. When he didn't, she finally said, "In that case, how about a rain check? We can always have dinner on another night. Besides, your family has to come first."

"Thanks for being so understanding, but then I knew you would be." He paused.

"Tell you what, how about tomorrow night instead?"

The invitation wasn't said with much enthusiasm which made her wonder if he'd used the old family emergency ploy to get out of the date to begin with. Maybe, like her, he'd had second thoughts as well. Then again, maybe like her, he had a case of the jitters. So, now what? Should she go or not go? Did she even want to go?

You're being ridiculous, and it's not like Mack is going to try to jump your bones or anything. It's just simply a dinner date. Nothing more, nothing less.

Before she could change her mind, she said, "Tomorrow evening would be fine. Just tell me when and where, and I'll meet you there."

"Is there some reason you don't want me to pick you up at your house?"

"No — no particular reason," she quickly assured him. "I just figured it would be easier all the way around if I drove myself."

"Yeah, you're probably right," he said after a moment. "It's been a long time since I was down here. I had to go downtown earlier and almost got lost. I'd forgotten how confusing all of the one-way streets can be. Anyway, there's a restaurant just down the block and across the street from the hotel."

"Yes, I know where you're talking about."

"Just meet me there around seven. I'll wait for you inside near the front door."

After Charlotte hung up the telephone, she wandered over to her little parakeet's cage. "Well, Sweety Boy, here I am, all dressed up with nowhere to go. All that worrying about what to wear for nothing," she grumbled.

She stuck her finger inside the cage, and the little bird quickly sidled over for her to rub the back of his head. "So much for my exciting dinner date. I'll just have to make-do with leftovers tonight instead. Guess I should look on the bright side, eh, Boy? Now I can get out of this garb and get comfortable."

But as she headed to the bedroom, she thought about Mack's rain-check dinner invitation again. Besides his lack of enthusiasm, there was something else that bothered her about it, something that hovered on the edge of her memory, but what?

Racking her brain for the illusive memory, she changed into her pajamas, but it was while she was eating a makeshift dinner of cold leftover chicken and a salad that it suddenly occurred to her what had been bothering her about her dinner date.

". . . the other reason I came by was to let you know that your father expects you to join him and the rest of the staff for dinner tomorrow evening."

The big staff dinner gathering scheduled for tomorrow evening was what had been bothering her. After thinking about the conversation between Belinda and Mack, she strongly suspected that Mack worked for Belinda's father, and that Mack, as well as the girl, would be expected to attend the dinner party as well.

While Charlotte cleaned up the kitchen, she debated on whether to cancel the date or keep it. Since there was a slight chance that she could be wrong, in the end she decided to give Mack the benefit of a doubt and keep the date.

Once the kitchen was clean, Charlotte decided to watch TV. Though she tried to stay awake until time for the television mystery series *Monk,* she kept nodding off. After she'd nodded off the third time, she gave up and switched off the television. In the bedroom she set her alarm clock an hour earlier than usual and climbed into bed.

Charlotte was just dozing off when she heard raised voices coming from Louis's half of the double. Not for the first time did she wish that the wall that separated her half from Louis's was thicker and more insulated. Though somewhat muffled, she could still hear every angry word whether she wanted to or not.

"Is this what you've been looking for?" Louis shouted.

"Give that back!" Joyce yelled.

"Not on your life. It's going down the drain."

"No! Don't!" Joyce cried. "It's mine. You have no right!"

"I have every right as long as you're under my roof," he retorted. "I'm warning you, either stop the drinking or get out."

For long moments, silence reigned, then Charlotte heard Joyce sobbing. Seconds later, like a shotgun blast, the front door slammed, and Charlotte jumped. Outside, a car engine roared to life, followed by the squealing of tires as the car pealed out of the driveway.

In the dark room Charlotte lay listening to Joyce's sobs, and though her instincts urged her to go next door and comfort the woman, her common sense agreed with Louis. Not that she agreed with his overbearing methods. But then, who was she to judge? Who knows, in his shoes she might do the same thing.

As she lay there, wondering where Louis had gone, at some point she realized that she no longer heard Joyce's sobs. Closing her eyes, she said a quick prayer for both Joyce and Louis, then finally dozed off into a fitful sleep.

"But I don't want you to go," she whispered, tears streaming down her face. Tomorrow he was leaving. Tomorrow he'd be on his way to Vietnam, clear across the world.

His arms tightened around her. "And I don't want to leave you," he whispered. "But don't you see? This way Uncle Sam will pay for me to go to medical school."

"There has to be another way," she cried. "We could borrow the money, and I can work while you go to medical school."

"Oh, honey, you know better than that. In the first place, no one is going to lend me that much money, and in the second place, without your degree, the kinds of jobs you'd qualify for would barely keep a roof over our heads."

"No," she sobbed. "Don't go . . . don't go . . ."

Charlotte came awake with a jolt, her face wet with tears.

"Dear Lord in heaven," she whispered, her insides still heavy from the throes of the dream. First, the nightmare about drowning during Katrina, and now she was dreaming about Hank. What in the world was going on?

Dreaming about the horrors of the hurricane she could understand, but why on earth would she be dreaming about Hank and something that happened over forty years ago?

Mack, she decided, blinking back tears as she pulled the covers to her chin and burrowed farther down in the bed to ward off a sudden chill. The combination of seeing Mack again, then hearing the argument between Louis and Joyce, must have stirred up all of the old, painful memories that she'd tucked away years ago, she decided.

Hearing Joyce and Louis argue had reminded her of the last night she'd spent with Hank before he'd left. It had been one of the few times that they had disagreed over anything. Too bad she hadn't realized then how sweet the making up afterwards could be or she might have instigated more arguments.

Relegating the memories back to where they'd come from, Charlotte turned her head to check the time. Reliving the past only made her sad. When she saw the numbers on the illuminated dial of the clock, she sighed. "Time to get up anyway," she grumbled. No sooner had the words left her mouth than the alarm buzzed.

When Charlotte stepped out on her front porch, she noticed that Louis's car was gone. As she locked the front door, she wondered if he had stayed out all night? If so, *where* had he stayed? Of course it was always possible that once he'd cooled off he could have come home then left again later. Though possible, not likely, she decided, as she crossed the porch, descended the steps, and headed for the van. Lately, any time he had to go out of town on business or catch an early flight, he let her know about it, just in case Joyce had an emergency.

With a shrug and reminding herself that what Louis did or didn't do was really no concern of hers, she unlocked the van, climbed inside, and drove to the hotel.

Most of Charlotte's day passed quickly without incident, and by midafternoon she only had one room left to clean before going home. She'd tried to clean it earlier but the occupant had put out the DO NOT DISTURB sign.

When she approached the door, she noted that the sign was gone, but just as she held up her arm and curled her fingers into a fist to give the courtesy knock, a woman from inside shouted, "I told you it was over, so leave me alone."

Charlotte dropped her arm and backed away from the door. Though muffled, she could still hear a man shout back at the woman. "And I told you that it's only over when I say it's over. I love you, and I don't intend for another man to raise my baby!"

"Well, I don't love you!" The woman cried. "And for your information, my baby will be raised by who I choose. And I don't choose you. Now, get out! Get out or I'll call the police!"

"Okay, okay, I'm going," the man yelled. "For now," he added. "But I'll be back."

The door abruptly opened, and a man stalked out into the hallway. Without a glance Charlotte's way, he stormed past her.

All that Charlotte could do was stare at the man, the same man whom she'd seen arguing with Lisa the day before. As she watched him disappear around the corner leading to the stairwell, she narrowed her eyes. *Christopher.* If she remembered right, that was what Lisa had called him. So, did that mean that the room belonged to . . .

"I don't need the room cleaned today."

At the sound of the woman's voice, Charlotte jerked her head around to see Lisa standing in the open doorway. The robe-clad woman's eyes were puffy and red. Probably from crying, Charlotte figured. Unable to help herself, her gaze lowered to Lisa's midsection. If Lisa was pregnant, she didn't show it yet. So, did Frank know about Lisa's condition?

"I *said* that I don't need the room cleaned today."

Lisa's words snapped Charlotte out of her reverie. "Yes, of course. Would you like for me to come back —" Before Charlotte had time to finish her sentence, Lisa slammed the door shut.

"Guess not," Charlotte muttered. Fine with her. She was tired anyway. Grabbing hold of the handles of the cleaning cart, Charlotte wheeled it toward the elevator. With one less room to clean, she could go home early and rest a bit before her dinner date with Mack. But as the elevator carried her to the ground floor, she couldn't stop thinking about the argument she'd overheard between Lisa and Christopher. And she couldn't stop wondering if Frank Morgan knew that his fiancée was carrying another man's baby.

Chapter 4

When Charlotte pulled into her driveway, she noticed that Louis's car was still missing, and later that evening, when she left again for her date with Mack, Louis still hadn't returned.

Where are you, Louis?

As prearranged, Mack was waiting for Charlotte inside the vestibule near the front door of the restaurant.

"You look gorgeous," he said as he took her hands and kissed her on the cheek. Charlotte bit her bottom lip to keep from laughing. Once again she'd opted for her little black dress, the gold chain, and gold hoops.

Though returning the compliment would have been the polite thing to do, "Thanks" was all that Charlotte said.

Personally, she thought that Mack looked like he'd been through the wringer. Besides having bags under his bloodshot eyes, his dark suit hung on him like a sack . . . or like he'd slept in it, his shirt was wrinkled, and unless she was mistaken, that spot on his tie looked suspiciously like dried-up ketchup or spaghetti sauce.

"You're welcome," he responded. Then, looking very uncomfortable, he said, "Before we go into the restaurant, I have a confession to make."

Uh-oh, here it comes.

"We'll be joining a few others tonight for dinner. I would have told you last night, but I was afraid you wouldn't come. Frank — he's my son-in-law — is having a dinner for the staff of his CPA firm, and since I'm the managing partner for the firm, I'm expected to attend as well."

Though Charlotte forced a smile, inside she was seething. If it had been anyone but Mack, she would have immediately turned around and gone home. "I don't like surprises, Mack," she warned.

A flush stole up Mack's cheeks, and he looked so uncomfortable that Charlotte took pity on him. "But what's done is done," she said. "Just don't ever do that again. Now, shall we join the others?"

The oblong table was located near the front of the restaurant in an alcove near huge windows that overlooked the sidewalk and street. The others they joined included Belinda, Lisa, two men, and another woman.

Mack escorted her to where one of the men was seated at the head of the table. On either side of the man, facing each other, were Belinda and Lisa.

Belinda smiled at Charlotte, but the expression on Lisa's face was anything but welcoming. And no wonder, thought Charlotte. Once Lisa had realized who she was, she had probably also realized that there was a good possibility that Charlotte had overheard the argument she'd had earlier with Christopher.

"Frank, this is Charlotte LaRue," Mack said. "She's the friend that I told you about. Charlotte, this is Frank Morgan." Mack's gaze slid to Lisa then back to Charlotte. "Frank is my son-in-law as well as the head of Morgan and Associates, the firm I work for."

When Frank Morgan smiled, stood, and Charlotte clasped the hand that he proffered, she suddenly realized why his wife Tessa was so obsessed with youth and beauty. Frank was an extremely handsome man in a dark brooding sort of way, and unless Charlotte missed her guess, he was also a bit younger than Tessa.

"Nice to meet you, Charlotte," he said, giving her hand a firm but gentle squeeze. "Glad you could join us tonight."

Charlotte nodded and smiled. "Nice meeting you, too."

When Frank released her hand, he faced the other guests at the table. "Listen up, everyone," he told the group. "We have a special guest joining us tonight, a friend of Mack's from his college days." He pointed out each person at the table. "Lisa, Belinda, John, and Tanya, this is Charlotte LaRue. Please make her feel welcomed."

All eyes turned toward Charlotte, and though she smiled, she felt her face grow warm with embarrassment.

Again, Belinda smiled at her, and again, Lisa simply glared at her, but the man named John and the woman named Tanya gave her a friendly acknowledging nod as Mack nudged her toward the other end of the table.

"I believe these two places are for us," Mack said.

Once they were seated, a waiter appeared to take their drink order.

"Unsweetened tea," Charlotte told him.

"A Bloody Mary for me," Mack said. Then he turned to Charlotte. "So, have you worked for the hotel long?"

"No, I haven't. I'm just filling in temporarily as a favor for an old friend. Actually, I run my own cleaning service, Maid-for-a-Day."

When a puzzled frown crossed Mack's face, Charlotte explained. "I employ two full-time maids and one part-time. We specialize in clients who live in the Garden District."

Mack shook his head in amazement. "How in the devil did you end up being a maid? Not that there's anything wrong with being a maid," he hastened to add. "It's just that with your brains, I always figured that you'd end up a college professor or something."

Coming from anyone else Charlotte would have been highly offended by Mack's assumption that only people of low intellect would choose to be a maid. "I never finished my degree," she told him bluntly. "I was finishing up my junior year when my parents were both killed in an accident —"

"I had no idea," Mack interrupted, his expression full of sympathy. "That's terrible."

Charlotte nodded. "Yes, at the time it was terrible. My father had never been able to afford life insurance, and their deaths left me with not only the welfare of my young son to think about, but also my younger sister to support. Thanks to Professor McGee — you remember her, don't you? She was an English Professor at Tulane." When Mack nodded, she continued. "Anyway, she was the one who suggested that I could make quite a bit of money cleaning houses, and she even recommended me to several of her more wealthy friends." Charlotte smiled. "Turned out she was right. And the rest is, as they say, history."

From the expression on Mack's face, Charlotte could already see questions forming. Still not comfortable talking to him about how she ended up with a fatherless son, she decided a subject change was in order. In her experience, asking the other person questions was the best way to change the subject. "So, what about you, Mack? How did you end up being an accountant?"

At that moment, the waiter returned with their salads. No sooner had he placed Charlotte's salad in front of her than a woman rushed through the door. Charlotte immediately recognized her as the same woman who had received a phone call from Tessa. Charlotte frowned, wracking her brain for the woman's name. Maybe Margaret. Yes, Margaret was her name.

"So sorry I'm late," Margaret gushed as she seated herself next to Belinda.

Frank nodded then cleared his throat. "Ah, excuse me." All eyes turned to him. "I believe most of you already know Margaret, my secretary and my right-hand man, so-to-speak. Of course rumor has it that she's really the one running the company."

As expected, everyone laughed at Frank's little joke, and a flush of embarrassment stole up Margaret's cheeks. When the laughter died down, Frank motioned toward the other end of the table where Charlotte and Mack were seated. "Margaret, meet Charlotte. She and Mack are old friends."

A spark of recognition lit Margaret's eyes as she and Charlotte nodded and smiled to each other. Then, Margaret turned to Frank. "Just so you know, I was able to finish typing that document you need for tomorrow's meeting."

Frank laughed. "That's my girl. Hey, everybody," he said, still laughing, "Not only does she run the firm, but she's got the fastest fingers in the south."

Again, as if on cue, everyone laughed again, but this time the laughter seemed even more forced than before, and it was all that Charlotte could do to keep from rolling her eyes.

Oh, brother. If this stuff gets much deeper, I'm going to need hip boots.

Appalled at her thoughts, Charlotte tucked her head and forked up a mouthful of salad. Thankfully, everyone else followed suit, then slowly, once again the murmur of conversation filled the room.

Afraid that Mack would resume giving her the third degree, Charlotte swallowed the bite of salad, then said, "Now, where were we? Oh, yeah, you were going to tell me how you ended up being an accountant."

Mack smiled. "After Nam, I finished up my degree and was working towards becoming a CPA when I met Joanne, Tessa's mother. Tessa was just a little girl at the time, and Joanne was struggling to hold on to the money that she'd inherited from her father. Joanne's first husband had turned out to be a drunk and had just about spent her inheritance before she realized what was happening. She'd already divorced him when we met, and — like I said — was struggling to hold on to what money she had left. Anyway, Joanne hired me to look after her investments. One thing led to another, we got married, then, together we worked until her finances were back on solid ground. Just as everything was looking up, Joanne discovered that she had breast cancer. Six months later she died."

His face bleak with sorrow, Mack paused and for several moments a muscle in his jaw quivered.

Remembering her own pain after Hank and her parents were killed, Charlotte could truly sympathize. "That had to be a painful time for you," she said softly.

Mack sighed then nodded. "Yes it was. Joanne was a wonderful woman, and I still miss her. But then you know all about that kind of pain, don't you?"

"Yes, I do," she said, realizing how much in common they had with each other. "But whether we like it or not, life does go on."

"I guess." Mack cleared his throat. "Anyway, when Joanne died, Tessa was a young teenager, and since she had no one else, I finished raising her."

"What happened to her father?"

Mack shrugged. "He was a loser. For Tessa's sake, I tried to locate him after Joanne died. It took several years to track him down, and when I finally found him, he was in prison. There was no way I could bring myself to tell Tessa that her father was a jailbird, so, like I said, I raised her."

"Raising a teenager by yourself had to be hard."

Mack simply shook his head. "Hard

doesn't begin to describe it. As a child Tessa had a stubborn streak, not to mention that Joanne and I had both spoiled her. After her mother's death, she was even worse — staying out to all hours of the night and constantly in trouble at school. Once, she even ran away, and for months I didn't know where she was or even if she was dead or alive. Then one day, out of the blue, she showed up at the front door. I don't know what happened to her during that time — and she's never told me — but whatever happened totally changed her. She went back to school, graduated with honors, and even went on to get a college degree. I'll tell you one thing, the day she graduated from college was one of the proudest days of my life."

At that moment two waiters showed up. While one of the waiters whisked away the salad plates, the other one served the entrées.

Immediately recognizing the dish, Charlotte's mouth watered: pecan-crusted catfish with Creole meuniére sauce. "I think I just died and went to heaven," she murmured.

Mack glanced her way quizzically. "Pardon?"

Realizing that she'd actually spoken her thoughts, Charlotte laughed. "Don't mind me. Just thinking out loud."

As she and Mack settled into a companionable silence while they ate, Charlotte caught bits and pieces of conversations going on farther down the table. While Tanya and John discussed the pros and cons of an advertising campaign, Margaret seemed enthralled by whatever Lisa was telling her. But even with the buzz of voices, Charlotte could still hear every word Frank said to Belinda, and it was disgustingly clear that he was badgering her about Tessa.

"She'd listen to you," Frank insisted. "Look, you know how miserable we've all been. If you could persuade her to sign the divorce papers, then maybe she'd get on with her life. Can't you see that it's the best thing for all of us?"

"You mean best for you, don't you?" Belinda retorted angrily. "The only reason everyone is so miserable is because of *her.*" Belinda shot Lisa a hateful look.

At that moment Tanya and John burst into laughter over something, and though Charlotte was unable to hear Lisa's retort to Belinda's jab, the furious look on her face said it all.

Charlotte quickly glanced down at the half-eaten catfish on her plate in an attempt to hide the sudden anger she felt and promptly lost her appetite. The very idea of a father pressuring his own daughter to go against her mother was reprehensible. What a sleazeball!

"Are you feeling okay?"

The sound of Mack's voice startled Charlotte, and for a moment she wondered if once again she'd spoken her thoughts out loud. "I'm fine," she answered, realizing that her cheeks were probably flushed. She looked up at Mack and forced a smile. How could he stand to be a part of the company when his son-in-law was making his daughter Tessa so miserable? "That last bite was kind of spicy." She reached for her tea and took several swallows.

Just as she set the glass down, at the other end of the table, Belinda suddenly shoved back her chair and stood. "I don't care what you say, I won't do it!" she shouted. "And you can't make me," she added, tears running down her cheeks. Then she turned and fled the room.

With Belinda's departure, for a moment the restaurant grew so quiet that Charlotte could hear pots and pans clanging back in the kitchen and felt every eye in the restaurant staring at their table. Then, just as abruptly, the other patrons seemed to lose interest and turned their attention back to their own tables.

Frank leveled a pointed look at Margaret. "Go after her, and see if you can talk some sense into her."

Margaret nodded, but as she pushed back her chair, Lisa said, "No, I'll do it." She motioned to Margaret's plate. "Go ahead and finish your meal." Before anyone had time to object, Lisa shoved her chair back and hurried toward the front entrance.

"Sorry about all of that," Mack said.

Charlotte shrugged. "Stuff happens even in the best of families."

Outside, Lisa hurried past the window, then disappeared out of sight. Just seconds later, a man hurried past, headed in the same direction that Lisa had taken.

Charlotte frowned. *Christopher.* Unless her eyes were playing tricks on her, she could swear that the man who had just gone past was Lisa's ex-boyfriend Christopher. Charlotte's frown deepened. Was it simply coincidence that he just happened to be passing by at that particular moment?

Not coincidence, Charlotte decided. In spite of Lisa's threat to call the police on him, he'd more than likely followed Lisa and had been waiting outside on the chance that he might get to talk to her again.

. . . it's only over when I say it's over . . .

and I don't intend for another man to raise my baby!

A sudden chill seized Charlotte at the memory of Christopher's words earlier that day. No, his being outside the restaurant was definitely not a coincidence, and for reasons she couldn't explain, she couldn't help thinking that Christopher was up to no good.

Chapter 5

Bananas Foster was one of Charlotte's favorite desserts, but not even the waiter flambéing the mixture of bananas, brown sugar, and cinnamon with banana liqueur and rum distracted her from wondering and worrying about Belinda, Lisa, and Christopher. She'd already witnessed one argument between Belinda and Lisa, and she'd overheard the altercation between Lisa and Christopher. Considering Belinda's frame of mind, together she and Lisa were a potential powder keg. Frank should never have allowed Lisa to go after Belinda. And adding Christopher to the mix could be just the spark needed to set off a dangerous explosion.

While one of the waiters set dishes of vanilla bean ice cream in front of each person at the table, another waiter came along behind him and spooned the banana mixture on top of the ice cream, then added whipped cream.

Charlotte sighed. No one else seemed worried about Belinda, Lisa, or Christopher. Certainly not Frank or Mack. So why should she be concerned?

She lowered her gaze to the dessert in front of her. Since becoming a diabetic, she was tempted on a daily basis by foods that were forbidden, and usually she was able to control herself. But surely just this one time, a bite or two of the sinful dessert wouldn't hurt.

Yeah, right. That's probably what Eve said to Adam just before he bit into the apple, and look what happened to him.

Ignoring the irritating voice of reason in her head, she quickly spooned up a bite and put it in her mouth. "Hmm," she groaned as she swallowed. "Now I know for sure that I've died and gone to heaven."

Beside her Mack chuckled. "Then I remembered right, didn't I?" He winked at her. "You do know that I ordered this particular dessert special, just for you."

"Remembered what right?" Charlotte asked, puzzled.

Mack grinned. "The first dinner date we ever had you ordered Bananas Foster."

Charlotte stared at Mack, her mind racing back over time. Then a slow smile pulled at her lips. "Mack Sutton, shame on you for telling such lies. The first dinner you ever bought me was a hot dog from a Lucky Dog vendor down in the Quarter."

Mack laughed. "Yep, same old Charlotte — mind like a steel trap. Never could fool you."

"Well," she drawled, "you know the old saying. 'Fool me once, shame on you. Fool me twice, shame on me.' But just for future reference, I'm not supposed to have sweets."

Mack's laughter died. "You're kidding, aren't you?"

Charlotte shook her head. "Nope, afraid not. I'm a diabetic."

"Well, in that case I'll remove the temptation." Mack reached out to take her dessert plate.

With a deft movement of her hand, Charlotte switched the fork to a knife grip and made a stabbing motion. "Touch that plate and you'll lose a finger," Charlotte warned.

Mack jerked back his hand. "Whoa! Whatever you say."

Charlotte and Mack were both still laughing when she saw Frank lean toward Margaret. "They should have been back by now," she heard him say. "Maybe you'd better go look for them. I'll take care of the check, then meet you back in the hotel lobby."

Evidently, Mack heard the exchange too. "Guess that's our cue that dinner is over," he said. "We could always go down to the Quarter to Café Du Monde for coffee."

Charlotte smothered a yawn with her hand. "Thanks, I'd love that, but not tonight. I'm tired and have to get up early tomorrow. Could I have a rain check?"

Mack nodded. "Any time." When he stood, Charlotte followed suit, and they walked over to where Frank was seated.

"Thanks so much for including me tonight," she told Frank. "The dinner was delicious."

At that moment, the waiter showed up with the bill. Distracted, Frank simply nodded. "Glad you could join us," he said. Then he turned his attention to the waiter.

With Mack's hand at the small of Charlotte's back, they headed for the entrance door. They had only taken a few steps when Mack suddenly halted.

Charlotte glanced up at him, but Mack was glaring at something or someone near the entrance of the restaurant. Alarmed by the hard, vicious expression on his face, she said, "Mack, what's wrong?"

When he didn't answer, her gaze followed his to where a lone man stood, glaring back at Mack. Though the restaurant was dimly lit, she could see well enough to know that the tall, stone-faced, rough-looking man gave her the heebie-jeebies. Then the man smiled and exited the restaurant.

Mack cursed and took Charlotte's hand. "We can leave now," he said.

Once outside, Mack glanced around, then took a deep breath, released it, and released her hand. Then he took another deep breath and sighed.

Recognizing the technique as the same one that she'd used many times to keep a hold on her temper, Charlotte said, "What on earth just happened in there?"

"Sorry about that," he said. "Remember that family emergency that I told you about?"

Charlotte nodded.

"That scumbag is to blame."

"Who is he?"

"His name is Ralph — Ralph Jones, and he's Tessa's long-lost father. Just got released from prison a couple of months ago from serving a second term, and he's been stalking Tessa ever since. Last night though, he went too far. He cornered Belinda and proceeded to introduce himself. When Tessa found out, all hell broke loose. Anyway, I tracked him down and had a little talk with him. But, as you can see, it didn't do a whole lot of good." Mack sighed and shook his head. "Never mind that though. Come on and let me walk you to your car."

"It's not far," Charlotte told him as they strolled down the sidewalk.

They'd only taken a few steps when Mack stopped. "Listen, guess I need to apologize again. Earlier, during dinner, Frank shouldn't have aired our family problems in front of you like that. I had hoped that he'd have better manners. Guess I should have known better."

"Here's my van," Charlotte told him, stopping beside it and fishing her keys from her purse. "As for what happened —" she shrugged. "Don't worry about it."

But Mack was eyeing her van. "Nice van," he said. "Being a maid must pay better than I thought it did."

"It's a living," Charlotte responded, purposely sidestepping the subjects of her pay and her van. Neither was his or anyone else's business. Even so, the new van was still a subject she wasn't comfortable even thinking about.

She was finally getting used to driving the vehicle and even enjoyed the luxury package that came with it, but she still hadn't gotten used to the fact that it had been given to her. And she still hadn't figured out whether she should view the van as a bribe or simply a gift from a grateful client. Just thinking about the van always brought to mind Mardi Gras and the horrible scene of Robert Rossi lying on the floor with a knife in his back, something she'd rather forget ever happened.

With a slight shiver, Charlotte relegated the memory to the farthermost recesses of her mind, and using her remote she unlocked the van. "Thanks again," she called out as she hurried around to the driver's side. Once inside, she slammed the door.

Just as she inserted her keys into the ignition Charlotte jumped at the sound of the sudden tap on her window. When she jerked her head around and saw that it was only Mack standing by the door, she willed her heart to slow down. He motioned for her to lower the window, and she hit the power window control. "You scared the daylights out of me," she said.

Mack bent down until his head was even with the open window. "Apology number three — or is that four? Sorry. Didn't mean to startle you." Then, without warning, he stuck his head inside, and before she realized his intentions, he kissed her.

As far as kisses went, it was more of a friendly type of kiss as opposed to the passionate type.

Before Charlotte could make up her mind which she would have preferred, Mack ended it, pulled back, and grinned. "Now what kind of date would I be if I let you leave without a proper good-bye?" He winked and slapped the side of her door. "Be careful driving home."

Once Mack was back on the sidewalk, and still trying to decide how she felt about the kiss, Charlotte pulled out into the street. Hoping for one last look at him, she glanced in her rearview mirror. Mack was walking in the opposite direction of the restaurant toward the hotel, instead of returning to the restaurant, as she would have expected him to do.

With an oh-well shrug, she turned her attention to driving. The hotel wasn't that far, so it stood to reason that Mack had chosen to walk instead of drive. Of course he could be going to look for the women since none of them had returned to the restaurant. Or he might even be looking for Ralph Jones. Either way, just because he'd kissed her, where he went or why, wasn't her concern.

Now if she were really paranoid she might suspect that Mack had only invited her to dinner to thwart Frank's campaign to enlist Belinda's help in persuading Tessa to sign the divorce papers.

Frank shouldn't have aired our family problems in front of you like that. I had hoped that he'd have better manners . . .

Charlotte frowned, recalling what Mack had said. "And I hope I'm wrong about Mack's motives," Charlotte grumbled. Given the lackluster kiss he'd planted on her lips and given the fact that he hadn't bothered to tell her that the dinner included other people, what other conclusion was there? He had probably thought that Frank wouldn't be so crass as to discuss such things with a complete stranger in the group, thus his earlier apology.

"So much for a love life," she murmured.

By the time Charlotte pulled into her driveway, she was more than ready to crawl into bed, and more than ready to forget the entire evening.

Gathering her purse and keys, she stepped out of the van, slammed the door, and locked it. She was almost to the front steps when the door to Louis's half of the double abruptly opened, and Louis strolled onto the porch.

From the look on his face Charlotte strongly suspected that he had been watching and waiting for her to come home. *What now?* She wondered, bracing herself. After the botched dinner date, she wasn't exactly in the mood to hear about Louis's problems with Joyce, not tonight.

"You look nice," he drawled, his eyes giving her the once-over. "Where have you been?"

Ignoring his question, she said, "Thanks," as she climbed the steps. Hoping he'd get the message that she wasn't in the mood for chitchat, when she reached the porch, she walked past him and headed straight for her front door.

"You in a hurry?"

Charlotte sighed. "Only to get to bed. I'm tired, it's been a long day, and I've got to work again tomorrow." *Not that it's any of your business,* she added silently.

"Want some company?"

Charlotte's hand froze as she inserted her house key into the lock. Surely he didn't say what she thought he'd just said, and even if he did say it, he didn't mean it like it sounded . . . Did he?

CHAPTER 6

Charlotte slowly turned to face Louis. "Company?"

A slow, wicked smile pulled at his lips. "I just thought that since it's a nice night out and the mosquitoes aren't too bad, we could sit out here for a while on the swing." He paused, the smile turning into a full-fledged grin. "Why? What did you think I meant?"

Caught. She was caught in a trap of her own making. Already she could feel her cheeks growing warm. "Exactly what you said," she replied a little more sharply than she'd meant to as she spun around to face the door. "Afraid I can't tonight," she said, striving for a more level tone of voice. "Like I said, I'm tired, and I've got to get up early."

She turned the key, and when the lock clicked she turned the doorknob and shoved the door open. "Maybe another time." She stepped inside and firmly closed the door behind her.

As Charlotte threw the deadbolt, she could have sworn that she could hear Louis laughing. "Well, just laugh then. Who cares?" She dropped the keys into her purse and placed the purse on the chair near the door. The whole misunderstanding about what Louis had said was all Mack Sutton's fault anyway. "Thanks, Mack, thanks a lot," she grumbled as she ignored Sweety Boy's squawks for attention and slipped the cover over his cage. If Mack hadn't kissed her, she wouldn't . . .

"Wouldn't what?" she exclaimed, realizing that she wasn't making sense.

"Just go to bed, Charlotte. Go to bed."

But even after her nightly ritual of changing into her pajamas, cleaning her face, and brushing her teeth, she couldn't stop thinking about Louis or wondering what he'd wanted to talk to her about as she climbed into bed.

"Probably just being nosy," she murmured, switching off the lamp beside the bed.

Only on extremely rare occasions did Charlotte ever schedule a job on Sunday. Sundays were always reserved for church and the weekly gathering of her family for lunch after the morning services. It was a tradition that she and her sister Madeline had begun when the children were young, and despite their hectic lives, the tradition still held, with Charlotte and Madeline taking turns hosting lunch. With the family count up to ten, and with yet another baby on the way, the Sunday lunch was no small matter.

Charlotte smiled as she pulled into the hotel parking lot. Just another couple of months and the newest addition to the family was scheduled to make his grand entrance into the world. At times Charlotte could hardly believe that it was actually going to happen, that her son was going to have a son, and that she would, at long last, finally be a grandmother.

Still smiling, she approached the lobby counter to get her room assignments for the day from Claire, the hotel's manager.

Claire was talking on the phone and held up her forefinger indicating that Charlotte should wait.

"Good news," Claire told her as she hung up the receiver. "Carrie sent over one of her former employees who has finally moved back and is ready to work again. Sarah is her name, and she'll be cleaning the first floor today, so all you have to worry about is the second floor."

"That is good news," Charlotte exclaimed, her mind racing ahead. Maybe, just maybe, she'd be able to finish up by lunchtime and make the Sunday family get-together after all.

After gathering the supplies she needed, Charlotte rode the elevator to the second floor. The first two rooms she approached had DO NOT DISTURB signs hanging on the doorknobs. When she realized the next room to be cleaned was room 201, her steps slowed as she pushed the cleaning cart down the hallway, and dread filled her. If she remembered right, 201 was Tessa's room. Maybe she'd get lucky and either Tessa would be out or she wouldn't want to be disturbed.

Since there wasn't a DO NOT DISTURB sign hanging on the doorknob, Charlotte raised her hand to knock on the door. Though muffled, she could hear a raised voice coming from inside.

"What's the meaning of this, Belinda?"

"Great," Charlotte muttered, as she dropped her arm. But even as she stepped back from the door, she could still hear Belinda's response. "You've been snooping in my things?" Belinda accused loudly. "How could you, mother?"

Charlotte grimaced. The last thing she

wanted was to walk in on an argument between mother and daughter. Maybe she should go on to the next room and come back to Tessa's room later. But as she stood there, trying to make up her mind, Tessa shouted, "Good thing I did. I swear I never thought I'd see the day that my own daughter was using drugs."

Charlotte froze. Belinda on drugs? Surely not, she thought. Surely the girl had more sense than that. At least Charlotte hoped she had more sense, for her own sake, as well as for Mack's sake.

"They're just diet pills," Belinda cried. "It's not like I'm shooting heroin or snorting cocaine. They were prescribed by a doctor, and besides, you're always on my case about losing weight. I'd think you'd be happy that I'm finally doing something about it."

Out in the hall Charlotte breathed a sigh of relief. Belinda wasn't on drugs after all. Just a misunderstanding.

"Happy?" Tessa screamed. "Happy that my daughter is a drug addict?"

"I am not a drug addict, Mother!" Belinda screamed back at Tessa. Suddenly, the door burst open, and Belinda stood in the doorway, her back to Charlotte. "I hate you!" She yelled at her mother, and with a sob, she whirled around and ran past Charlotte down the hallway toward the stairs.

"You come back here!" Tessa yelled as she hurried to the door. But when she stepped out into the hallway, the sight of Charlotte brought her up short.

Realizing that Charlotte had witnessed the altercation, a deep flush darkened Tessa's cheeks, and she stiffened. An awkward moment passed, then, Tessa seemed to get control of herself again. "You might as well come on in," she told Charlotte.

"I can come back later," Charlotte offered.

Tessa shook her head. "No, now is as good a time as any." She waved in the general direction of the stairs. "Kids! Nowadays, they have no respect for anyone."

Sounded like the pot calling the kettle black to Charlotte. After all, from what she'd heard, Tessa was the one who had gone snooping through her grown daughter's things.

Tessa sighed heavily. "What's a parent to do?" With a shrug, she turned and walked back inside the room.

Having experienced Tessa's wrath herself, at that moment Charlotte would have rather eaten worms than be in the same room with the woman. Even so, there was no way she could refuse to clean Tessa's room without seeming rude. Bracing herself, she gathered up the cleaning supplies she needed from the supply cart and stepped inside.

Tessa was staring at her reflection in the dresser mirror as she adjusted the red scarf she wore around her neck. "Do you have children?" she asked.

"Yes — a grown son," Charlotte answered as she headed for the bathroom.

"Humph! Just be glad you don't have an ungrateful daughter for a child, though I suppose that technically she's grown too. At least she should be, but sometimes I find it hard to believe, especially when she acts more like a two-year-old throwing a temper tantrum than an eighteen-year-old."

Children learn what they live . . . Monkey see, monkey do.

The moment the old adages popped into Charlotte's head, she bit her bottom lip to keep from voicing the thoughts out loud. *Shame on you, Charlotte LaRue. Judge not lest ye be judged.*

Charlotte rolled her eyes. In her opinion, there were some people who needed to be judged.

But not by you.

Releasing a large sigh, Charlotte finally conceded the argument with her conscience and busied herself cleaning the mirror, the countertop, and the sink. While Charlotte finished cleaning the bathroom, the phone in the bedroom rang a couple of times, but she was grateful that Tessa spoke so low that she couldn't hear her side of the conversation.

By the time Charlotte was ready to start cleaning the bedroom, Tessa had turned on the television. When Charlotte began stripping the sheets off the beds, Tessa seemed to be totally engrossed in the movie she was watching, an old black and white one starring Jimmy Stewart.

"Do you like old movies?" Tessa asked, and without waiting for an answer said, "I love them. And so does Belinda." She waved at a stack of video tapes next to the television. "She found those down in a little shop in the Quarter yesterday."

"There are a few I like," Charlotte said as she shook out a fresh, folded fitted sheet and tugged it onto the mattress. "In fact, Jimmy Stewart was one of my father's favorite actors of all time."

At that moment someone knocked on the door. Tessa pressed the pause button on the TV remote, then called out, "Yes, who's there?"

"Tessa, it's Margaret," a muffled voice answered.

"Oh, well, so much for watching movies," Tessa grumbled as she shoved out of the chair, walked to the door, and opened it.

"I wasn't sure you'd be in," Margaret said as she stepped into the room. "I figured you'd be on the tour with the rest of the group this morning."

"Yes, well, I was scheduled to go, but Belinda and I had words, then the maid showed up to clean, and —" She shrugged as if that explained it all.

Margaret glanced Charlotte's way and Charlotte paused, her gaze meeting Margaret's. Margaret blinked twice, then, without so much as a smile, she turned her attention back to Tessa.

The fact that Margaret didn't acknowledge that they had officially met the night before only bothered Charlotte marginally, as she turned her attention back to straightening the bedspread. It had been her experience that most people usually ignored the maid.

"Have a seat." Tessa motioned toward the chair that she'd just vacated. "Shall I order up some coffee or tea?"

Margaret shook her head as she sat down. "Nothing for me. It hasn't been that long since I had breakfast."

Tessa seated herself in the other lounge

chair. "So, what brings you here this time?" she asked. Motioning towards the briefcase that Margaret had brought in with her, she said, "I guess Frank keeps you hopping these days, what with this expansion and everything. I had thought that you and I would have a chance to visit more while we're here, maybe go to lunch again."

"Yeah, me too," Margaret said. "I'm afraid this isn't a social call though this time." She reached down, opened the briefcase, and extracted two folders from within. Handing one of the folders to Tessa, she said, "This is that background information you asked me to get for you on Lisa, but I've also brought some papers for you to sign."

"Thanks for this." Tessa waved the folder then leaned over and placed it on the nearby desk. "I owe you big time." When she straightened, she tilted her head, narrowed her eyes, and held out her hand for the other folder. "What kind of papers?"

"You know what kind of papers, Tessa. The divorce papers."

Tessa quickly withdrew her hand and shook her head. "Uh-uh. No way. You can just take those right back to him," she retorted. "I don't intend on signing anything without my lawyer's approval. And between you and me, I don't intend on signing any divorce papers period, even if my lawyer does approve. If Frank wants a divorce, he can file for it, instead of making it look like I filed for it."

Margaret reached out and patted Tessa's hand. "I know, and I told him that's what you'd say. I'm just sorry that he's using me as the go-between."

Tessa shook her head. "Don't blame yourself. I don't. I blame Frank. You and I have been friends for a long time — long enough for me to know that this wasn't your idea. You don't like this any more than I do."

"No — no I don't," Margaret concurred. "Between you and me, I think that woman is nothing but a little gold digger."

Though there was no way Charlotte could ignore the conversation, she kept her face as emotionless as possible as she smoothed out the bedspread on the second bed. When seconds later she felt her cell phone vibrating in her pants pocket, she was grateful for an excuse to leave the room. Grabbing up the bundle of dirty sheets off of the floor, she hurried out into the hallway. Dropping the sheets, she pulled out the phone and pressed the TALK button.

"Maid-for-a-Day, Charlotte speaking."

"Charlotte, this is Louis. I-I thought I'd

better let you know what's happening."

Charlotte could count the times on one hand that Louis had called her on her cell phone, and that alone set off alarm bells. "What's wrong?"

"It's Joyce, Charlotte. I'm at the hospital. I had to go to the office this morning, and when I got back home, she was still in bed. When I couldn't wake her, I called 911. The EMTs took her to the Touro."

"Oh, Louis, I'm so sorry. How bad is she?"

"How should I know?" he snapped. "Some doctor I've never heard of is in with her, and no one will tell me anything."

Charlotte winced at the anger she heard in his voice. She'd known Louis long enough to know that when he was really worried about something, the only way he seemed able to express his worry was through anger. Joyce's condition had to be really serious.

"The thing is," he continued, "I've been trying to get in touch with Stephen. He's out of town on business until tomorrow. Either his stupid cell is off or he doesn't have it with him. I left a message on his voice mail and at the hotel where he's staying, but there's no telling when he'll check his messages . . ." Louis's voice trailed away.

"Listen, you hang in there," Charlotte told him. "All you can do — all anyone can do at this point — is pray and hope for the best. Just keep trying to get in touch with Stephen, and —" Charlotte paused. She wanted to offer to go sit with him and be there for him, something she'd do for any friend. But Louis was a proud man, and she wasn't sure how to word the offer without seeming pushy or intrusive. She took a deep breath. *Just do it, Charlotte.* "Would you like some company?"

After what seemed like forever, he finally said, "Yeah," and Charlotte released her breath in a sigh of relief.

"I could use some company about right now," he admitted. "If it's not too much trouble," he added.

Dear Lord in heaven, have mercy, she thought, and for a moment she was speechless. She could hardly believe that Louis had actually just admitted that he needed something or someone.

Charlotte swallowed hard. "Well, th-th-then," she stammered. "It will take a little while, but I'll see you as soon as I can get there." Feeling as though she'd just walked through a minefield, Charlotte pressed the disconnect button and dropped the phone into her pocket. With another sigh, she stared at the door leading to Tessa's room, and her mind jumped into high gear.

All she really had left was dusting and vacuuming Tessa's room. A mental picture of the room flashed through her head. Nothing really looked all that dusty, so maybe she could skip doing that today and just vacuum. Vacuuming wouldn't take long, and once she finished, then, she'd have to find Claire, explain the situation, and hope that leaving would be okay.

Ordinarily, she wouldn't have considered leaving a client in the lurch, but with the arrival of the other maid that Claire had told her about, she figured that just this once would be okay.

"Best get to it," she muttered, eyeing the pile of sheets on the floor. As she was stuffing the sheets into the bag attached to the supply carrier, the door to Tessa's room opened and Margaret backed out into the hallway.

"See you later," she called out to Tessa.

"Thanks again," Tessa replied.

Margaret pulled the door closed behind her, and when she turned and saw Charlotte, she stiffened and her eyes widened with surprise. "Oh, hi. I thought you had left."

"No, I'm not quite finished yet." Charlotte reached for the vacuum cleaner.

"Your name is Charlotte, isn't it?"

"Yes, it is," Charlotte responded.

"Well, listen, Charlotte, I didn't mean to be rude to you in there or ignore you. It's just that Tessa is really touchy about Frank's relationship with Belinda and Mack, and I wasn't sure if she knew that Frank had invited Belinda to join us for dinner last night."

Charlotte shrugged. "No problem. I understand."

"Oh, good." Suddenly Margaret frowned thoughtfully. "Hmm, now that I think about it, I wonder if that was the reason she and Belinda had words earlier. It would be just like Belinda to tell Tessa all about the dinner." She paused, and, staring at Charlotte, she narrowed her eyes. "You didn't happen to overhear what their argument was about, did you?"

Charlotte had several rules that her employees had to abide by, and any infraction of those rules was grounds for immediate dismissal. One of the most important ones was that whatever they overheard was privileged information and not to be repeated or gossiped about.

Instead of answering Margaret's question with an outright lie, Charlotte hedged. "They must have been arguing before I got here."

Margaret's face fell with disappointment. "Oh, well, whatever the problem is I'm sure they'll work it out. Anyway, it was nice seeing you again." And with a too-bright smile she turned and hurried down the hallway.

Since Margaret didn't strike Charlotte as exactly the friendly confiding type, she wasn't quite sure what to make of Margaret's little tête-à-tête. But she didn't have time to worry about it. Louis was waiting.

A minute later and armed with the vacuum cleaner, Charlotte reached for the doorknob and twisted, but the doorknob wouldn't budge. "Great," she muttered, and in her mind's eye she saw Margaret pulling the door shut when she left the room. She'd forgotten that the door automatically locked. With a growl of frustration, Charlotte knocked on the door.

"Yes, who is it?" she heard Tessa call out.

"Hotel maid, ma'am. I still need to vacuum."

"Oh, okay, just a minute."

A few seconds later Tessa opened the door. Giving Charlotte an impatient look, she did an about face and headed for the desk.

While Charlotte quickly vacuumed, Tessa sat at the desk and thumbed through the contents of the file that Margaret had left her.

Charlotte finished vacuuming and unplugged the machine, her mind on finding Claire. She was winding the chord onto the handle when there was suddenly a loud banging on the door.

"Mama, open the door!" Belinda banged on it again. "Open the door!"

"Oh, for pity's sake," Tessa grumbled. "What now?" Shoving out of the chair, she marched over to the door.

The moment she opened it, Belinda rushed into the room, her face flushed and her eyes wide with terror. "She's dead, Mama!"

"What?" Tessa stiffened. "What are you talking about?" She grabbed Belinda by the shoulders. "Who's dead, Belinda?"

"Lisa, Mama! Lisa's dead!"

Charlotte froze, and the color drained from Tessa's face.

Chapter 7

"Oh, dear God," Tessa whispered. Her eyes bright with tears, and her voice shaking, she said, "Are you sure?"

Belinda nodded. "One of the hotel gardeners just found her. Someone said — they said she'd been st-strangled to death."

A momentary look of fright crossed Tessa's pale face and she slowly shook her head from side to side. "This can't be happening," she said, her voice barely above a whisper. Releasing her grip on Belinda, Tessa squeezed her eyes closed and unconsciously rubbed her arms with her hands. "They're going to think I did it."

Still stunned by Belinda's news and her heart heavy over the senseless death of such a young woman, Charlotte watched as Tessa suddenly opened her eyes, turned, and stumbled toward the desk. Her hands were visibly shaking as she began to shove the papers back into the file; half the papers sailed off the desk, scattering on the floor. When Tessa immediately scrambled to pick them up, Charlotte bent down to collect the ones that had landed at her own feet.

Once Charlotte had them in hand, she stood, and with intentions of straightening them before handing them to Tessa, she glanced down at the top page. She hadn't meant to read any of the pages, but the word *adoption* was boldfaced and jumped out at her, piquing her curiosity. Before she had a chance to read more though, Tessa snatched the papers out of her hands and quickly stuffed them back inside the file.

"Mama, what's going on?" Belinda asked, clearly confused at her mother's reaction.

Ignoring Belinda, fresh tears filled Tessa's eyes as she closed the file. Clasping it to her breasts, she turned, and blinking back the tears, she glared at Charlotte. "Are you finished?"

"Ah, yes — yes I am."

"Then, if you don't mind —" Tessa raised one eyebrow expectantly.

At that moment, there was a knock on the door. "Now what?" Tessa moaned.

"Tessa, it's Margaret."

Tessa hurried to the door and opened it. Margaret grabbed Tessa's arm. "Brace yourself," she said. "I was on my way back to my room when I heard that —"

"Lisa was murdered," Tessa said flatly, finishing Margaret's sentence. "Come in. Belinda just told me." She stepped aside for Margaret to enter, then glanced over at Charlotte. "Didn't you say you were finished?"

"Yes, ma'am." Never one to stay where she wasn't welcome, Charlotte grabbed hold of the handle of the vacuum cleaner, walked quickly to the door, then pulled it out into the hallway. Before she could turn to close the door, it shut with a firm click behind her.

Still a bit stunned by what she'd heard and witnessed, Charlotte attached the vacuum to the cleaning supply cart. But as she headed for the elevator, she couldn't stop thinking about Tessa's weird reaction or the papers that she had been so determined to put away out of sight once she'd heard about Lisa's death.

Unless she was mistaken, and she didn't think she was, the scattered papers had been in the same file that Margaret had brought her.

This is that background information you asked me to get for you on Lisa.

At the time, Charlotte hadn't thought too much about why Tessa would want background information on Lisa. But now, after seeing the word "adoption" on one of the papers that she'd picked up, the file had to be important, so important that Tessa had felt that it would somehow incriminate her. But why?

After stashing the cart and supplies in the maintenance closet and retrieving her purse, Charlotte went in search of Claire. She had to keep reminding herself that what Mack's family did or didn't do was none of her business. Nor was Lisa's death, adoption, or anything else any of her business. Right now, she needed to concentrate on Louis and Joyce. Even so, there was no way she could completely shrug off what had happened. A young woman's life had been snuffed out. And if that wasn't enough, everywhere Charlotte looked, hotel guests were gathered in groups buzzing with speculation about the murdered woman, and uniformed police roamed the hallways. As she passed by the entrance to the lounge, she recognized Frank Morgan seated near the doorway. Across from him was yet another policeman.

When she finally located Claire in the lobby, there were several people surrounding her. Charlotte recognized two of the men as NOPD detectives, and she suspected that at least three out of the group were reporters. She figured that the others hanging around the fringe of the group were, more than likely, hotel guests.

As Charlotte stood, waiting and hoping for a chance to talk to Claire, she admired the way the young manager handled herself. Instead of wringing her hands and looking harassed as someone else in her position might have done, Claire seemed composed and completely in charge of the situation.

Several minutes passed before Charlotte finally caught Claire's eye. Claire nodded at Charlotte, then said, "Excuse me just a minute," to the man she had been talking to. Without waiting for his permission, she stepped over to where Charlotte was standing. "Yes, Charlotte, what do you need?"

"First of all, is it true? Was a guest found strangled on the premises?"

Claire nodded. "Afraid so. She was found in the middle of the azalea bushes near the patio extension of the hotel restaurant."

"When do they think it happened?"

"From what I'm hearing, they think it happened around nine o'clock last night."

Charlotte swallowed hard. Lisa was murdered not long after she had volunteered to go after Belinda. And Christopher had followed her.

"Is there anything else?"

Charlotte shook herself out of her reverie, and though she suspected that she already knew the answer, she decided to ask anyway. "I need to leave — an emergency of sorts — but I can come back and finish up here later."

Claire sighed and shook her head. "Sorry, but that won't be possible, not for a while anyway. The entire hotel, the guests, and the employees have been sequestered for questioning. Now, if there's nothing else —"

"In that case, should I keep cleaning?"

Claire shook her head. "No, I don't think so. I think the detectives want to search the rooms. But that's a good question." She held up her forefinger. "Tell you what, let me check on that and get back to you. Wait right here just a minute."

Charlotte watched as Claire walked over to one of the men she'd been speaking with earlier. After talking to him a moment, she turned toward Charlotte and slowly shook her head. "No cleaning," she mouthed.

With a grimace, Charlotte nodded to let Claire know that she understood. "Now what?" she muttered, tapping her foot impatiently as she glanced around for a place to sit. Would the detectives question the guests first or the staff? Selfishly, she hoped they questioned the staff first so that she could leave.

Since all of the seats in the lobby were taken, she headed for the restaurant. Inside, the crowded restaurant was noisy with the buzz of voices and the clatter of dishes. As Charlotte scanned the room for a vacant table, Simone the hostess approached her. As before, Simone was decked out in all black. "Sorry, Charlotte," she said, "but all of the tables are full, and there's a waiting list a mile long."

"Even the patio?" Charlotte asked.

Simone visible shuddered. "No one's allowed out there. That's where they found that poor woman's body."

Charlotte smacked her forehead. "Well, duh, of course it is. I don't know what I was thinking."

"Tell you what though," Simone said, "you might find an extra chair available in the lounge next door down. That's where most of the staff is hanging out."

"Thanks," Charlotte said.

When Charlotte entered the lounge, she immediately spotted an empty chair at the bar and made a beeline for it. Since Charlotte had only worked at the hotel a couple of days, she really didn't know any of the staff, so she couldn't tell if the man on her right and the woman on her left worked there or were guests. Since neither did more than nod, she didn't feel obligated to make conversation.

After ordering a cup of coffee, Charlotte fingered the cell phone in her pocket. Should she call Louis and let him know why she was delayed, or should she just wait and hope that one of the detectives got around to questioning her pretty soon? If she called him though, he might know something about Joyce's condition by now. Suddenly she frowned. Had Louis called on his cell phone or from the hospital phone?

Charlotte knew there were ways of finding the phone number of the last call on her cell phone, but she'd only read the book that came with the phone just enough to know how to make and answer calls. Any other functions of the cell would be just guesswork on her part. Of course she could always find a phone directory and look up the hospital number that way.

She was still debating whether to look for a phone directory when the bartender set a cup of coffee in front of her. "Thanks," she told him.

Charlotte was on her second cup of coffee, and having decided against calling, she was growing more impatient with each passing minute when she felt a tap on her shoulder.

With a frown, she swiveled around. At the sight of the man standing behind her, a feeling of dread lodged in the pit of her stomach. In her mind she could still hear what he'd said to her during their last encounter. *Ah-ha! Now I know why your name sounds so familiar. You're that maid.*

"That maid" indeed, she thought, cringing as she remembered the night that she and homicide detective Gavin Brown had met. Then, like now, was because of a murder, and from the expression on his face, this time wasn't going to be any better than the other time.

"Why, Ms. LaRue," he drawled, "why am I not surprised to find you at the scene of another murder? Seems you have a knack for being in the wrong place at the wrong time."

Same sarcastic jerk, she thought. Never mind that he was right, but that wasn't *her* fault.

The only reason you aren't being arrested too is because of your niece Judith.

Again, recalling their last meeting and how nasty he'd been, Charlotte glowered at him.

Gavin Brown's lips thinned with disapproval. "So, what brings you to the Jazzy?"

he sneered.

"I work here," Charlotte retorted.

Narrowing his eyes, his expression grew grim. "That's what I was afraid you were going to say. Come on then." He tilted his head toward the door. "We might as well get this over with."

"The sooner the better," Charlotte muttered. Pulling the strap of her purse over her shoulder and coffee in hand, she followed the detective to one of the two rooms on the ground floor that had been designated as office space. Once inside, Gavin Brown closed the door and motioned for Charlotte to be seated in the chair facing the desk.

Instead of taking a seat behind the desk, he crossed his arms and perched on the front edge of the desk so that he towered over her, forcing her to look up at him.

Immediately recognizing the ploy of intimidation from all the mystery books she'd read and the TV reruns of *NYPD* and *Law and Order* that she'd watched, it was all that she could do to keep from laughing at him.

"So how long have you worked here?" he asked.

"Counting today, three days," she responded.

"Kind of a step down for you, isn't it, after

working for the mob?"

Charlotte ground her teeth at his jibe. In an attempt to keep her temper under control, she silently counted to ten. Losing her temper would only drag things out. Finally, with a forced smile and attempting to keep her voice steady, she simply said, "Like the job I had for the Rossis, the hotel job is *temporary.* I'm doing a friend a favor until her regular help comes back."

"So, Charlotte, what can you tell me about the woman who was murdered?"

She could have told him plenty. She could have told him that Lisa was a married man's mistress, and she could have told him that she suspected that it was possible Lisa was blackmailing Mack.

We could always make this Lisa person disappear . . . Permanently . . . We could do it and no one would be the wiser.

Charlotte almost smiled. She could also tell him about the Red Scarf women plotting Lisa's demise.

But Louis was waiting and she was anxious to see if Joyce was okay. Besides, she didn't like Gavin Brown. He was an arrogant, sarcastic, pain in the butt, and everything she knew about Lisa was hearsay anyway, just second-hand information. As for the Red Scarf women, even the thought of them actually murdering someone was ludicrous.

Charlotte simply shrugged. "Sorry, but I'm afraid I can't tell you anything. I don't know the woman who was murdered. I'm just the maid."

But Gavin Brown didn't give up so easily. For the next twenty minutes he continued grilling Charlotte, asking the same stupid questions over and over until she began to suspect that he was doing it just to be hateful.

"Okay," he finally told her. "You can leave now." He held out his business card. "But if you think of anything — anything at all, call me."

"What? No threats to have me arrested if I leave town?" The minute she uttered the words, she wished she hadn't.

"Well," he drawled, "that can be arranged."

Charlotte snatched the card, but as she hurried from the room, a slow smile pulled at her lips. Maybe she would call him later. She could say that she'd thought of something to tell him. Then she could tell him that he was a scumbag jerk and hang up the phone.

Shame, shame, shame on you . . . do unto others . . .

Charlotte immediately sobered as the golden rule came to mind. When had she become so intolerant? After all, a woman had been murdered, and whether she liked him or not, whether she approved of his methods or not, the detective was just doing his job.

"Charlotte! Hey, Charlotte, wait up."

Recognizing the booming voice as belonging to Carrie Rodgers, Charlotte stopped. When she turned, sure enough, Carrie was walking towards her.

Charlotte had always thought that Carrie matched her voice perfectly. A tall, stout woman in her fifties, with short, salt-and-pepper hair, she was aggressive and had a no-nonsense business attitude that had served her well despite her heart of gold.

"Hi, Carrie. What are you doing here?"

"Bad news travels fast," Carrie said. "So, what's the scoop? Know anything about the dead woman?"

Ever aware of the passing time, Charlotte shook her head. "Not really, just hearsay and a bit of gossip."

Carrie frowned. "Sarah — the other maid I'm using temporarily — said the same thing. Have you met Sarah yet?"

Charlotte shook her head. "No, I haven't — not yet."

"Well, do me a favor and make it a point to meet her. I'm thinking about keeping her on full-time and would love to get your impressions of her."

"Will do," Charlotte agreed. "Listen, I hate to run off, but I'm in kind of a hurry."

"Nothing's wrong, I hope. Your family's okay?"

"Everyone's fine. It's just that a friend of mine has had an emergency, and I promised I'd help out."

Carrie nodded. "See you later, then. And call me once you've met Sarah."

"Sure thing," Charlotte said. Glancing at her watch, she groaned and hurried out the door. Two hours had passed since she'd told Louis that she would come to the hospital as soon as possible. By now, anything could have happened. Charlotte shuddered, and dread mingled with sadness weighed heavily on her heart and mind. By now, Joyce could even be dead.

She picked up her pace, almost to a slow jog. By the time she reached the hotel parking lot, she was breathing hard, a reminder that of late she'd been neglecting her daily walk.

Earlier, when she'd parked her van, the parking area had been almost empty, but now it was full.

Charlotte stopped to catch her breath. If she remembered right, she'd parked on the far side of the lot near the Dumpster. Sure enough, once she crossed the lot she immediately spotted the van. As she hurried around to the driver's side, she suddenly froze in her tracks.

A woman standing on a small ladder was digging in the Dumpster, and though the woman was bent over the edge with her back to Charlotte, Charlotte still recognized her. "Judith?" she called out.

Charlotte's niece froze. "Aunt Charley?" Judith glanced over her shoulder, a puzzled look on her face. "What are you doing here?" She dusted her gloved hands, then stepped down off of the ladder and walked over to Charlotte.

Charlotte gave Judith a brief explanation of her temporary job at the hotel, and then motioned toward the Dumpster. "What are you looking for?"

"You know about the murder."

Charlotte nodded. "Yes, that rude detective Brown has already interrogated me."

"Now, Aunt Charley, Gavin is just doing his job. Besides, we don't *interrogate* possible witnesses. We question them."

"Hmph! Says you."

"Aw, come on, Auntie."

Charlotte sighed. "Oh, all right." Not really wanting to discuss Gavin Brown, she motioned again at the Dumpster. "So what does the Dumpster have to do with the murder?"

"I'm looking for a stolen security tape," Judith explained. "The brass has pulled out all the stops on this one, and I was drafted to help."

"How is Brian? I haven't seen him in a while." Brian Lee was Judith's partner, a nice-looking young man with sad, world-weary eyes.

"He's fine now. He had some surgery though and had to take a few weeks off."

Charlotte nodded then motioned at the Dumpster. "So what about the security tape?"

"The hotel has security cameras that scan the grounds of the hotel," Judith continued, "but the particular tape to the one that scans the murder vicinity is missing. It's possible that the perp might have thrown it away. We've already searched all the trashcans inside the hotel, so that leaves only the Dumpster as a possibility."

"Wouldn't that be kind of stupid? Surely the killer would know that the Dumpster would be searched?"

Judith laughed. "You'd be surprise at how

stupid most criminals are."

"Maybe so, but isn't it more feasible that the killer would have taken it with him and disposed of it elsewhere? And as for the hotel trashcans, there are at least a thousand other places a tape could have been hidden in the hotel besides trashcans."

Judith sighed with impatience. "Yes, Auntie, I realize that, but we have to start somewhere, and as we speak, we've got uniforms searching room by room."

Charlotte frowned, her mind going back over what Judith had said earlier. "Surely there was someone monitoring the cameras?"

"Yes, there was — a security guard."

"Well, he should know what happened to the tape, shouldn't he?"

Judith sighed again. "Ordinarily he would, but either unfortunately, or by design, he was called away for a disturbance inside the restaurant."

"What kind of disturbance?"

"Not that it's really your concern — and don't you dare interfere with this investigation — but two women were arguing. Bottom line is, the tapes were left unguarded for a short while. Since the original tape was replaced with one that only started recording after the time frame in which the murder occurred, we figure that the murderer switched the tapes."

Charlotte suddenly felt a chill. "If that's true, then it means that whoever murdered Lisa must have planned it down to every little detail. And for your information, young lady, I have never interfered with an investigation, not on purpose."

"Yeah, right."

"Well, almost never."

Judith narrowed her eyes suspiciously. "You called the dead woman by name. Sounds like you knew her. Did you tell Gavin that you knew her?"

Immediately realizing her mistake and wishing she'd kept her mouth shut, Charlotte shook her head. "No, I didn't tell him I knew her because I don't. Not exactly."

"And just what does "not exactly" mean, Auntie?"

Charlotte lowered her gaze and pretended to examine her thumbnail. She was caught. *Now what?* "Well . . ." she drawled, her mind racing as she stalled for time to think. Should she or shouldn't she? Maybe if she only admitted part of the truth, she wouldn't have to listen to a lecture from Judith. Deciding that her niece would probably find out anyway, she finally said, "I did have dinner with her last night."

"What!"

"Not exactly with *just* her," she quickly added. "I met an old friend the other day, and he invited me to dinner last night. But the dinner turned out to be a business thing that included several other people, and Lisa was one of those people."

"And what else, Auntie?"

"What do you mean?"

"You know good and well what I mean. What else do you know about the dead woman? And how did you know that the woman at the dinner was the same one who was murdered?"

Charlotte shrugged. "I don't." When Charlotte saw the skeptical look on her niece's face, she said, "Listen, Judith, like I said, I don't know anything else. Since I was the outsider, I was introduced to everyone, including a woman named Lisa. I just assumed that since it was a business dinner that all of the dinner guests were staying at the hotel, just as I assumed that the woman I met was the same Lisa who was murdered. Now, I really need to go. Louis called me earlier and Joyce is in the hospital in critical condition. I told Louis that I would come sit with him."

"Did you tell Gavin about having dinner with the dead woman?"

"No, but she wasn't dead when I had dinner with her."

"Aunt Charlotte, you know good and well that's not what I meant. You're just being stubborn. As usual," she added, clearly frustrated.

"Yeah, well, sorry, hon, but I do have other things on my mind right now, and we can talk about this later. Can I go now?"

"Go then. For now. But we will definitely talk about this again, Auntie. My gut tells me that you know more than you're telling."

"Maybe it's just gas. Try some Pepto-Bismol."

The look on Judith's face was priceless.

Charlotte chuckled. "Sorry, I couldn't resist."

Judith pointed at Charlotte's van. "Go! Go now, before I forget that you're my aunt and that I love you."

As Charlotte turned and hurried around to the driver's door, Judith called out, "Give my best to Louis, Auntie, and let me know how Joyce is doing."

Though the drive to the hospital was a short one, and she should have been concentrating on Joyce and Louis, Charlotte couldn't stop thinking about Lisa. Granted, what she knew about the woman was only hearsay and speculation, but if even half of it were true, then there were plenty of suspects, Tessa for one. After all, an older woman trying to hang on to her younger husband has a lot of motive. Still, there was Christopher, Lisa's ex-boyfriend. Maybe he'd decided that if he couldn't have Lisa, then nobody could. And she did see him follow Lisa when Lisa went after Belinda, just an hour or so before Lisa was murdered.

Charlotte turned into the hospital parking lot and parked the van.

And what about Mack? Unless she'd misunderstood the conversation between Mack and Belinda, it sounded like Lisa could have been blackmailing Mack. But why?

Though Charlotte couldn't completely dismiss her old friend from the suspect list, she felt like a hypocrite even thinking that he could be the murderer.

With a sigh, she climbed out of the van and locked the door. As she headed across the parking lot, a thoughtful frown marred her face. Though she hated to think it, another prime suspect was Belinda. The girl evidently loved her parents but was being used as a pawn by both of them — a daughter caught in the middle of warring parents — and all because of Lisa.

Then, there was Margaret, Frank's so-called "right-hand-man." Like Belinda, Margaret was another victim caught in the cross-fire between Tessa and Frank: employed by Frank, but friends with Tessa. The only problem with Margaret being a suspect was motive, and at the moment, Charlotte couldn't think of one. It wasn't like Frank's affair with Lisa presented any threat to Margaret's employment or anything.

Charlotte's forehead furrowed in a frown. But there was another problem as well. Lisa would have put up a fight, wouldn't she? Whoever killed her would have had to overpower her, not to mention that strangling her would have required that the killer have strong hands. Not that she'd had any first-hand experience, but she imagined that strangling someone would take a lot of strength . . . a man's strength? If that were the case, then wouldn't that fact alone eliminate any of the women as suspects? Then again, some women were a lot stronger than they appeared to be . . . especially if several had ganged up on Lisa.

A mental image of the Red Scarf group surrounding Tessa came to mind. "Don't be stupid," she whispered. The women had been joking. Besides, they'd be too afraid of breaking a fingernail to do anything as physical as choking someone to death.

Charlotte could feel the beginnings of a headache. Maybe like Miss Scarlett O'Hara in *Gone with the Wind,* she'd think about it all tomorrow.

With a shake of her head, she entered the hospital and went in search of Louis.

Chapter 8

Thoughts about Lisa's murder weren't as easy to dismiss as Charlotte would have hoped. Like a dog that wouldn't let go of a bone, she mentally reviewed each of the suspects and their motives again. When the elevator dinged a second time, she suddenly realized that she'd missed getting off on the floor where the ICU was located and had to ride the elevator all the way to the top floor, then back down again. When she finally located the ICU waiting room, it was empty except for Louis.

The moment she saw him, sympathy seared her heart. He was seated on a small vinyl sofa and slumped forward, his elbows propped on his thighs and his hands supporting his bowed head.

Charlotte hurried over and sat down beside him. "Oh, Louis, I'm so sorry."

He removed one of his hands and turned his head sideways to look at her.

"It took longer than I'd expected to get away," she explained.

For several moments she waited, hoping that he would volunteer information about Joyce's condition or at least say something, but his only reaction was a slight shrug, as if to say, no big deal.

Though his attitude stung a bit, especially after all the trouble she'd had getting there, for the moment she ignored it.

"So — how is Joyce?"

"She'll recover," he finally answered, his tone flat, his expression grim.

"Well, now, that's good news, isn't it?"

"Yeah, right, just peachy-keen news."

Totally bewildered by his sarcastic attitude, she said, "For Pete's sake, Louis, what's wrong with you?"

Louis abruptly straightened in his chair and crossed his arms over his chest. His eyes narrowed and a muscle tightened in his jaw. "Don't push, Charlotte." His words were clipped and his voice deadly soft. "Right now I'm so mad I could chew nails."

Charlotte swallowed hard. She'd seen Louis angry before. She'd even been the object of his anger on several occasions. But this was different. This was a side of Louis that she'd never seen before, a very scary side. "What on earth is going on?" she whispered.

Louis switched his gaze to stare straight ahead and heaved a sigh. "When she was admitted through the ER, they couldn't get in touch with her regular doctor. He was off to some medical convention or something. Anyway, the admitting doctor took over her case." He paused. A muscle jumped in his jaw and his hands doubled into fists. "She's not dying," he finally said. "She's been faking it all along."

"What!" Charlotte was stunned. "What do you mean, 'she's been faking it?' "

He turned to glare at her. "It was a scam from the beginning. She was broke and tired of eating out of garbage cans. She knew that having a terminal illness was the only way I'd take her back. And she was right.

"Like a moron I fell for it. The only thing wrong with Joyce is that she's a drunk, a lousy lying drunk who needs to be put away to dry out." He let loose a bark of self-deprecatory laughter. "Know why I couldn't wake her up?" Without waiting for an answer, he said, "I couldn't wake her because she'd drunk herself into a stupor then passed out cold. By the time I got there she was near comatose."

"But didn't you talk to her other doctor?" Charlotte asked, not quite able to take it all in. "Surely he wouldn't have lied about her condition. And she looked so sick all of the time."

Louis shook his head. "The other doctor didn't lie, but then I never talked to him, not directly. All of my information came second-hand from Joyce. As for Joyce really looking sick, she's a makeup artist. That's what she did when she first moved to California before she became a drunk. She worked as a freelance makeup artist."

Charlotte's head was spinning as she tried to wrap her brain around what Louis was saying. "So — let me get this straight. Joyce doesn't have cirrhosis of the liver, and this whole time she's been faking it?"

"You've got it."

Charlotte could hardly believe her ears. What kind of woman would lead her ex-husband, her son, and even her granddaughter to believe that she was dying? "That's horrible."

"Tell me about it."

For several moments neither of them said anything. Charlotte waffled between being furious with Joyce and feeling sorry for Louis. He was such a proud man, one on whom the jacket of humiliation didn't fit well at all.

Charlotte reached out and squeezed Louis's arm. "I'm so sorry you've had to go through this. So what now?"

"Right now I'd like to wring her scrawny neck and choke the life out of her."

Charlotte shuddered as Louis's angry words conjured up a mental image of Lisa. Someone had wrung her neck and choked the life out of her. "Don't, Louis," Charlotte told him. "Don't even think like that."

"Can't help but think it. Doesn't mean I'd do it. I ought to throw her out and be done with it, but for Stephen's sake, I'll make sure she gets into one those detox programs. After that, I'm done with her, and she's on her own."

"Speaking of Stephen, what will you tell him?" In addition to her other sins against her son, now Joyce had added the lie of all lies to the list.

Louis shrugged. "I honestly don't know. Stephen's a grown man, but he seems to have a blind spot where Joyce is concerned. Even knowing what she did before — deserting us and all when he was a kid — he still loves her." Louis's expression turned hard. "One thing I do know: I plan to do everything within my power to make sure that she never gets the chance to hurt him again."

Charlotte winced at the venom in Louis's

voice, and swallowed hard. Time to change the subject. Past time. "Have you had anything to eat today?"

He shrugged. "I can't remember, but I'm not hungry."

"Well, that's just too bad." Charlotte stood, reached down, grabbed his hand, and tugged. "Come on. I'll buy you a late lunch. I hear the cafeteria here has pretty decent food."

All through lunch, the temptation to tell Louis about Lisa's murder nagged at Charlotte. According to Judith, Louis had been one of the best homicide detectives the NOPD had before he'd retired.

But Charlotte resisted. In addition to being a cracker-jack detective, she knew for a fact that Louis was also a die-hard chauvinist who believed that civilians like her should mind their own business and leave the detective work to the professionals. Besides which, he had enough on his mind dealing with the ramifications of Joyce's deceit.

Though Louis more or less picked at his food, by the end of lunch he seemed to be a bit more calm and in control.

"I really appreciate you coming by, Charlotte," he told her as they rode the elevator back up to the ICU waiting room. "But there's no use in you hanging around here if you've got something else to do. If it weren't for Stephen, believe me, I'd be gone in a heartbeat."

Charlotte wasn't quite sure how to answer him. She didn't want to be in the way, but she really hated for him to sit and stew about the situation all by himself.

The elevator dinged and the doors slid open. "I'll stay for a little while," she finally said as they stepped out of the elevator. "Who knows, maybe Stephen got your message and is on his way back even now."

"It's possible, I suppose. He was just going up to Baton Rouge for a couple of days. Some of his paintings are in a gallery there, and there was going to be a showing tonight."

Louis reached and pulled the waiting room door open, then he froze and uttered a rude expletive.

"What's wrong?"

With his head, he motioned toward the inside of the room. "Stephen's here. I knew I shouldn't have left," he muttered. "I knew it."

Stephen was seated in the waiting room, his back to the door. Seated beside him was his wife, and across from him was a man dressed in a white coat.

"I was hoping to talk to him first," Louis said, "before the doctor got hold of him."

"My fault," Charlotte murmured. "I'm so sorry. Maybe I should go, and leave you and Stephen to sort this out.

For an answer, Louis placed his hand firmly against the small of her back and nudged her through the doorway.

"Guess I'll stay," she said. Whether he was unable or unwilling to outright say he needed her support, she knew that the gesture was his way of telling her that he did, and there was no way that Charlotte could refuse to go with him.

By the time Charlotte left the hospital that evening, she felt as if she'd been wrung out to dry. She'd run the gamut of emotions, first with finding out about Lisa's murder, and then, dealing with Louis and his anger. But the worst was witnessing Stephen's stunned reaction upon discovering his mother's deception.

But now, away from it all, guilt reared its ugly head. Just as no one was all good, Charlotte had always believed that no one was all bad either. For as far back as she could remember she'd been taught that no one was beyond redemption. Even prisoners on death row could be redeemed. They still had to pay for their crimes against man, but their souls could be redeemed.

She also believed that without forgiveness, all that was left was bitterness. From experience she knew that bitterness only festered, ruining the lives of those who were unwilling to forgive.

She should have said as much to Louis and to Stephen. Still, maybe it wasn't too late. Maybe, when the time was right and she got over her own urge to join Louis in wringing Joyce's neck, she'd get another chance. At least she prayed she would, not only for Joyce's sake but also for Stephen and Louis's as well.

As for Lisa's murder, for once she should listen to Judith and Louis, and let the professionals handle things.

Home never looked so good, as Charlotte unlocked the front door, went inside, and switched on the light.

"Hey, Sweety, did you miss me?" Charlotte locked and bolted the door, set her purse on a nearby chair, then slipped off her shoes and stepped into her moccasins.

The little parakeet ruffled his feathers and sidled over towards the door of the cage. But instead of his usual chatter, he simply stared at her expectantly.

"What? The cat got your tongue? Or are you pouting?" She poked her forefinger into the cage and rubbed his head. Guilt tugged at her conscience. Normally, every day or so, she'd let him out of his cage to fly around the room for a while, but lately, there just didn't seem like enough time to do anything but work.

"Sorry, boy, can't let you out tonight. I'm going to bed, just as soon as I get a bite to eat and check my messages. Soon though, I promise."

Withdrawing her finger and ignoring Sweety Boy's squawks of protest, she headed for her desk. When she saw that the light on her answering machine was blinking, she sighed, and for a moment she was tempted to ignore it.

"Maybe something to eat first," she muttered. But as she headed for the kitchen, she did an about face and went into her bedroom instead. "Pajamas first, then food."

As she undressed, her gaze strayed to the bathroom door. Normally, after working all day, the first thing she did when she got home was take a shower, but tonight she was just too tired to even think about it.

In the kitchen she warmed up a can of soup and made herself half a turkey sandwich. In hopes of taking her mind off the day's events, she took the food and a glass of skim milk into the living room and switched on the television. After channel surfing for several minutes and finding nothing of interest, she finally settled for watching the rebroadcast of the local news as she ate her food.

Halfway through her meal and bored with the news, her gaze strayed to her desk and the blinking light on her message machine. According to the number of blinks, she had at least four messages.

Curiosity, along with a healthy imagination, had always been one of Charlotte's failings. At least that's how she viewed it. And now was no exception. Once she'd entered the hospital, she'd had to turn off her cell phone. What if her family had called? There could have been an emergency . . .

Setting her plate down, she pressed the MUTE button on the remote, then walked over to the desk and pressed the PLAY button on the answering machine.

"Mom, just checking in with you. We missed you today. Love you."

As the brief message ended, Charlotte smiled. "I missed you too, son." Then the machine beeped, and the next message played.

"Hi, Auntie."

Judith. Charlotte grimaced.

"I don't have but a second," Judith said, "but I was wondering how Joyce was doing and how Louis was holding up? Let me know what's happening when you get home. Love you. Bye."

Charlotte glanced at the cuckoo clock hanging behind the sofa. Eight o'clock wasn't that late. She could return Judith's call. Charlotte grimaced. She loved her niece like a daughter, but Judith was the last person she wanted to talk to at the moment, especially since there was a good possibility that Judith probably would grill her again about Lisa's murder.

The machine beeped. "Charlotte, this is Carrie. Claire called me and said that the police are still snooping around. One of the detectives told her that they'd be finished by noon tomorrow, so, bottom line, don't bother going into work until noon. Thanks, and see you soon. Hmm, guess I'm a poet and don't know it."

Carrie's little joke made Charlotte smile. Then, the machine beeped again, and after the mechanical voice stated the time and date, for several seconds no one talked. Figuring that the caller must have hung up, she reached for the DELETE button. Then she heard the sound of breathing and her hand froze in midair.

"Oh, wonderful," she grumbled. "Just what I need tonight — a heavy breather." Tapping her foot with impatience, she listened for a few seconds longer in hopes that she was wrong, but the breathing only grew louder.

Just as she was trying to figure out whether the breather was male or female, the call abruptly ended, and the mechanical voice of the message machine voice said, "You have no more messages." But as she listened to the various options, then pressed the DELETE button, an uneasy feeling crawled up her spine.

"You'd think people would have better things to do," she muttered. Still glaring at the message machine, Charlotte's eyes narrowed in thought. Unlike in the past, nowadays there were ways to find out who called. If she remembered right, all she had to do was dial star sixty-nine to get the phone number of the last person who placed the call. Or she could probably find it on her caller I.D., if she knew how to operate the ding-dang thing.

Since figuring out the caller I.D. would require reading the directions in the booklet she'd gotten, Charlotte picked up the receiver and tapped out star sixty-nine instead. Then she grabbed a pen and notepad and waited.

"The last number that called your line was . . ."

Along with the date and time, Charlotte scribbled down the number on the notepad.

"To call this number, enter one," the voice continued. "Otherwise, hang up now."

Still staring at the number, Charlotte hung up the receiver. "Different area code," she murmured, not recognizing the phone number.

Maybe if she actually called the number . . .

And say what?

"I don't know," she muttered. She could always simply say, who is this? But if the breather had caller I.D. and saw that she was calling, he wasn't likely to fess up and tell her his name. Then again, though highly unlikely, she just might recognize the voice when he said, hello.

"Don't be stupid, Charlotte. They wouldn't say hello if they see your number on the caller I.D. They probably wouldn't even answer the call."

Finally, with a shrug of annoyance, she walked over to the sofa, picked up the remote, and turned off the television. Having lost her appetite, she took her dirty dishes to the kitchen. After dumping the uneaten food into the trashcan, she loaded the dishes into the dishwasher. Once she'd finished her nightly chores of preparing the coffeepot and covering Sweety Boy's cage she headed for the bathroom.

By the time that Charlotte finally climbed into bed, all she wanted was to forget everything and sleep. But as she lay there in the dark, she couldn't stop thinking about the heavy breather or the other events of the day . . . Lisa . . . Joyce . . . Louis and Stephen . . .

As for the heavy breather, who knew what that was all about? The breather could have been just someone waiting in hopes that she was screening her calls and would pick up.

Nothing is ever as it seems or as it first appears to be.

"Yeah, yeah," she mumbled as the phrase swirled in her head. But sometimes, things were exactly as they seemed, she countered. Then, punching her pillow, she tried to find a more comfortable position in the bed.

She was just beginning to relax when she heard the sound of a car door slamming. Charlotte went stone still, her ears tuned to any sound out of the ordinary. What if the heavy breather wasn't just someone waiting for her to pick up the phone? What if the breather was a thief checking to see if she was home so that he could rob her?

Yeah, right. If someone was bent on mischief, they wouldn't be slamming a car door and they'd see that her van was parked in the driveway. Besides, Louis was just next door, and all she had to do was scream . . .

But Louis wasn't next door. He was still at the hospital.

"Oh, for pity's sake." She threw back the cover and tiptoed quietly into the living room. The car door slamming was probably just Louis coming home from the hospital, but she'd never rest until she checked it out.

Just as she reached for the curtain to peek out of the front window, the front porch creaked and she froze.

Chapter 9

Outside, the porch creaked again, and Charlotte held her breath until she heard the jangle of keys. A lock clicked, and a door opened and closed.

Louis.

Charlotte gasped for air. For Pete's sake, it *was* only Louis, after all. Duh!

Feeling like a fool and aggravated that she'd let the silly breather call get to her, Charlotte headed back to the bedroom. Praying that she could fall asleep, she climbed into bed again. Nights like this one made her wish that she had a prescription for sleeping pills.

On Monday, by the time that Charlotte turned into the hotel driveway, she felt as if she'd already put in a full day's work. Like Sweety Boy, her house had been neglected of late, and she'd spent her morning off cleaning it.

As she drove back to the parking area, the first thing she noticed was the yellow and black crime scene tape that cordoned off the area around the azaleas.

Once she'd parked, she headed for the lobby in search of Claire. Claire was surrounded by a small group of hotel guests.

"I can assure you that everything is under control," Claire told the group. "We've brought in extra security to patrol the grounds."

Once Charlotte caught Claire's eye, Claire excused herself from the group and walked over to where Charlotte was standing. Up close, Charlotte couldn't help noticing the dark circles beneath Claire's eyes. "Rough night?" she asked.

Claire gave her a tired smile. "I've had better, but thank goodness most of our guests have decided to stay, in spite of what happened."

"Did the police ever find the missing security tape?" Charlotte asked.

"How did you know about that?"

"My niece is a detective with the NOPD, and I ran into her yesterday as I was leaving."

Claire frowned in thought. "So that's why she looked so familiar? I nearly drove myself crazy yesterday trying to place where I had seen her before, and now I know."

Charlotte smiled. "Yes, we've been told that we favor each other." The fact that Judith favored Charlotte in looks more than she favored her own mother had always been a sore subject with Madeline. "So, did they find the tape?"

Claire shook her head. "Not as far as I know."

"That's too bad," Charlotte murmured.

"Yes, it is. Catching the murderer would put everyone's mind at ease. Anyway — let's get you your room assignments."

Charlotte followed Claire to the front desk where Claire retrieved a clipboard. "By the way, the guest in this room —" Claire pointed to one of Charlotte's assigned rooms, and Charlotte immediately recognized the room number as the one in which Tessa and Belinda were staying. "She called and said that her trashcan is missing and she needs a new one for her room."

Charlotte frowned. "Why on earth would a trashcan come up missing?"

Claire shrugged. "What with the police searching everything, they probably just forgot to put it back yesterday. Anyway, there are some extras in the storage closet."

Charlotte nodded, and when she left Claire, she went to the storage closet to collect her cleaning supplies. Once she'd loaded the cart with the supplies she'd need, along with fresh towels, washclothes, and sheets, she added an extra trashcan to the cart then headed for the first room on her list.

Since there was no DO NOT DISTURB sign on the door, she knocked, and called out, "House Cleaning." Waiting a few minutes, she knocked again, just to be sure. When no one responded, she let herself inside with a master key.

At first glance the room wasn't a total wreck, just a bit messy. But it smelled.

Charlotte walked over to the bathroom and peeked inside. For several moments, all she could do was stare in horror.

Dirty towels and washcloths had been carelessly thrown on the floor, the sink countertop was smeared with toothpaste and what appeared to be dried shaving cream, and flecks of God only knew what dotted the mirror. The bottom of the bathtub was coated with a fine layer of grime, but worst of all, either the toilet was broken or the occupant simply hadn't bothered to flush it . . . or close the lid.

Wrinkling her nose against the smell and trying not to gag, Charlotte pulled on a pair of rubber gloves. Wishing she'd thought to bring a biohazard suit like the ones they'd used in the aftermath of Hurricane Katrina, she reached out and flushed the toilet.

Nope, the toilet wasn't broken. It flushed just fine. "Disgusting," she grumbled as she poured bowl cleaner into the toilet. "Totally disgusting."

Once the toilet was clean, she started on the rest of the room. Though she tried concentrating on Louis's situation with Joyce, her mind kept straying to the different events that had led up to Lisa's murder.

The first thing that came to mind was Tessa's hissy fit on that first day, and all because she'd run into Lisa and Lisa had bragged about being engaged to Frank. Then, there were the threats that Tessa's little group had made.

We could always make this Lisa person disappear . . . Permanently . . .

Charlotte shook her head. "No way," she whispered. "They were just kidding."

Charlotte sprayed the bathtub with cleaner, but as she scrubbed out the tub the strange conversation between Belinda and Mack came to mind. To her it had sounded like Mack was being blackmailed by Lisa, but blackmailed about what?

Then there was Margaret. Charlotte straightened from her kneeling position by the bathtub and paused. There was something about Margaret nagging at the back of her mind. But what?

Satisfied that the bathtub looked 100 percent better, she stepped over to the sink and countertop, sprayed the mirror with window cleaner, then wiped it clean.

As Charlotte removed the toiletries from the countertop, she noted that there were no feminine products like makeup or hairspray, just a bottle of men's cologne and shaving items.

"Should have guessed," she grumbled as she wiped down the sink and countertop. With few exceptions, men proved to be a lot messier than women.

As she replaced the toiletries, in her mind she replayed the visit Margaret had paid Tessa in hopes of remembering what was nagging her. Then, like a light bulb going off, she remembered.

The papers.

Margaret had brought Tessa two file folders. One contained divorce papers, but the other one, as best as she could tell, contained papers about an adoption.

The divorce papers had upset Tessa, but she'd seemed truly grateful for the other file. But why would Tessa want a file about an adoption? Whose adoption?

This is that background information you asked me to get for you on Lisa.

Lisa's adoption? But why would that interest Tessa?

"And what does that have to do with the price of tea in China?" She grumbled, as she set out a new bar of soap, a bottle of shampoo, crème rinse, and lotion.

Last but certainly not least, there was Christopher. And there was Ralph Jones. She frowned. Offhand she couldn't think of any motives that Ralph Jones could possibly have, but Christopher was another matter altogether. He had both motive and opportunity.

At that moment Charlotte's cell phone rang. Pulling off her gloves, she reached into her pocket, took out the tiny phone, and answered the call.

"Maid-for-a-Day, Charlotte speaking."

"Charlotte, this is Claire. Listen, one of the guests — a man named Mack Sutton — wants you to call him as soon as possible. He didn't say what he wanted, but he did say to tell you that he's in room 210."

"Thanks, Claire." And because Charlotte could tell from Claire's voice that she was dying of curiosity about Mack's call, she explained, "Mack is an old friend of mine from college. He probably just wants to meet for coffee or something."

"Well, that's a relief. For a moment there I was afraid that you might be earning money on the side, if you know what I mean?"

"Claire! Get your mind out of the gutter. The very idea!"

Claire giggled. "Gotcha! Just kidding, Charlotte. Just kidding."

Rolling her eyes, Charlotte said, "Bye," and pressed the END button. Slipping the cell phone back inside her pocket, she walked into the bedroom to the hotel phone on the bedside table, picked up the receiver, and dialed room 210.

The phone only rang twice before Mack answered. "Hello."

"Mack, this is Charlotte. I was told that you were trying to get in touch with me."

"That was fast."

"Yes, well, Claire said that you told her as soon as possible. Is everything okay?"

"Everything is fine. I just wanted to catch you before you made lunch plans. You haven't made any yet, have you?"

It was just as she'd thought. With a sinking feeling and knowing what was coming, Charlotte said, "No, I haven't."

She liked Mack. He was an old friend, and she would forever be grateful that he'd introduced her to Hank all those years ago. But she wasn't sure if getting more involved with him and his family — especially his family — was such a good idea. She'd already seen and heard way more than she was comfortable with.

"Good," he replied. "Then would you let me buy you lunch today?"

After a moment's hesitation, Charlotte said, "The bad news is that I only get thirty minutes for lunch. The good news is, if we eat here at the hotel, I get to eat free, since I work here."

"Only because you just have thirty minutes, and not because you can eat free, I guess I'll have to settle for eating at the hotel restaurant. Would noon be okay?"

"Noon would be just fine."

"See you then."

Charlotte hung up the receiver. So much for not getting involved, she thought.

She eyed the entrance to the bathroom. All that it needed now were clean towels, washclothes, hand towels, and an extra roll of toilet paper. Once she'd vacuumed and mopped, she'd be finished in there.

"Thank goodness," she murmured.

After Charlotte finished the bathroom, she stripped the beds, then dusted the furniture in the bedroom. The small desk in the room had a stack of yellowed newspaper clippings on top, along with a laptop computer. She was moving the stack of newspapers to one side to dust beneath them when the headlines of the top paper caught her eye.

LOCAL GIRL GRADUATES WITH HONORS.

Out of curiosity, Charlotte skimmed the first paragraph then frowned. The article was all about Tessa. She glanced at the date at the top of the page, did a quick mental calculation, then nodded. Yes, the date would be about right, and the article was from the *Shreveport Times.* And Tessa lived in Shreveport . . .

Her curiosity aroused even more, she lifted the newspaper and glanced at the one beneath. Sure enough, it was another article about Tessa, one announcing her engagement to Frank, and the one beneath that one was about her marriage to Frank.

Charlotte's frown grew deeper. Why would anyone have collected old articles about Tessa?

. . . released from prison about a month ago, and he's been stalking Tessa ever since.

As Mack's words came back to her, a shiver ran up Charlotte's spine. An estranged father might collect old newspaper articles, especially a father who had been locked up in prison for years.

Charlotte glanced around the room. This had to be Ralph Jones's room. She swallowed hard. What if he walked in and recognized her as the woman who had been with Mack at the restaurant? He might think that she was snooping for Mack.

"Not if I can help it," she whispered.

Within record time, even for Charlotte, she finished cleaning the room and was out of there. Just as she was about to knock on the door of the room next to Ralph's, the elevator dinged down the hallway, the doors slid open, and out stepped Ralph Jones.

"Oh, no," Charlotte whispered.

Chapter 10

Coward, a tiny voice whispered inside Charlotte's head. *What on earth is wrong with you? You have every right to be here. You work here. And just because he's stalking his own daughter doesn't mean that he's an ax murderer.*

Duly chastised by the voice of her common sense, Charlotte stiffened, took a deep breath, then turned her back to the hallway and knocked on the door.

"Housekeeping," she called out. Waiting a moment, she knocked again, and as she called out, "Housekeeping" again, Ralph Jones walked by behind her and kept walking until he reached the door to his hotel room.

As Charlotte inserted her key into the keyhole of the door, she slid her eyes sideways. Without even a second glance her way, Ralph unlocked the door to his room and went inside.

Now see, all that worry for nothing.

"Yeah, yeah," she grumbled as the lock clicked and she opened the door.

By noon, Charlotte was more than ready for a break. Her feet ached and she was hungry. It seemed that every room that she'd cleaned was a bigger mess than the one she'd just cleaned.

"Must have been a full moon last night," she muttered as she stepped out of the elevator.

Expecting to see Mack waiting for her near the entrance of the restaurant, she froze in her tracks when she spotted Louis standing near the doorway instead.

At the same time that she saw Louis, he saw her and waved. "Hey, Charlotte," he called out.

Charlotte walked over to where he was standing.

"I was hoping I'd find you," he said. "The manager told me that you would probably take your lunch break about now."

"What are you doing here?" she blurted out, still stunned to see him there. "How did you even know that I'm working here to begin with?" She was pretty sure that she hadn't told him about her hotel job.

Louis grinned. "I talked to Judith this

morning, and she told me that you were working here."

"Oh — I see."

"Yeah, well, I thought that maybe we could have lunch together."

"Well — I — er — I kind of have a prior commitment." No sooner had the words left her mouth than, out of the corner of her eye, she spotted Mack coming through the hotel entrance door, and momentary panic seized her. Telling herself that she was being a silly old woman, she took a deep breath and tried to relax.

Louis frowned. "A prior commitment?"

Charlotte nodded, just as Mack reached her side.

"Sorry I'm late," Mack said. "I got caught up in a traffic jam downtown."

Louis narrowed his eyes and stared at Mack.

In size, the two men were equal, but Charlotte figured that Mack outweighed Louis by a good thirty pounds. Even so, Louis had kept himself more fit and was more muscular than Mack looked to be, despite Mack's size.

Charlotte swallowed hard. "Louis Thibodeaux, this is Mack Sutton. Mack is an old friend who's in town on business." She turned to Mack. "Louis is — he's —"

To her horror, she couldn't think of how to introduce Louis. Introducing him as simply her friend or her tenant seemed somehow lacking, not quite enough, but when all was said and done, that's all he was to her and all he could be since Joyce had come on the scene.

As if sensing her dilemma, Louis stepped up and offered his hand to Mack. "I'm a friend of the family and Charlotte's tenant," he told Mack.

Though Charlotte was sure that Mack didn't notice, she didn't miss the smirk on Louis's face that was meant for her. Darn his hide, he was enjoying her discomfort.

Mack shook Louis' hand. "Nice to meet you. We were about to have a bite of lunch. Why don't you join us?"

At that moment, Charlotte would have loved nothing better than to kick Mack for even suggesting such a thing.

Louis grinned. "Thanks, I think I will."

Charlotte glared at Louis and decided that kicking him would be even better.

Mack stepped inside the entrance to the restaurant. "Table for three," he told Simone.

Since neither man hadn't bothered to consult her about their decision to eat together, she was sorely tempted to tell them both to have a nice meal without her, then leave.

When Charlotte looked up and saw the knowing, amused look on Simone's face, she felt her face grow warm with embarrassment. Only another woman would catch on to what she was feeling.

Be nice, Charlotte.

Charlotte took a deep breath and let it out slowly; then, ignoring both Louis and Mack she followed Simone to a table for four in the corner of the room.

When each of the men pulled out a different chair on opposite sides of the table for her to sit in, Charlotte pulled out a different one for herself and sat down.

Mack, looking a bit embarrassed, chuckled self-consciously, then seated himself in the chair that he'd pulled out. Though Louis sat in the chair that he'd pulled out too, Charlotte could tell from the gleam in his eyes that he was enjoying her discomfort enormously.

"Your waitress will be with you in a moment," Simone told them.

They all picked up the menus at the same time. Louis was the first to lower his. "So, Mack, what kind of business are you in?"

"I'm an accountant." Mack lowered his menu. "The firm that I work for is opening up a branch here in New Orleans. And you?"

"I work for Lagniappe Security."

Mack frowned in thought. "I've heard of them before. That's a good company. I hear that they mostly employ retired cops."

Louis nodded. "Yeah, I was with the NOPD before I retired a couple of years ago."

At that moment, the waitress approached their table. "What can I get you folks to drink?" she asked.

After giving the waitress her drink order, Charlotte said, "And I already know what I want to eat. I'll have a shrimp po-boy —"

The waitress grinned. "Extra lettuce and tomato, and no mayonnaise."

Charlotte nodded, pleased that the girl had remembered.

"The house salad and a bowl of seafood gumbo for me," Mack said.

"That sounds good to me too," Louis told the waitress.

When the waitress left, Louis turned to Charlotte, "By the way, I never did get around to asking you yesterday how Carol is doing."

"Who's Carol?" Mack asked.

"Carol is Charlotte's daughter-in-law," Louis told him, "and she's expecting Charlotte's first grandchild."

Mack grinned. "Well, congratulations, Charlotte. You never mentioned you were about to be a grandmother."

Knowing what was coming next, a sinking feeling settled in the middle of Charlotte's stomach. "Thanks," she said to Mack, then she glared at Louis. "Carol is doing just fine."

Louis's eyes narrowed. "But didn't Hank say that she was —"

Mack stiffened. "Hank?"

Heat rushed up Charlotte's neck. She never had gotten around to telling Mack about Hank Junior, but worse, she'd never told Louis that she'd never married Hank's father.

"Hank is Charlotte's son," Louis told him. He turned to Charlotte. "I thought you said that you and Mack were old friends. So, why doesn't he know about Hank and Carol?"

"He doesn't know because —"

"You have a son named Hank?" Mack interrupted.

Charlotte lowered her gaze to stare at her plate and nodded. "Yes, Hank Junior."

"Oh, Charlotte, why didn't you tell me?"

Louis, clearly baffled, said, "Yeah, why didn't you tell him?"

Both Mack and Charlotte ignored Louis.

"I assume that Hank Junior is Hank Senior's son. Did he know he had a son?" Mack asked.

Charlotte shook her head. "No," she whispered, still unable to meet Mack's gaze. "He was killed before I was able to tell him." *Or before we were able to marry,* she added silently.

"Does your son know about his father?"

Charlotte lifted her head and stared hard at Mack. "My son knows that his father was a good man and that he was a soldier. He knows that his father died a hero. And that's all he needs to know."

For long moments Mack held Charlotte's gaze, his eyes probing as if trying to read her mind. Then, finally, he nodded. "I understand."

To give Louis credit, he didn't interrupt or ask questions, and moments later the waitress arrived with the food. Charlotte stared at the shrimp po-boy that was set in front of her, but she no longer had an appetite. Only because she knew how dangerous it could be for a diabetic to skip a meal, she forced herself to eat.

Mack was the one who finally broke the uncomfortable silence at the table. "Hank Senior was my best friend and roommate when we attended Tulane," he said to Louis. He chuckled. "Charlotte and I had had a couple of dates, but then I made the mistake of introducing her to Hank. After that —" He shrugged, but he didn't complete the sentence. "Anyway," he said, "Hank wanted to be a doctor, but like me, it was all that he could do to swing college. Just before graduation, he got this bright idea that he'd let Uncle Sam send him to medical school. Only problem, he had to survived Vietnam first. We both did. Only Hank didn't make it."

Louis nodded. "Yeah, I know a little about that war myself — Marines, Fourth Regiment. I served two tours over there."

Charlotte couldn't remember Louis ever mentioning that he'd been a Marine or that he'd gone to Vietnam, but a lot of men who had gone there never talked about it. As she picked at her food and the two men swapped war stories, listening to them brought back all of the old painful memories that she'd tried so hard to forget. Decades had passed, and though the pain of remembering wasn't as sharp, it still hurt.

In the past, she'd found that the best way to combat the pain was hard, physical work, and now was no exception. She made a show of glancing at her watch. After wiping her mouth with her napkin, she placed it beside her plate. "If you gentlemen will excuse me, I have to get back to work." Without waiting for either of them to comment, she stood.

Both men immediately jumped to their feet like a couple of jack-in-the-boxes.

Gentlemen to a fault, she thought as she turned and headed for the door. Too bad they didn't know when to keep their mouths shut.

By the time that Charlotte had retrieved the cleaning cart from the supply closet, her mind had cleared somewhat, and a tiny jab of guilt made her sigh. To be fair, the whole fiasco had been her own fault for not sharing her past before now with either man.

Maybe Tessa and her Red Scarf Sorority sisters had it right after all with their tell-all sharing policy. At least that way, there were no surprises.

Yeah, and what about Lisa?

"Well, almost no surprises," she whispered as she pushed the cart off the elevator and headed for the next room on her list.

Just as she was about to enter the room, her cell phone rang. When she answered it, it was Claire.

"That same man wants you to call him again," she said. "And Charlotte, it's not that I mind being the go-between, but this time, why don't you give him your cell phone number."

"Of course, Claire. I should have already done that. Sorry for the inconvenience."

"No problem. Would you like for me to go ahead and connect you to his room now?"

"Yes, please."

After a moment, the phone rang, and Mack answered.

"Mack, this is Charlotte."

"Whew! I was afraid that after all that went on during lunch you wouldn't call."

"My fault," Charlotte told him. "I don't like talking about that time in my life. It's just too painful."

"I can understand that. After losing Joanne, it was hard for me to talk about her for a long time too. Anyway, what I'm calling about — besides apologizing — is Hank. Your son," he clarified. "I would really like to meet him, Charlotte. But only if it's okay with you," he hastened to add. "And I wouldn't mention anything that you weren't comfortable with," he assured her.

Charlotte bit her bottom lip as she wrestled with her conscience. All of her son's life, he had been eager for any little tidbit of information he could get about his father. Though she'd told him what she had considered the important things and had shown him pictures, Mack could tell him so much more.

"I think he would like that very much, Mack. And by the way, he's a doctor, a surgeon in fact. Hank would have been so proud of him. Anyway, he has a pretty busy schedule, so I'll have to check with him and get back to you."

"Thanks, Charlotte."

"No, thank you for being willing to talk to him. But listen, before I forget, let me give you my cell number."

Once she'd given him the number, she said, "I'll be in touch soon."

By midafternoon, Charlotte had cleaned all of her assigned rooms except for one. She'd purposely saved Tessa's room for last in hopes that she'd be out and about somewhere. But first, she needed to replenish several of her cleaning products and pick up two more sets of clean sheets.

As Charlotte rolled the cart toward the supply closet, she heard a commotion near the elevator in the entrance hall. Wondering what on earth was going on, she walked to where the short hallway to the supply closet met the entrance hallway, then peeked around the corner to take a look.

In stunned silence, Charlotte froze. Standing in front of the elevator were Gavin Brown, two uniformed policemen, and Tessa. The uniformed policemen stood on either side of Tessa, each with a firm grip on her arms. Tessa's hands were handcuffed behind her back and she was crying.

"Why are you doing this?" she sobbed, as the policemen escorted her toward the entrance of the hotel. "I keep telling you that I didn't do anything. I didn't kill her."

"Oh, no," Charlotte whispered, and all that she could think of was Mack. He would be crushed.

At the same time that the front door closed behind the police and Tessa, the stairwell door opened, and Mack stepped out. When he headed toward the entrance, Charlotte went after him. By the time he reached the entrance though, the police were already putting Tessa into the squad car.

As Charlotte approached him, the squad car was pulling onto St. Charles Avenue. The look on Mack's face as he watched the car reminded her of a distraught lost child.

"Mack? Are you okay?"

Mack simply shook his head. "She didn't do it. I don't know how they could think that she did."

Charlotte was at a loss as to what to say to Mack, so she simply took his hand and squeezed it.

Though Mack continued staring at the retreating squad car, his lower lip quivered and a lone tear roll down his cheek.

Charlotte immediately wrapped her arm around his waist and said, "Come on with me, Mack, and let an old friend buy you a cup of coffee. There's a small coffeehouse just a block over where we can talk."

Mack nodded. "Thanks, Charlotte. I could use a friend about now."

A few minutes later, over a cup of steaming café o'lait, Charlotte asked, "Why Tessa, Mack? What evidence could they possibly have against her?"

Mack sighed heavily. "They found an earring belonging to Tessa at the murder site. And that ignoramus son-in-law of mine went and told the cops that the earring belonged to Tessa. Also, with all of us at the dinner on Saturday night, there was no one to give her an alibi at the time they think Lisa was murdered. They also suspect that Lisa was strangled with something like a tie or scarf." He rolled his eyes and shook his head. "It would be just Tessa's luck if it turns out to be one of those stupid red scarves that she wears. But that's not all.

They found the remains of what appears to be some kind of tape or something in Tessa's trashcan."

"Oh, no," Charlotte whispered. "The missing security tape."

"Security tape?"

After Charlotte explained about the security cameras and the missing tape, Mack groaned. "They claim that she'd tried to destroy it, that she broke it up first, then tried to burn it."

Mack swallowed hard then stared straight into Charlotte's eyes. "I don't care what they found though. She didn't do it, Charlotte. There's just no way Tessa would ever murder anyone. She's all bark and no bite. And she's not that stupid. Considering the circumstances, with her and Frank being separated and Frank shacking up with Lisa, Tessa has sense enough to know that if she did such a thing, she would be the number one suspect."

They're going to think I did it.

Recalling Tessa's initial reaction to the news of Lisa's murder, Charlotte nodded her agreement. Mack was right. In the first place, Tessa's stunned reaction wasn't faked. And in the second place, Tessa was too intelligent to think that she could get away with such a thing. Besides which, Charlotte couldn't imagine that Tessa would be physically strong enough to overcome a woman almost half her age.

"I'm telling you right now, she's been set up."

"By who?" Charlotte asked.

"Who else?" he answered. "That lousy husband of hers. Either he did it himself or he paid someone to do it."

Charlotte frowned. "But why? Why would Frank murder Lisa, then set up Tessa to take the fall?"

Mack grimaced. "Money. Why else? When Joanne died, she left everything to Tessa in a trust."

Everything? Surely not everything, Charlotte thought. What about Mack? He was Joanne's husband, and according to what he'd already told her, not only had he been responsible for saving his wife's inheritance, but he'd helped raise her daughter as well. Wouldn't she have left something to him?

"Once Tessa turned twenty-one," Mack continued, "she got it all. She's always held the purse strings in the family since then. When she married Frank, he had to sign a prenupt, and even when she financed his CPA firm, he had to agree to certain stipulations, one being that he would lose it all if he ever divorced her. But there were loopholes. If she becomes incapacitated to the point that she can't handle her own affairs, then Frank and his firm would be free and clear. And if I remember right, there was also a morals clause, and I'm pretty sure that would cover her being convicted of murder."

"But what about Belinda? If Tessa were convicted of murder or became incapacitated, wouldn't Belinda inherit it all?"

Mack shook his head. "Like Joanne had done for Tessa, Tessa put aside a special trust fund for Belinda when she was born. She'll get it when she turns twenty-one."

Charlotte's frown deepened. "That still doesn't explain why Frank would murder Lisa. Why not just kill Tessa?"

Mack hesitated, as if thinking through what he was about to say. "Maybe he had qualms about killing her himself, what with her being Belinda's mother."

Charlotte shook her head. "That doesn't make sense. He'd be willing to make his daughter's mother a jailbird, but not kill her?"

It was if Mack hadn't heard her. "I think that Frank was just using Lisa all along," he said. "By framing Tessa for Lisa's murder, then he'd be free and clear."

"I guess that's possible." But even as

Charlotte murmured the words, her mind raced. She had always considered herself a fair judge of character. She'd only been around Frank that one time, during her dinner date with Mack. Though Frank had struck her as a relatively intelligent, albeit somewhat shallow man, unless it was all an act, she had her doubts about him being capable of the type of deviousness that Mack was talking about.

So why would Mack come up with — suddenly, the hair on the back of Charlotte's neck stood on end.

Mack.

Charlotte tucked in her head and stared into her coffee cup. For Mack to even come up with such a scenario was farfetched at best, but it was also suspicious, almost as if he'd conjured up the scenario to hide something . . . to hide his own guilt?

What if Mack, not Frank, was the one who had killed Lisa and set up Tessa to take the blame? After all, it wasn't as if Mack was Tessa's real father; he was only her stepfather. He'd readily admitted that Tessa's mother had left everything to Tessa, and that she held all of the purse strings in the family. Having handled his wife's finances for all of those years, then to end up just another employee working for Tessa's husband, had to be humiliating for him. But was it humiliating enough to commit murder and set up his stepdaughter to take the blame?

Then, there was that conversation she'd overhead between Mack and Belinda?

Did you talk to Lisa . . . If she goes through with it and calls in the cops I'll be ruined . . . there's no way I can do what she wants.

What was that all about, if not blackmail?

No, no, no, don't even think it, not about Mack.

But Charlotte couldn't help but think it.

Chapter 11

When Charlotte looked up, Mack was staring off into space with unseeing eyes. A lot of years had passed since they were students at Tulane. If she'd changed, and she had, didn't it stand to reason that Mack might have changed too? Pity was, not all changes were necessarily for the better. Some people changed for the worse.

Charlotte's cell phone rang, and with a whispered apology for the interruption, she pulled it out of her pocket, and pressed the TALK button. "Maid-for-a-Day, Charlotte speaking."

"Are you avoiding me on purpose, Aunt Charley?"

Charlotte slid her gaze to Mack, but he was still staring off into space. "I really can't talk right now," she told Judith. "I'll call you back later."

"But that's what you said —"

"I know, hon, and I'm sorry. Why don't

you come by the house this evening? I'll even spring for pizza."

After a pregnant pause, Judith said, "Okay, but you'd better be there."

Charlotte disconnected the call. "That was my niece," she said, but from the blank look on Mack's face, he was still lost in his own thoughts.

Though Charlotte didn't like what she was thinking about Mack, she couldn't completely dismiss it either. Maybe putting some distance between them would give her a better perspective on the situation. Besides, just thinking about her old friend being capable of murder was giving her a headache.

As she searched for an excuse to leave, she suddenly remembered that she still had one room left to clean back at the hotel before she could call it a day. Tessa's room. Of course it was possible that the police could have secured it and wouldn't let her clean it anyway, but there was only one way to find out.

"Mack, I really hate to, but I need to leave. I've still got work left to do back at the hotel. Are you going to be okay?"

As if someone had thrown a switch in his brain, Mack blinked several times, then frowned. "Sorry — what did you say?"

"I've still got work to do back at the hotel," she repeated. "I have to leave."

"Oh, sure, of course. I understand."

"Are you going to be okay?"

"I'll be fine," he assured her. "And thanks — thanks for your support, Charlotte. Just one more thing, if you don't mind. You wouldn't happen to know the name of a good lawyer, would you?"

The way Mack asked the question made Charlotte wonder if he was asking for himself or for Tessa.

Paranoid. Now you're really being paranoid.

Charlotte took a deep breath then sighed. Of course he was asking for Tessa. Reaching inside her pocket she pulled out a notepad. "My nephew is an attorney with a large firm in the city." She scribbled down Daniel's name and office number. "If he can't help you, he can recommend someone who can. Just tell him that I told you to call." She tore the sheet out of the notebook and slid it across the table to Mack.

Mack picked up the piece of paper. "Thanks."

Charlotte stood. "Take care of yourself, Mack, and let me know if there's anything else I can do."

Outside, the afternoon sun beat down relentlessly and the air was so thick with humidity that it was hard to even breathe. Though the walk back to the hotel didn't take long, by the time she reached it she was sticky with sweat. Anticipating the relief of air-conditioning, she stepped into the lobby, then halted in her tracks.

"What in world is going on?" she whispered.

The lobby was chaos, crowded with mostly women trying to check out of the hotel. She frowned. The majority of the women were wearing the signature red scarves around their necks.

Your pain is our pain.

Yeah, right, thought Charlotte, recalling the scene she'd witnessed in Tessa's room. "Bunch of hypocrites," she muttered.

Her mouth pursed tight with disapproval, she made her way through the noisy crowd. So much for their "one for all and all for one" philosophy. If they were really the kind of friends they had claimed to be, they would stick around and lend Tessa the moral support she needed right now instead of deserting her.

Halfway through the lobby, Charlotte decided she should ask Claire about cleaning Tessa's room. Claire would know if the police had secured it or not, and possibly save her a wasted trip.

Ignoring the pointed glares of the women standing in line, Charlotte pushed her way through to the front desk. Claire had just finished checking out a woman when Charlotte caught her eye. Claire motioned for Charlotte to meet her at the end of the front desk.

"What is it, Charlotte?" she asked a moment later.

"I just wanted to check with you first. I have one last room to clean, and it just happens to be the one that Tessa Morgan was staying in. Did the police secure that room or is it okay for me to clean it?"

Claire shrugged. "As far as I know, it's okay to clean it. Ms. Morgan's daughter is still in it. She hasn't checked out yet." Claire motioned toward the women waiting in line. "Unlike the rest of the guests."

Belinda.

Charlotte's breath caught in her lungs. She'd completely forgotten about Belinda. And so had Mack, evidently.

"The hotel is taking a big hit," Claire continued. "Most of these women were booked until the end of the week. Still, I guess I can't really blame them. Ms. Morgan was the president of the group, and she's the one who had arranged for the get-together to begin with. Without her —"

Claire shrugged.

Charlotte disagreed about blaming the women for checking out but didn't say so. In her opinion, Tessa's arrest was all the more reason for the group to stick around and lend their support.

"You know," Claire went on, "I only spoke to Mrs. Morgan a few times, but she seemed like a nice enough lady. I'd have never guessed that she could kill anyone."

"I'm not so sure that she did," Charlotte murmured, remembering the conversation she'd just had with Mack.

"Did your niece tell you that?"

Realizing her mistake, Charlotte quickly shook her head. "No, my niece doesn't tell me anything about the cases she works on." Not if she can help it, she added silently.

Claire nodded thoughtfully. "Guess that makes sense. Anyway — about the room — I guess you should go ahead and clean it." Claire's gaze shifted to the long line of women. "And I need to get back to work."

Charlotte found the cleaning cart exactly where she'd left it. Once she'd replenished the cleaning products and picked up the two sets of clean sheets she needed, she rolled the cart toward the elevator.

When she knocked on the door to Tessa's room a few minutes later and called out,

"Housekeeping," no one answered, so she knocked again. When no one answered the second time, she used her master key and let herself inside.

The moment Charlotte opened the door, she wrinkled her nose against the acrid smell that permeated the room. Burnt plastic had a distinct odor all it's own, an odor that was hard to get rid of, and what she was smelling was definitely the leftover stench of burnt plastic.

Charlotte frowned remembering what Mack had said. *They claim that she'd tried to destroy it, that she broke it up first, then tried to burn it.*

Shaking her head, Charlotte stepped back out into the hallway and retrieved the new trashcan that she'd brought for the bathroom. Anyone with sense would know that the smell would be a dead give-away. Tessa had her faults, but she didn't strike Charlotte as lacking common sense.

Too many things didn't add up, and Charlotte was beginning to agree with Mack that someone had set Tessa up for the fall. But was that someone Mack?

Again Charlotte shied away from the thought that Mack, not Tessa, was Lisa's killer. But if not Mack, then who? Frank?

This is not your problem, Charlotte . . . none

of your business. Just get it cleaned and go home.

"Yeah, yeah," she grumbled. As if scrubbing harder and working faster would make the nagging suspicions go away, she began cleaning the bathroom.

She had just finished the bathroom when she heard the lock of the entrance door click. Seconds later Belinda appeared in the bathroom doorway.

One look at Belinda's ravaged face, and sympathy for the girl welled within Charlotte. Belinda's eyes were puffy and red-rimmed from crying, and her hair was a mess.

"I-I was hoping th-that you'd be the one cleaning," Belinda said in a fragile, shaky voice. "Do-do you know where my grandfather is? I-I've been looking for him everywhere."

Charlotte nodded. "The last time I saw him was at that little coffeehouse just down the street from the hotel. It was just after —" She swallowed hard. "It was just after the police took your mother away."

"Then he does know about my mother?"

Charlotte nodded. "Yes, hon, he knows."

Belinda's face collapsed into sheer misery and fresh tears filled her eyes. "She didn't do it, you know. She didn't kill Lisa." She covered her face with her hands, sank down to the floor and sobbed.

Charlotte rushed over to the girl and knelt down beside her. "Of course she didn't," Charlotte soothed, patting Belinda on the back. "Everything will be okay."

Belinda shook her head. "N-nothing will ever be okay again," she cried. "Everything is-is all screwed up and I don't know what to do."

Filled with pity for the girl and not knowing what else to do, Charlotte gathered Belinda in her arms, and simply sat there, holding her as the girl sobbed her heart out.

Though Charlotte didn't mind lending comfort when it was needed, nor did she mind that she had been elected for the job by default, she couldn't help thinking that it should have been Mack or Frank there instead of a stranger. After all, Mack was her grandfather, and Frank was her father. But wasn't it just like a man to be so absorbed in his own problems that . . .

Not true, and you know it. Not all men are like that.

Belinda's sobs had been reduced to snuffling, then the occasional sniff. A moment more passed, and she finally pulled away from Charlotte. "Sorry," she whispered.

Charlotte smiled. "No problem, hon."

"I think I need to find Granddaddy now." She got to her feet and Charlotte did the same.

"If I were you I'd try his room first," Charlotte suggested. "If he's not there, then check the coffeehouse. It's been a while, but he could still be there."

Belinda nodded. "Thanks, I will." She walked over to the sink, and after blowing her nose, she turned on the faucet and rinsed her face. After drying off, she reached for a small makeup bag.

Charlotte figured that the fact that Belinda cared about how she looked was a good sign. Satisfied that the girl would be okay for now, she went into the bedroom and began stripping the sheets and blankets off of the beds.

A few minutes later, Belinda, looking much better, emerged from the bathroom. When she reached the entrance door, she paused and turned to face Charlotte. "Thanks again, Charlotte," she said, then she was gone.

Once the beds were made, Charlotte began dusting, starting with the dresser. As she removed each item on the dresser, her thoughts were on Belinda and Tessa. The last item she removed was a small stack of neatly folded red scarves. With a grimace of distaste, she reached for the scarves. Who would have thought that such a small piece of material could be used as a murder weapon?

Charlotte tilted her head and frowned as she stared at the scarves. Something about them looked different. She picked up the top scarf to examine it more closely. The tiny gold embroidered TM was there, but when she rubbed the scarf between her forefinger and thumb, she realized that it didn't feel the same as the other ones Tessa had. These had a more silky feel to them. Silky . . . silk . . . The first set of scarves had been polyester, but these were silk.

The dye in the new scarves I just bought bled through.

Charlotte's frown grew deeper as she remembered Tessa complaining about the scarves. Still staring at the scarf, she tried to remember if anyone had mentioned whether the one that had been used to strangle Lisa was silk or polyester. Whether silk or polyester, what difference did it make? But as she placed it back on the top of the stack, she couldn't shake the nagging feeling that her discovery was somehow important.

The last piece of furniture Charlotte dusted was the desk. On top of the desk was a stack of file folders and several old videos. Charlotte reached to move the file folders, but her hands froze in midair, as, once again, she remembered Tessa's strange reaction when the papers had scattered on the day that she'd learned about Lisa's murder.

Charlotte could feel the tips of her fingers just itching to open the files. Squeezing her hands into fists, she fought the temptation.

But surely just one little peek couldn't hurt.

Don't you dare.

Why not? Who would know?

You would know.

So what? she countered.

For as long as she could remember she'd been both blessed and cursed with the aggravating inner voice of her conscience that tried to keep her on the right path of life. More than once over the years she'd been tempted to snoop through a client's things. Most of the time she listened to her conscience and resisted the temptation.

But this time is different, she argued. What if she found something that could help prove Tessa's innocence? After Tessa's reaction to the scattered papers, they had to be important, and there was only one way to know for sure.

With her ear tuned to any unusual noise

in the hallway, Charlotte grabbed the stack of file folders, and before she had a chance to change her mind, she quickly went through them.

The first one contained information pertaining to the Red Scarf Sorority: hotel receipts, workshop schedules, and such. The second folder contained the divorce papers. Nothing there but a bunch of legalese gobbledygook.

Charlotte set aside the first two folders and opened the third one. Though the pages were out of order, it didn't take long for her to realize what they were all about. Someone, more than likely Tessa, had hired a private detective to do a background check on Lisa.

Charlotte frowned as she skimmed down the pages. But if Tessa had hired a private detective, why had Margaret brought her the folder? Maybe because Tessa had Margaret hire the private detective through Frank's company. But why had Tessa hired a private detective to begin with?

For the obvious reasons, Charlotte decided. Tessa was trying to save her marriage and had hoped to find something that she could use against Lisa.

According to the file, Lisa had been adopted by an older couple when she was just days old. Though not exactly wealthy, the couple was financially sound. Then her adoptive father died without leaving any life insurance or security, and her adoptive mother came on hard times, just barely able to make ends meet. Though Lisa graduated from high school, she couldn't afford to attend college. With the help of loans, she took some business courses, and finally landed a job with Frank's company as a secretary.

As Charlotte skimmed the rest of the pages, she found nothing more out of the ordinary than some speeding tickets. Even Lisa's credit report checked out just fine.

Charlotte frowned as she rifled through the pages. Where was that page she'd seen with the word adoption on it? Then she found it.

As she quickly read the page, halfway down, her breath caught in her lungs. "Oh, no," she groaned. Surely there was a mistake.

Taking a deep breath, she reread the paragraph. There was no mistake. "Oh, dear Lord in heaven," she murmured.

Chapter 12

"Not possible," Charlotte whispered as she quickly skimmed the rest of the sheet of paper. But there it was in black and white.

Charlotte continued staring at the paper with unseeing eyes long after she'd finished reading it.

Once, she even ran away, and for months I didn't know where she was or even if she was dead or alive. Then one day, out of the blue, she showed up at the front door. I don't know what happened to her during that time — and she's never told me — but whatever happened totally changed her.

As Mack's words spun through her mind, Charlotte shook her head in disbelief. Giving birth to an illegitimate baby, then giving that baby up for adoption would certainly change a teenage girl, and according to the copy of the adoption paper she was holding in her hand, Tessa had done just that. During the time that Tessa had run away, she'd given birth to a baby girl. She'd given birth to Lisa. Lisa was Tessa's daughter.

Still stunned by what she'd discovered, Charlotte suddenly realized that she'd been standing there, staring at the paper for a long time. Her gaze shifted to the door. Too long. Any minute now, Belinda could return, and the last thing she wanted was to get caught snooping.

Charlotte quickly gathered the detective's report and slipped it back inside the file folder. Now, even more than before, she was convinced of Tessa's innocence. There was just no way that Tessa could have murdered her own flesh and blood, not after the supreme sacrifice she'd made as a teenager of giving Lisa up for adoption.

Charlotte's mind whirled with random thoughts, as she quickly finished dusting then began vacuuming.

Besides Tessa, the private detective, and possibly Margaret, who else could have known about Lisa being Tessa's daughter, she wondered?

Not Mack, she decided. He'd already admitted that he didn't know where Tessa was when she had run away, and nothing he'd said had indicated that he even suspected that she was pregnant or had a baby.

What about Belinda though? Charlotte

doubted that Belinda would have known . . . unless she'd read the files. But given how she felt about her mother snooping through her things, it was unlikely that she'd snoop through her mother's things.

And what about Frank? Frank couldn't have known. Not even a sleaze like Frank would have knowingly had an affair with his wife's daughter. Would he?

Charlotte shut off the vacuum, and as she gathered the cord, she added Ralph Jones to the list. She still hadn't figured out how he fit into the mix, but she couldn't dismiss him. But how would Ralph know about any of it? He'd been locked away in prison for years. All that he knew about Tessa had been gleaned from newspaper articles. The fact that she'd had an illegitimate baby wasn't exactly the type of thing he would have read in the newspapers. More to the point, why would he care anyway whether a daughter whom he barely knew had an illegitimate child or not?

Charlotte sighed as she glanced around the room one last time. Something about the whole situation just didn't add up, but the thing that bothered her most was the connection between Lisa and Tessa. What were the odds that out of all of the young women in the world, Tessa's illegitimate daughter would be the one having an affair with her husband?

"A hundred billion to one, maybe," Charlotte muttered as she left the room. But as she closed the door behind her and the lock clicked, an uneasy feeling crawled up her spine.

What if Lisa had known that Tessa was her birth mother? What if she'd somehow discovered that Tessa was her mother and had decided to get even with her for giving her away? According to the detective's report, Lisa and her adoptive mother had a hard time surviving after the death of her adoptive father. If, and when, she found out about Tessa, she might have resented the fact that her half-sister Belinda had grown up in the lap of luxury while she'd had to live in near poverty.

Charlotte shook her head. She'd always had a healthy imagination, but even for her, the idea of such a thing was a real stretch. Instead of conjuring up off-the-wall scenarios, she should be thinking about what, if any of this, she should tell Judith.

Down the hallway, as Charlotte waited for the elevator, something kept nagging her, something that Mack had said to Belinda about Belinda being friends with Lisa.

I just thought that with you and Lisa being

old friends she might listen to reason if you talked to her.

Old friends? How long had Belinda and Lisa been so-called friends? What if Belinda knew or suspected that Lisa was her half-sister? That, along with Lisa's affair with Belinda's father and Lisa's threat against Mack just might be enough to push Belinda over the edge.

The elevator dinged, the doors slid open, and Charlotte pushed the cart inside and stepped in behind it. She was doing it again. She was getting dragged into yet another murder investigation that she had no business getting involved in.

As the elevator doors closed, she began humming the tune to an old song. Suddenly realizing what she was doing, she laughed. How appropriate, she thought, that she'd end up humming, *Why me, Lord.* She'd always been taught that everything happened for a reason, that there were no accidents in life, so was it fate that she was always in the wrong place at the wrong time? Or was it simply the fact that the older she got, the nosier she became?

Then, a third possibility occurred to her. If she truly believed that everything happened for a reason, and she did, then wasn't it also possible that she was exactly where she was supposed to be? Wasn't it possible that this was a way that she could use her gift of discernment for good?

The elevator door dinged, the doors slid open. Thinking about the other times that she'd helped solve a murder, Charlotte pushed the cart out into the hallway. Once she'd put it away, she headed for the hotel entrance, but as she passed by the door leading into the restaurant, out of the corner of her eye she spotted Mack and Belinda seated at a table.

Charlotte's steps slowed. From the looks of things, Mack seemed to be doing his best to comfort and reassure Belinda.

"Good," Charlotte whispered. "That's what he should have been doing all along."

When Charlotte pulled into her driveway, the first thing she saw was Louis sitting on the porch swing.

"Great," she grumbled. Just what she needed. Didn't the man have anything better to do than sit around waiting for her?

Of course there was always the possibility that he wasn't waiting for her, that he was just relaxing on the front porch.

"Yeah, right," she whispered. Sitting on the front porch in ninety-degree-plus weather, just to relax. No way. First lunch and now, here he was again.

Thinking about lunch, Charlotte frowned as she climbed out of the van. Strange that not once during the entire meal had he brought up the subject of Joyce. Why hadn't he mentioned her?

Charlotte slammed the door and locked it. It occured to her that he probably didn't wanted to air his problems in front of a complete stranger.

"Got a minute?" Louis called out as she climbed the steps.

"Not really," she told him. "Judith's supposed to come by and I promised her pizza." She threw up her hand, palm out. "And before you ask, no, you're not invited." There was no way she wanted to get caught between Louis and Judith over yet another murder investigation.

Though Louis looked a bit hurt, he had the good sense to look embarrassed as well. "Yeah, well, I guess I owe you an apology for horning in on your lunch date — sorry about that." His expression hardened. "But it's your own fault about that other business. How was I to know that you had shacked up with Hank's father then didn't marry him?"

Anger, like the heat of a flash fire, shot through Charlotte's veins. "Not that it's any of your business, but I did not 'shack up' with Hank's father."

"Well, there's only ever been one virgin birth, and it didn't involve you."

Momentarily speechless, all Charlotte could do was stare at him as she fought to hold on to her temper. Leave it to Louis to come up with such a derogatory label for the one night that she'd shared with the man that she'd loved with all of her heart.

After counting to ten, between gritted teeth she finally said, "I think that's the meanest, most insensitive thing that you've ever said to me." Curling her fingers into fists, she spun away from him and stomped across the porch to her door.

"Aw, come on, Charlotte, don't leave. I'm sorry. Okay? Don't be mad."

Ignoring him, Charlotte rammed her key into the lock and twisted it.

"You know I didn't mean anything."

Charlotte whirled to face him. "Then why say it?"

A muscle in his jaw jumped and his expression grew tight with strain. "I don't know why. This business with Joyce has got me so tied up in knots that I don't know why I'm doing anything lately."

Part of her wanted to keep yelling at him, just on general principle, for being such a jerk. But in her heart of hearts, she couldn't do it. It was obvious, at least to her, that he was hurting, and hurting badly. Unfortunately for her, she was the handiest person around for him to take out his frustration on.

You always hurt the one you love.

Charlotte felt her checks grow warm. Where had that come from? Louis didn't love her. Why, he'd only kissed her once during the entire time that she'd known him. Yes, he'd flirted with her and teased her, but that's what friends did. And they were friends — just good friends. Never mind that she'd had thoughts that their relationship might become more than that. But that was before Joyce had shown up.

With a sigh, she left her key in the door, walked over to the swing, and sat down beside him. "What's going on, Louis?"

"Joyce is missing."

"Missing? How could she be missing? When I left last night she was still in a coma."

"Yeah, that's what we all thought. But after you left, they told us that she was awake and that they were moving her to a regular room. Then, when Stephen and I went to her new room, she was gone."

"But where on earth could she go without

any clothes or money? Surely someone would have seen a woman walking out in a hospital gown."

"As best as we can figure, she got hold of some hospital scrubs. We found her gown in a storage closet near the OR. As for money —" He shrugged. "She'd been living on the streets for years out in California. Street-savvy people know how to get along without it."

"So what's being done about it? Did you file a missing person's report?"

Louis shook his head. "Can't, not for twenty-four hours, and besides, there's no reason to believe that foul play is involved and she's a grown woman. Except for when I saw you at lunch, Stephen and I have spent most of the day canvassing the homeless shelters. But no luck. That's one of the reasons I came by the hotel. Joyce liked you — she respected you. It was a long shot, but I was hoping that she might have tried to get in touch with you somehow."

"But why, Louis, why would she do such a thing — just up and disappear — unless . . ." Charlotte narrowed her eyes. "Unless she overheard you talking to the doctor about putting her in detox to dry her out."

Louis nodded. "My thoughts exactly." He turned sideways and stared hard at her.

"You would tell me if she had tried to contact you, wouldn't you?"

"Yes, of course I would. Joyce may not be dying, but she's still a sick woman who needs help. I —" Charlotte suddenly went stone still.

"What?"

Charlotte shook her head. "It may not be anything, but last night, I had this strange message on my answering machine when I got home."

"What kind of message?"

She shook her head again. "Not a message exactly, more like a heavy breather." She reached up and rubbed the back of her neck. "At the time it kinda scared me, but thinking about it now — do you think it could have been Joyce?"

"What time did the breather leave the message?"

"I don't remember — but wait —" Charlotte hopped out of the swing and headed for her front door. "I did one of those star sixty-nine call-back things and wrote down the time, date, and number in a notebook. I think that notebook is still on my desk."

Ignoring Sweety Boy's vie for attention, once Charlotte was inside she headed straight for her desk. When Louis followed her a few seconds later, Sweety Boy went wild, squawking and flapping his wings.

Charlotte picked up the notebook, handed it to Louis, then hurried over to the little parakeet's cage. "Calm down, boy," she murmured to the little parakeet. "Just calm down before you hurt yourself."

But the little bird was beyond soothing. "Louis, either go back out on the porch or go to the kitchen," she told him.

"That's one rotten little bird you've got, Charlotte." With a shake of his head, Louis headed back toward the kitchen.

It took several minutes, but once Sweety Boy settled down, Charlotte went to the kitchen. When she entered, Louis was seated at the kitchen table, his cell phone to his ear.

"The call came from the hospital," he said, lowering the cell phone and switching it off.

Charlotte was both relieved and disturbed. "So it's a pretty good bet that Joyce did try to contact me."

Louis nodded. "If she calls again, try to get her to meet you somewhere, then call me."

"I'll try. But Louis, you can't force Joyce to go into detox, can you?"

"No, I can't force her, and to tell the truth, I don't care if she goes one way or another. She can rot on the streets —"

"Louis!"

"Okay, okay." He sighed. "Bottom line, Stephen and Amy care, and that's the only reason I'd try to talk her into anything."

With the mention of Louis's little granddaughter, Charlotte smiled. "And how is Amy?"

"Growing like a weed and getting a sassy mouth on her."

Charlotte nodded. "I can hardly wait to have one of my own."

"Too bad Amy can't have someone like you for a grandmother instead of a lush like Joyce."

Unsure whether Louis's comment was simply a compliment or if it held a deeper meaning, Charlotte was at a momentary loss for words.

"Guess we can't choose our relatives though," Louis continued. "Not those by blood anyway."

Time to change the subject, Charlotte decided. She glanced at her watch. "Listen, I don't mean to be rude, but I need to get some things done before Judith shows up."

As Louis stood up, a car door slammed outside. "Okay, I'm leaving," he said.

"Aunt Charley?" Judith called out from the living room.

Louis shrugged. "Uh-oh, too late."

Ignoring Louis, Charlotte called out, "In the kitchen, hon."

A minute later, Judith entered the room. "Why is the front door open — oh, hey, Louis."

"Hey, yourself, little girl."

Judith made a growling sound. "I wish you'd stop calling me that."

Louis chuckled. "So how goes it?"

"Same old, same old," Judith retorted.

Charlotte cleared her throat. "Ah, excuse me, but I hope you aren't expecting to eat immediately. I've still got to order the pizza, and I thought I'd make a salad to go with it."

As if Charlotte hadn't spoken, Judith said, "You're staying to eat, aren't you, Louis?"

Louis only hesitated a moment. "Guess that's up to your aunt. I've already horned in on her lunch date today, and I'm not so sure that she'd appreciate me doing it again."

"Lunch date? Aunt Charley had a date?"

"Yeah, some man she knew back when she was at Tulane."

"What man?" Judith asked him.

"Said his name was Mack Sutton."

"Ah, excuse me! But I am standing right here." Charlotte glared first at her niece and then at Louis.

Judith rounded on Charlotte. "Aunt Charley, why didn't you tell me that you knew Tessa Morgan's stepfather?"

"Who's Tessa Morgan?" Louis asked.

Charlotte crossed her arms and lifted her chin. "I told you that I had dinner with an old friend," she said, ignoring Louis.

"But you conveniently left out who your old friend was," Judith shot back.

"Who's Tessa Morgan?" Louis asked again.

"I didn't think it was relevant at the time," Charlotte retorted, not liking Judith's attitude one bit.

Judith stepped forward and glared at Charlotte. "What's relevant or not relevant is not your decision, Aunt Charley. From now on why don't you let *me* determine what's relevant."

Suddenly Louis let loose a shrill whistle. "Time out!" He stepped between Charlotte and Judith. "You!" He pointed to Charlotte. "Go order the pizza. And you!" He shook his finger at Judith. "Sit down and tell me what the blue blazes is going on."

Both Charlotte and Judith glared at him, but Louis glared right back. Finally, with a shake of her head, Charlotte stomped out of the kitchen. "I knew this would happen," she complained, as she headed for the telephone on her desk. "I just knew it."

Behind her, she heard the scrape of the kitchen chair against the floor. "Now sit down," she heard Louis tell Judith.

In the living room, Charlotte tapped out the numbers to the pizza place with more force than necessary. While waiting for someone to answer, her gaze strayed to the front door. She could just leave. She could pick up her purse and keys and walk right out the door. That would show them.

"Domino's Pizza."

Charlotte gave the order for a hand-tossed large pepperoni with mushrooms and onions and extra sauce, then gave her address. But as she hung up the phone, she released a sigh of frustration. It would be just her luck that Judith had parked behind her van and she wouldn't be able to get out of the drive way.

Then, another idea occurred to her. If she couldn't leave, she could demand that Louis and Judith leave. After all, this was her house.

Get a grip, Charlotte. You know that you won't do any such thing.

"Nice thought though," she muttered. With one last longing look at the front door and dragging her feet, she headed for the kitchen.

Louis was seated across from Judith and was grilling her about Lisa's murder. Ignoring them and hoping they would ignore her as well, Charlotte opened the refrigerator and removed the ingredients for a garden salad: lettuce, tomatoes, carrots, cucumbers, and green onions. From the cabinet, she took a large salad bowl, then began washing and chopping up the ingredients, all the while listening as Louis and Judith talked.

"How big of a woman is this Tessa?" he asked.

"Not that big. About my size."

"And how big is the vic?"

"About the same, only skinnier, and, hey — I know what you're thinking. I thought the same thing. It takes a lot of strength to strangle someone. But the way I figure it, if she had the vic face down, on the ground, she'd have enough leverage to do it. The autopsy's in the morning, and we'll know more after that."

Louis nodded. "Look for ground-in grass, dirt, and such on the vic's face and chest, and look for bruising on her back. The only way the perp could get enough leverage would be a knee in the vic's back to keep her down."

"Yeah, I know, but —"

"But what?"

Judith shrugged. "It's just a feeling, but it all seems too easy, too pat: the earring, the scarf, and now the tape. What kind of fool would try to burn the tape in her own room? She had to know that all the rooms would be searched." She shook her head. "Frankly, I think Gavin Brown jumped the gun arresting her — too many loose ends. But it wasn't my call. The chief was being pressured from city hall to make an arrest, and Gavin is bucking for a promotion. He seemed to think that Tessa Morgan was our best bet."

Not if he knew what I knew, Charlotte thought as she chopped up the green onions.

Almost as if Judith had heard Charlotte's thoughts, she added, "Unless Aunt Charley knows more than she's telling. Which I suspect she does," she said.

Though her back was to them, Charlotte could feel both Judith and Louis staring at her.

A loud knock reverberated from the living room.

Charlotte breathed a sigh of relief. Saved by the pizza man . . . for now. "That's probably the pizza," she said.

"I'll get it," Louis told her. "My treat and

no argument."

"Fine," Charlotte retorted. Why not let him pay for it? After all, he had invited himself to dinner.

That's not true. Judith invited him.

Yeah, yeah, Charlotte silently argued. But he didn't have to accept the invitation.

When Louis left the room, Judith walked over to where she was standing at the cabinet. "What can I do to help?"

"Put ice in the glasses for tea," Charlotte told her. "Unless you'd prefer Coke instead. I may have a bottle of diet Coke in the pantry."

"No, tea is just fine. And just so you know, I still intend to have a little talk with you."

Forewarned was forearmed, thought Charlotte. But she had a few questions of her own as well.

Chapter 13

Throughout the meal, Judith and Louis seemed content to eat without grilling her about Lisa's murder, much to Charlotte's relief. She figured if she could sidestep the whole subject long enough, maybe Louis would go home.

Louis and Judith were playfully quibbling over the last piece of pizza when Judith's cell phone rang. After several moments of monosyllabic answers into the tiny phone, Judith finally told her caller, "I'm leaving now. ETA not more than ten minutes."

When Judith disconnected the call, she said, "I hate to eat and run, Auntie, but duty calls. There's been a shooting on Louisiana Avenue."

"No problem, hon," Charlotte told her. "Just be careful."

Judith nodded, then wiped her mouth with a napkin, stood, and took her plate and glass to the sink. "We still need to have that talk though." She glanced at her watch. "If this doesn't take too long, I may be back." She walked back over to Charlotte and hugged her neck. "Thanks for dinner."

"Watch your back out there, little girl," Louis told Judith when she headed for the kitchen door.

Judith paused at the doorway, and with a smile twitching at her lips, she said, "I always do, *old man*." Then she was gone.

With a shake of his head and a chuckle, Louis turned to Charlotte, "Are you sure that she's not your daughter?"

Charlotte smiled. "I'll take that as a compliment. Anyway, guess you get the last piece of pizza after all."

"Nah." He shook his head. "I just like giving the little girl a hard time." He sighed. "And speaking of time, I've got one last place I want to check out before calling it a night. Like your niece, I hate to eat and run but —"

"And like I told her, no problem."

"Thanks, Charlotte." He wiped his mouth with a napkin, and then he carried his plate and glass to the sink. "You won't forget to let me know if Joyce tries to call you again?"

"I won't," she assured him.

Louis eyed the doorway leading into the living room, then said, "Guess I've terrified your bird enough for one day, so I'll just go out the back."

"You don't have to do that."

He nodded. "It's the least I can do. Lock up now, and I'll talk to you later."

Charlotte locked the back door behind Louis, then finished cleaning off the table. She'd just put the last of the dishes in the dishwasher when her phone rang.

"Now what?" She grumbled as she hurried into the living room. Charlotte picked up the receiver. "Maid-for-a-Day, Charlotte speaking."

"Ch-Charlotte?"

"Belinda?"

"Yes-yes ma'am."

The girl was crying so hard that she could hardly talk. "What's wrong, hon?"

"I-I didn't know who to-to talk to," she cried. "Who-who to call. I —"

"Okay, okay, just calm down," Charlotte said gently. "Take a deep breath and calm down."

Long seconds passed, and from what Charlotte could hear, Belinda was trying to get control of her emotions.

After what seemed like forever, the girl finally said, "Could I talk to you, please?"

"Sure you can, hon. Where are you? Where's your grandfather?"

"I'm-I'm at the hotel, but I-I'm scared. I can't stay here. Could you come get me?"

Scared? Scared of what? "Belinda, what's happened?"

"Please, Charlotte. Please just come get me."

Unnerved by the girl's pleas, Charlotte drummed her fingers against the desktop. What to do? What to do? "Okay," she finally responded. "Tell you what, I can be there in about ten minutes or so. I'll just swing through the driveway at the entrance. Watch for a light gray van."

"Okay, but please don't tell anyone that you're picking me up. Especially not my grandfather or my father," she added.

As Charlotte hung up the receiver, an uneasy feeling nagged her. Something or someone had scared the girl. Picking up Belinda for a talk was one thing, but the girl's plea for her not to tell anyone about it sent up red flags. Why wouldn't she want Mack or her father to know where she was? Charlotte narrowed her eyes. Two reasons immediately came to mind: either she was afraid of them because one of them had actually killed Lisa, or someone, possibly the police, was after her because she murdered Lisa.

Charlotte sighed. Of course there was

always a third possibility. Belinda could simply be overreacting to something that happened.

Whatever the reason, Charlotte couldn't shake the uneasy feeling she had. But what to do about it?

Then, Charlotte got an idea. Grabbing a piece of paper, she scribbled a note to Louis telling him where she was going and whom she was picking up. He wouldn't exactly understand why she'd left him the note, but she could always come up with some excuse later, and at least someone would know where she'd gone, just in case there was trouble.

After taping the note to Louis's door, Charlotte drove to the hotel. The Jazzy had two driveways: one that led behind the hotel for guest parking, and a half-circle driveway directly in front of the hotel. When she first pulled into the half-circle she didn't see Belinda, so she drove up to the curb near the entrance, slid the gear into park, and waited with the van idling.

Almost immediately a bellhop approached. Charlotte hit the automatic window button, and shaking her head, she waved him away. "I'm just picking someone up," she told him. She'd just rolled the window back up when, out of the corner of her eye, she saw a figure carrying a small suitcase step out of the shadows near the end of the portico and hurry over to the van.

Once again an uneasy feeling slid through Charlotte's veins. Was Belinda hiding from someone? Was someone after her? But even more worrisome, why was she carrying a suitcase?

Belinda opened the back door and quickly shoved the suitcase inside. Then she climbed into the passenger seat, shut the door, and hit the lock switch.

"What in the world is going on, Belinda? Were you hiding just now?"

Belinda nodded, turning her head from side to side as if she were searching for someone or something. "Yes, ma'am."

"From who?"

Instead of answering her, Belinda said, "Could we please just leave?"

Charlotte hesitated a moment, then with a resigned sigh, she finally said, "Sure." Slipping the gear into drive, she pulled away from the curb and out onto St. Charles Avenue. "Is there anywhere in particular that you want to go?"

Belinda was half-turned in the seat, her gaze on the disappearing hotel behind them.

"Anywhere but the hotel," she whispered tearfully.

As Charlotte's mind whirled with places they could go to talk, only one place appealed to her. "My house okay?" When Belinda didn't immediately answer, Charlotte glanced over at her. Even in the dimly lit van she could tell that the girl was crying again, but her silent tears were somehow even more disturbing than if she'd been sobbing aloud.

Charlotte took a deep breath and prayed for the right words. "Listen, hon, I realize that something or someone has upset you and you're scared, but I can't help unless I know what or who. And crying won't do anything but make you sick."

She reached over and squeezed Belinda's forearm. "You need to get a grip and dry it up," she said, using the same no-nonsense voice that she'd often used when Judith had gone through teenage crying jags. "There's some Kleenex in the glove compartment," she said."

Several long moments passed in which Belinda didn't respond, but as Charlotte turned onto Milan Street, the girl opened the glove compartment. She grabbed several tissues, and blew her nose.

"Good, girl," Charlotte whispered.

A few minutes later Charlotte pulled into her driveway. "Here we are," she said. "Home sweet home."

Belinda glanced around. "This is your house?"

Charlotte nodded. "Like I said, home sweet home." She parked the van, switched off the engine, then opened her door. "Get your suitcase, and let's go inside."

As Charlotte led Belinda up the steps into her house, the girl remained silent. Though Sweety Boy did his regular routine vying for attention, Belinda only spared him a glance.

"This-this is nice."

"Thank you. You can leave your suitcase here." She pointed at the table near the doorway. "Now, have a seat." She motioned toward the sofa as she closed and locked the front door. "Are you thirsty? Hungry? I've got a slice of pizza leftover from dinner."

"No, ma'am," Belinda murmured as she settled near the end of the sofa.

After divesting herself of her purse and slipping into her moccasins, Charlotte joined the girl on the sofa. Turning toward Belinda, she took the girl's hands into her own. "Okay, now out with it."

Blinking back fresh tears, Belinda said, "After I left you cleaning the room, it took a while, but I finally found granddaddy down in the hotel bar." She lowered her gaze to stare at their joined hands. "I've never seen him drunk before," she whispered. "Never even seen him take a drink." After a moment she swallowed hard and raised her gaze level with Charlotte's. "He-he started talking about Lisa's murder and about my mother, then he started in on my father. Charlotte, he has this whole theory about how my father set up my mother . . ." Her voice trailed away.

Charlotte nodded. "Yes, I know. He told me all about it."

"Well, it's just not true. None of it's true. But when I argued with him about it he got angry and started saying all kinds of things."

"What kinds of things?"

Belinda shrugged. "All about how he'd tried to hold the family together, but all he'd ever gotten was misery. He went on and on about my grandmother, and about how my grandfather — my real grandfather — had almost ruined her, and now my father was trying to do the same thing to my mother."

Well, at least Mack's story was consistent, thought Charlotte. "And that's what has you so scared?"

Belinda shrugged. "Partly."

"How so?"

Belinda shook her head. "I can't," she whispered. "I promised —"

Charlotte narrowed her eyes as the conversation between Belinda and Mack came to mind. "Is this about your grandfather? Is it something you promised him?"

Belinda nodded.

Charlotte squeezed Belinda's hands. "Does it have anything to do with Lisa blackmailing your grandfather?"

Belinda's eyes widened in astonishment. "But-but —" She sputtered. "How-how did you know about that?"

"So it is true? Lisa *was* blackmailing him?"

Belinda hesitated, then slowly nodded. "Lisa found out that my grandfather was diverting funds from one of my father's accounts. She threatened to call in the cops if he didn't help convince my mother to give my father a divorce. When I confronted Granddaddy about it, he told me that Lisa had never liked him because he always took my mother's side against my father. Granddaddy had found out that my father kept a secret bank account. He said that it was money that rightfully belonged to my mother and that he'd only done it to protect her and me. But Lisa caught him transferring some of the money and threatened to call the police."

Once more tears filled Belinda's eyes. "If I didn't know better, I'd think that my granddaddy — and not my mother — killed Lisa. I don't want my mother in jail, but I don't want Granddaddy in jail either."

Since Charlotte had had the same thoughts about Mack herself, there was little she could say in his defense, so she opted for a change of subject. "Earlier you said that talking with Mack was only partly why you were scared," she reminded Belinda. "What else happened?"

Belinda visibly swallowed. "It-it was when I went back up to the room that I really got scared. It's like, I know that you cleaned it and left it all straight and everything, but I could tell that someone had been in there. It wasn't a wreck — it was still clean — but stuff was out of place, like someone had been searching for something but didn't want anyone to know they'd been looking for it. And since no one else has a key but my mother and me, then someone must have broken in."

Belinda paused. A shadow of fear darkened her eyes, and she took several quick breaths. "But that's not even the really scary part. While I was trying to decide whether to call the hotel desk and report it, I heard someone outside the door. I could tell that they were trying to turn the doorknob, so I ran over and put that security bar thing on. I guess maybe whoever was out there heard me, because after that, the noise outside stopped."

"Maybe it was just someone who had the wrong room."

"Maybe, but I don't think so."

"Why didn't you call the front desk? They have security people there at the hotel."

"I tried to call, but no one answered. Then I tried to call my father and Granddaddy, but neither of them answered either. I didn't know what else to do, and that's when I called you."

Charlotte frowned. "How did you know my home phone number?"

"The other night at dinner, I heard you talking to Granddaddy about your maid service, so I looked it up in the telephone book."

Charlotte nodded. "That makes sense. But let's go back and take this situation one step at a time and see what we can figure out. First of all, about things being out of place. Sometimes when I clean, I have to move things in order to dust. I try to put the stuff back exactly like I found it, but sometimes I don't succeed. What exactly was out of place?"

Belinda shrugged. "Mostly the stuff on the desk — all of Mother's files and things."

See, that's what you get for snooping.

Charlotte felt her face grow hot and could only hope that Belinda didn't notice. "I do remember moving them around," she said, "but I thought I put them back in a neat stack where I found them."

"That's just it!" Belinda exclaimed. "The files weren't in a stack. They were sort of fanned out, and I'm pretty sure that one of them was missing."

Something in Belinda's tone made Charlotte suspect that the girl knew more than she was telling. "Do you know which one was missing?"

It was Belinda's turn to blush with embarrassment, and after a moment she nodded. "Yes, ma'am. I don't usually make a habit of going through my mother's things," she said defensively, "but I was hoping that I'd find something that would help her. One of the files was about Lisa. From the looks of it, my mother had hired a private detective to check her out."

The uneasy feeling Charlotte had felt before returned with a vengeance. "So you read what was in the file?"

"No, not all of it. Just a few pages."

Charlotte was itching to ask Belinda if she'd read enough to know that Lisa was her half-sister, but if she asked her, she'd have to admit that she'd snooped and read the file herself. "So you're sure that particular file was missing?"

When Belinda nodded, Charlotte sighed. Maybe there was another way of finding out how much Belinda knew about the file. "Do you have any idea why that file would be important to someone else?"

"The only thing I can think of is that there was something in there that might prove that my mother was innocent."

"My thoughts exactly," Charlotte murmured.

"And now that we're talking about it," Belinda continued, "it makes me think that maybe Granddaddy's conspiracy theory might be right. Not about my father," she quickly added. "I just can't believe he'd do such a thing. But maybe about someone else. Whatever, I just know that I'm scared to stay at that hotel. I mean, what if whoever took the file figures out that I read it?"

Charlotte nodded thoughtfully. "Yes, I can see your point. Tell you what — why don't we ask my niece about all of this. She's a police detective, and —"

"No! No police! Please, Charlotte, please."

Charlotte threw up her hand. "Okay, okay, just calm down and hear me out. The police need to know about that file being stolen. It could help your mother's case."

Belinda shook her head. "They might think I stole it, or that my grandfather stole it, because it could incriminate my mother even more."

Not if I told them about the adoption paper, Charlotte thought. But again, she'd have to admit that she'd been snooping. Still, if it helped save an innocent person from being convicted of murder, maybe she had a moral obligation to tell them what she knew. But how on earth could she convince Belinda without revealing she'd snooped?

Charlotte sighed. She couldn't, not without owning up to what she'd done.

Suddenly, the weight of the day seemed to close in around Charlotte, and all she wanted was to climb into bed and forget that she'd ever met Mack's family.

She glanced up at the cuckoo clock on the wall behind the sofa. Almost nine. She returned her gaze to Belinda. "Listen, it's been a long day. I don't know about you, but I'm very, very tired. Maybe if we sleep on it, things will look better in the morning. I've got a spare bedroom and you're welcome to —"

The shrill ring of the telephone made them both jump. As Charlotte stood, it suddenly occurred to her that the caller could be Mack. Then another thought occurred. What if the caller was Joyce?

She walked over to the desk, and only after she picked up the receiver did it occur to her that she should have checked the caller I.D. first. "Hello."

For several seconds no one responded, then, "Aunt Charlotte, I'm not going to make it back over tonight. I just thought I'd let you know so that you wouldn't be waiting up for me."

When Charlotte heard Judith's voice, relief washed through her. "Okay, and thanks, hon."

"But this doesn't let you off the hook, Auntie. I'll be around the Jazzy tomorrow, so why don't you plan on having lunch with me — say around twelve or so?"

Before Charlotte could answer, Judith said, "Got to go now. Love you."

As Charlotte hung up the receiver, she suddenly remembered the note that she'd left on Louis's door. If she retrieved it now, then she wouldn't have to come up with an excuse as to why she'd left it there in the first place.

Charlotte turned toward Belinda and sighed. Belinda was curled up on the end of the sofa asleep. In sleep she looked much younger and more vulnerable. Poor thing, how horrible all of this mess must be for her, what with her mother being arrested and her mixed feelings about her father and grand father . . . unless *she* murdered Lisa.

Charlotte grimaced, then shook her head as if the action would clear it of all of her ugly suspicions.

The note. Just go get the note.

"Okay, okay," she whispered. She'd retrieve the note first and then she'd put Belinda to bed. As quietly as she could, Charlotte went to the door, eased it open, and then hurried across the porch. Once she had the note in hand, she hurried back to her own door and slipped inside.

Quietly folding the note into a small square, she dropped it into the wastebasket near her desk. With her eye on Belinda, she walked over to the sofa. "Belinda?" She gently shook the girl's shoulder. "Wake up, hon."

Suddenly, Belinda's eyes flew open and widened in alarm. "What? Where — ?" She sputtered. Then, just as suddenly, recognition lit her eyes. "Oh, Charlotte." She struggled to a sitting position then yawned.

"Sorry, I guess I must have dozed off."

"You've had a long day," Charlotte soothed. "I really hated to wake you, but I think you'd be more comfortable in a bed. Come with me, and I'll show you to the spare bedroom."

Belinda nodded, and after retrieving her suitcase, she followed Charlotte to the spare bedroom.

Once Charlotte had settled Belinda in the guestroom, she undressed, slipped on her pajamas, and went through her nightly routine of washing her face and brushing her teeth. As she climbed into bed, her gaze settled on her bedroom door.

In spite of everything that Belinda had told her, she really didn't know a lot about the girl. She felt like the girl was telling the truth about it all, but for all she knew, Belinda could have made up the whole scenario about the file being stolen and about someone trying to get into her hotel room. And if she wasn't telling the truth, then there was only one reason to go to such elaborate measures . . .

Hating the fact that she was so paranoid, she decided that, one way or another, she'd rather be safe than sorry. Better to be paranoid than dead.

Climbing back out of her bed, she went to

the door, closed it, and locked it. Then, as an extra precaution, she wedged the extra kitchen chair that she always kept in her bedroom beneath the doorknob.

With one last look at the makeshift security measures that she'd taken, she climbed back into bed, set her alarm, and then switched off the bedside lamp. Surely the girl wasn't that good of an actress . . . all that crying and carrying on.

Charlotte punched her pillow to fluff it up and snuggled down farther into the bed. If Belinda had been faking it though, then she'd missed her calling and should have been an actress, Charlotte decided.

Just as Charlotte was about to doze off, she heard a car door slam. Seconds later, she heard the porch creak, then the door to Louis's half of the double open and close. Only then did she realize that she'd completely forgotten about Louis and Joyce. But now that she thought about it, question after question pounded through her head. Did Louis find Joyce? If he did find her, then where did he find her, and what did he do with her?

Charlotte yawned, and once again, fatigue swept through her. Tomorrow would be soon enough to find out. For tonight though, just knowing that Louis was within screaming distance if she needed his help was enough to ease her concern about Belinda's presence in her home.

Feeling much more rested than she had the night before, on Tuesday Charlotte went about her regular morning routine, all the while figuring that Belinda would eventually wake up.

By the time she was ready to leave for work, Belinda was still asleep. Though Charlotte hadn't quite figured out what to do with the girl while she was at work, she was still hesitant about leaving a virtual stranger in her home without her being there. Any other time she might have been tempted to call in sick and stay home, but the hotel was already short-handed as it was.

Charlotte glanced at her watch. She still had a few minutes before it was time to leave. "Maybe, just one more cup of coffee," she murmured. And maybe Belinda would wake up and decide to return to her hotel room.

After pouring the coffee, Charlotte settled at the kitchen table and stared out of the window. Outside was overcast and thunder rumbled in the distance. Wondering if it was supposed to rain all day, she reached out for the newspaper that she'd retrieved earlier off the front steps. Then, she went through it until she found the page with the weather forecast. Sure enough, rain and thunderstorms were predicted throughout the day and into the evening.

"Great," she muttered. Every time it rained there were always certain streets that held water, and depending on how well the pumps could keep up, driving could be hazardous.

With a shrug and knowing that there was nothing to be done about it, she pushed the newspaper away.

But the weather didn't hold her attention long, and she was back to worrying about what to do with Belinda. If Belinda didn't wake up before she left, should she wake her up or let her sleep? Even if she woke her up, what then?

Charlotte had almost finished her coffee and was still debating her options when she heard the toilet flush.

"Finally," she whispered.

Moments later, wearing an oversized T-shirt for a nightgown, a sleepy-looking Belinda appeared in the kitchen doorway.

"Good morning," Charlotte told her.

"Morning," Belinda grumbled, then headed straight for the coffeepot. Once she'd poured herself a cup, she sat down at the table opposite Charlotte.

Charlotte cleared her throat. "Ah, I was wondering what your plans are for today," she said. "I have to leave in a few minutes to go to work, but I can wait until you get dressed if you need me to drop you off somewhere."

Confusion clouded Belinda's eyes, then they widened with panic. "But-but I thought that I could stay here. Just until I figure out what to do," she added.

When Belinda's lower lip began quivering and a lone tear rolled down her cheek, Charlotte didn't have the heart to refuse her, in spite of her misgivings about leaving the girl alone in her house.

"Of course you can stay," she said. "I just thought — I —" She shrugged. "I don't know what I was thinking."

The relief on Belinda's face made Charlotte feel even more rotten than she did before. "There's cereal in the pantry for breakfast. Or if you'd rather have eggs, there are plenty in the refrigerator. And there's lunch meat in there too for sandwiches later." Shoving her chair back from the table, she stood and carried her cup to the sink. "Just make yourself at home," she said over her shoulder.

Charlotte opened a drawer and took out a

notepad and pen. "This is my cell phone number." She jotted down the number, and then, with a quick smile, she handed it to Belinda. "Just call if you need anything. And if, for any reason, you decide to leave for a while, there's a spare key beneath the ceramic frog in the front flowerbed. Be sure and lock up if you do go somewhere."

But as Charlotte turned to leave, another thought occurred to her and she paused. "If the phone rings, just let the answering machine take the call."

This time Charlotte made it to the kitchen door before yet another thought came to mind. She turned to face Belinda. "And don't mind Sweety Boy — he's my parakeet. He'll probably squawk and carry on, but he'll eventually calm down."

By the time Charlotte pulled into the hotel parking lot, fat drops of rain were splattering against her windshield, and she'd thought of at least another half a dozen things she should have mentioned to Belinda. Telling Louis about her houseguest, for one. If Louis heard someone moving around in her half of the double and didn't see her van parked in the driveway, he might think she was being robbed or something. Besides, telling him about her houseguest would give her an excuse to ask about Joyce.

As soon as Charlotte parked the van, she pulled out her cell phone and called Louis. The last thing she needed was for him to scare Belinda even more than she was already.

The phone rang in her ear several times. When Louis's answering machine picked up the call, Charlotte frowned. Either he'd left right after she had or he was in the shower. Now she'd have to wait until later to learn if he'd found Joyce yet.

Charlotte waited impatiently for the beep, then left her message. "Louis, this is Charlotte. I just thought I'd better let you know that I have an unexpected guest staying at my house, just in case you hear her moving around. Her name is Belinda. She's Mack's granddaughter. Also, did you have any luck finding Joyce last night? Talk to you later. Bye."

Thunder rolled in the heavens and the raindrops turned into a deluge. "Wonderful," Charlotte grumbled as she twisted in her seat and searched for her umbrella.

At the hotel entrance, she shook the umbrella and closed it.

"Try this, ma'am." The bellhop handed her a clear, tubular-shaped plastic bag.

"Thanks," she told him, and once she'd

slipped the dripping umbrella into the bag, she entered the hotel. The moment she stepped inside, she immediately spotted Mack at the front desk. From the looks of him, he was angry about something, and poor Claire was on the receiving end of his tirade.

Charlotte's steps slowed as she approached the desk.

"I need to get inside that room," Mack insisted.

Claire shook her head. "I'm sorry, sir, but I keep telling you that I can't let you do that. It's against hotel policy."

"But you don't understand. I —"

Charlotte tapped Mack on the shoulder. "Mack, what's wrong?"

Mack whirled to face her. His eyes were bloodshot, and he looked as if he'd slept in his clothes. "A better question would be what's not wrong?" With a sigh, he reached up and rubbed the back of his neck. "Sorry. Didn't mean to snap at you, but Belinda's missing, and this —" He motioned toward Claire. "This moron won't let me in her room."

To give Claire credit, she didn't flinch in the face of Mack's anger.

Charlotte spared the young woman a sympathetic look, then she grabbed Mack's arm. "Mack Sutton, shame on you," she told him as she pulled him away from the desk. "There's no need to get nasty. Claire is just doing her job. Besides, Belinda is okay." At Mack's dubious expression, she repeated, "Belinda is okay. Read my lips, Mack. Your granddaughter is just fine."

"You've seen her?"

Charlotte nodded. "Yes, I have, but she doesn't want to see you right now."

"Where is she?" Mack shot back.

"I said, she doesn't want to see you right now," Charlotte repeated.

Mack bowed his head and stared at the floor. "My fault," he muttered. "I should have kept my mouth shut."

"Yes, you should have," Charlotte agreed. "What were you thinking, telling her all that stuff about her father? Now, she doesn't trust you or her father. And with her mother in jail, now she has no one — no one to depend on, no one she can talk to."

Mack raised his head and gave Charlotte a pointed look. "No one except you, evidently," he drawled in a mocking tone.

Charlotte glowered at him and silently counted to ten in an attempt to keep her anger under control. "Just give her some time," she finally said, emphasizing each word slowly. "If you give her some time, she'll come around eventually."

"Yeah, well, easy for you to say," he sneered. "It's not your granddaughter who's missing with a killer running loose."

"And they say I'm stubborn," she muttered. Trying to get through to Mack was like talking to a brick wall. Holding on to her temper by a thread, Charlotte said, "Look! Believe it or not — that's your choice — but I'm here to tell you that Belinda is safe. She is not missing."

"If she's not missing then where is she?"

Charlotte rolled her eyes to the ceiling, then with a shake of her head she said, "Forget it. Just forget it. I give up." Turning her back on him, she stalked over to the desk to get her room assignments from Claire for the day.

"Thanks, Charlotte," Claire told her as she handed over her list of room assignments for the day.

"Don't mind him," Charlotte said. "He's just upset right now." And though she had her doubts, she said, "I'm sure that once he thinks about it, he'll apologize."

When Charlotte approached the second room she'd been assigned to clean, she cringed, remembering the last time that she'd been in Ralph Jones's room.

Charlotte stared long and hard at the doorknob as if doing so would make a DO NOT DISTURB sign miraculously materialize. Too bad she didn't have an extra one that she could hang on the door. She could always claim that there was a sign, but then she'd have to feel guilty about lying.

Think positive.

But the only positive thing she could come up with was the remote possibility that Ralph Jones had checked out and that someone else was now occupying the room. Either way, like it or not, the room had to be cleaned.

Charlotte reached up and knocked on the door. "Housekeeping," she called out. Waiting a couple of minutes, she knocked again. "Housekeeping."

Finally deciding that no one was in the room, she pulled out her master key and unlocked the door. The moment that she opened the door, a strange smell assaulted her senses. And the room was pitch black. Evidently, Ralph had closed the room-darkening curtains when he'd gone to bed last night and had neglected to open them this morning before he left. The curtains being closed, along with the cloud cover and rain outside left the room even darker than it would have been ordinarily.

The first thing she intended to do was open up the curtains, and let what little light there was outside in. But not until she turned on the lights. No way was she going to feel her way through that dark room. All she needed was to stumble over something, fall, and break an arm or a hip.

She slid her hand along the wall until she located the light switch, then flipped it on. Waiting a minute for her eyes to adjust, she stepped inside.

What was that smell? Wrinkling her nose and intent on opening the curtains, she headed for the windows on the far side of the room. But as she rounded the end of the bed, she suddenly froze.

Panic welled in her throat and blood roared in her ears. "Dear Lord in heaven," she whispered.

Chapter 14

Charlotte felt a scream clawing in her throat. For what seemed like forever, she couldn't move as she stared at the man on the floor beside the bed. Fully dressed in jeans and a short-sleeved shirt, he lay half on his side and half on his back, facing the bed. From where she was standing though, she couldn't see his face.

She'd seen dead people before, but not often enough to tell if they were dead just by looking. Maybe he'd just passed out or something.

Her gaze zeroed in on his chest, and she stared at it, willing it to move or show some sign that he was still breathing.

After a moment though, she began to panic. If he wasn't breathing, was it possible that he could still have a pulse? Maybe all he needed was CPR.

Move, Charlotte. Get your butt in gear and move. See if the poor man still has a pulse.

There was only one way to determine if he had a pulse, and though she didn't remember moving, she found herself kneeling beside Ralph Jones. With a shudder of revulsion, she reached out and placed her fingers just below his jaw near the side of his neck. His skin was cold to the touch . . . dead cold. And there was no pulse.

But there was blood . . . the strange odor. The blood explained the strange odor.

Charlotte snatched her hand away. There didn't seem to be a lot of it. Most of it had probably soaked into the carpet between the body and beneath the bed.

After a moment, she stumbled to her feet and backed away from him.

She took several deeps breaths and willed her legs to stop trembling. *Why me?* she thought. Why did I have to be the one to find him?

Because you were meant to find him.

Still not totally willing or convinced that she was meant to use her so-called gift for discernment to solve murders, her gaze shifted to the door. She could simply leave and let someone else find him. She could walk out, close the door behind her, and pretend that she'd never gotten around to cleaning his room.

You should be ashamed. For Pete's sake,

get a grip, Charlotte.

"Yeah, yeah," she whispered as the irritating voice of her conscience hammered in her head. Besides, with her luck, someone was sure to find out, and then she'd have to explain why she hadn't reported finding a dead body.

Taking yet another deep breath, she stepped over to the telephone on the bedside table, picked up the receiver, and dialed the front desk.

"Front desk. How may I help you?"

Charlotte immediately recognized Claire's voice. "This is Charlotte. I'm in room 208. I really hate to tell you this, but you need to call the police. The guest who's staying in this room, Ralph Jones, is dead."

After Charlotte hung up the phone, she left the room. When she stepped out into the hallway, she decided against completely closing the door and left it just slightly ajar.

Without warning, her knees suddenly went weak. Grabbing the wall for support, she sat down on the carpeted floor. Crossing her legs Indian style, she closed her eyes and leaned back against the wall.

She was still sitting on the floor when she heard the ding of the elevator. Opening her eyes, she turned her head and saw two men wearing hotel security shirts step out of the elevator down the hallway and hurry toward her.

The taller of the two men stopped and knelt down beside her. "Are you Charlotte?"

When she nodded, he said, "I'm Tom Nelson, hotel security. Are you okay?"

Again she nodded. "Just a little weak in the knees," she told him.

"Why don't you wait right here for a minute? I just need to check inside, and then I'll escort you to the bar downstairs. When the police get here, they'll want to talk to you."

When Charlotte nodded, he got to his feet and opened the door. With the other man trailing along behind him, they went inside. Within minutes, they both reappeared at the doorway.

"Stand guard until the police arrive," Tom Nelson told the other one. He turned to Charlotte. "Ready to go now?"

Charlotte nodded.

"Need some help?" He held out his hand.

"No, I don't think so." She waved his hand away, uncrossed her legs and got to her knees. So far, so good, she thought, and using the wall for support, she stood up.

Though her legs still felt a bit shaky, she finally decided that they would support her.

"Ready?"

Charlotte nodded. Then she frowned and eyed the cleaning cart. She should probably return it to the storage closet.

"Don't worry about it for now," he told her. "Just leave it."

She made it to the elevator just fine, but once inside, she leaned against the wall. "What happened to him?" he asked.

The security guard shrugged as he pushed the first floor button. "Looks like he's been shot."

The elevator doors slid closed and they began the descent to the first floor.

A few minutes later the elevator slid back open, and Tom Nelson escorted her to a corner table in the bar. Except for the bartender, the room was empty.

"I need to go wait for the police," Tom said. "Just stay here for now." He patted her shoulder. "Will you be okay?"

Grateful for his concern, Charlotte smiled and nodded. "I'll be fine."

"Probably be best if you don't talk to anyone about what you found, at least until the police get here."

Again Charlotte nodded. "I understand."

After the security man left, the bartender approached her. He was a young man, probably in his thirties, Charlotte decided, and he had a kind face.

"You're Charlotte, aren't you?"

Charlotte nodded.

He waved toward the doorway where Tom Nelson had disappeared. "What's going on?"

"There was a problem in one of the rooms on the second floor," she told him. Before he could ask what kind of problem, she said, "You wouldn't happen to have some coffee would you?"

"Yes, ma'am. I just brewed a fresh pot."

"Could I please have a cup?"

"Sure. Be back in a minute."

When he returned with her coffee, he motioned to the chair opposite her. "Mind if I sit down?"

Charlotte minded, but besides not wanting to be rude, she decided that talking to him might be a good distraction for the moment; better than dwelling on Ralph Jones. She shook her head, indicating that she didn't mind.

"Things are always slow this time of morning," he said once he was seated. "By the way, my name is Patrick."

"Nice to meet you, Patrick."

"Same here." He paused a moment, then said, "Is it true?"

Confused, Charlotte frowned. "Is what true?"

"Is that lady homicide detective that's been nosing around your niece?"

When Charlotte didn't answer immediately but simply stared at him, a flush stole up his cheeks. "I overheard Claire talking to Miss Carrie," he explained, "but I just wanted to make sure."

Charlotte's suspicious nature kicked in and her frown deepened. "Why?"

Patrick shifted uneasily in his chair, and the flush on his cheeks darkened. "I-I thought — I —" He sighed heavily. "I was hoping that you could tell me if she's seeing anyone? I don't figure she's married — at least I didn't see a ring, but —" He shrugged.

All of Charlotte's suspicions immediately disappeared, and she felt a smile tugging at her lips. Deciding to take pity on the poor man, she said, "Sorry, but she is seeing someone."

"Is it serious — I mean, like, are they engaged or anything?"

"They're not engaged — at least not that I know of — but I think you'd need to ask her about it being serious."

Patrick nodded. "That's cool, as long as she isn't married or engaged." Suddenly his gaze shifted to the doorway and Charlotte followed it. "Uh-oh, the police again," he said. His gaze pinned Charlotte and he narrowed his eyes shrewdly. "Just what did happen upstairs?"

"I'm not supposed to discuss it until I talk to the police."

"Don't tell me that there's been another murder."

"Okay, I won't."

"Which means there was."

Charlotte shook her head. "I didn't say that." She threw up her hand. "And don't ask."

"It's a shame about that other one. She was a real looker." He sighed. "If this keeps up, I'll be out of a job. No one will want to stay here." He shook his head. "First that maid who was caught stealing, then with that woman being strangled, and now . . ." He stared at Charlotte expectantly. When she stared back at him, he repeated, "And now . . ."

"Nice try," she finally said, "but I told you that I can't talk about it, so stop fishing around for information."

"Hey, can't blame a body for trying."

Charlotte smiled at him indulgently, but something he'd said suddenly pricked her memory and her curiosity. "Ah, Patrick, you didn't happen to know the maid who was caught stealing, did you?"

"Not really."

"What did she steal?"

"I think one of the guests accused her of taking some jewelry or something like that."

Jewelry . . . Tessa's missing earring . . . the earring found at the murder scene . . . Mack's theory about Tessa being set up . . . What if there was a connection between the jewelry that the maid stole and Tessa's missing earring? What if Mack was right after all? What if someone had set up Tessa to take the fall for murdering Lisa?

"Charlotte?"

Charlotte blinked when Patrick waved his hand in front of her face.

"For a minute there you zoned out on me. Where did you go?"

She blinked again. "I-er-I was just thinking," she said. "Sorry."

"So what were you thinking?"

Out of the corner of her eye, Charlotte saw someone enter the lounge. "I was thinking that you have a new customer."

Patrick glanced over at the bar then eyed Charlotte suspiciously. "Yeah, well, guess I'd better get to work then." He shoved out of his chair and headed for the bar.

As Charlotte watched Patrick greet his customer, she made a mental note to ask Claire about the maid who'd been fired.

As if the thought of Claire had conjured her up, Claire entered the lounge and glanced around. When she spotted Charlotte seated in the corner, she headed straight for her table.

"Sorry I didn't get around to checking on you before now," she told Charlotte as she sat down across from her. "Are you doing okay?"

Charlotte nodded. "I'm okay. The police got here pretty quickly."

Claire nodded. "Yeah, they did. That's the good news." She rolled her eyes. "The bad news is that we had to call them at all."

Charlotte was fairly certain that Ralph Jones had been shot to death, but she decided to ask anyway in hopes that Claire could shed some light on what happened. "I saw blood. Has anyone said what he officially died from yet?"

"No, not officially. But I did overhear one of the detectives tell another one that it looked like he was shot early yesterday evening, probably around six or seven."

After a moment, the significance of the time frame suddenly dawned on Charlotte, and a cold knot formed in her stomach. "Six or seven?" she asked, her voice barely above a whisper. "Are you sure, Claire?"

When Claire nodded, all Charlotte could

do was stare at her. Six or seven was right about the time that Belinda had called her . . . Belinda upset, crying . . . scared. Though she kept telling herself that it was nothing but coincidence, the knot in Charlotte's stomach twisted tighter.

Claire suddenly reached out and gripped Charlotte's hand. "Are you sure you're okay? You're as pale as a ghost, and your hands are like ice."

When she didn't immediately answer, Claire turned toward the bar. "Hey, Patrick, bring a fresh cup of coffee over here, and make sure it's hot."

Hearing the panic in Claire's voice, Charlotte forced her lips into a stiff smile, squeezed, and slid her hand out of Claire's grip. "I'm okay," she assured her. "Guess I'm still a little shook up is all."

"Well, of course you are. Who wouldn't be?"

Patrick appeared by her side and replaced the half-empty cup of cold coffee with a steaming one.

"Thanks." Charlotte gave him a quick, polite smile as she wrapped her hands around the warm cup.

"Listen," Claire said. "Just as soon as the detectives finish questioning you, I want you to go home and get some rest."

Charlotte shook her head. "I'll be fine. Besides, you're already short-handed as it is."

Claire gave her a stern look. "I insist. Besides, it's about time that new girl Sarah began earning her pay."

Sarah. With the mention of the new maid's name, Charlotte suddenly remembered her conversation with Carrie in which Carrie had wanted her opinion about Sarah. But it also reminded Charlotte of the maid who had been fired as well.

"Claire, can I ask you something?"

"Sure."

"The other maid — the one that you had to fire for stealing — what was that all about?"

Claire sighed. "One of the guest turned in a complaint — said that she'd caught her red-handed stealing some of her jewelry."

"Do you remember the name of the guest who made the complaint?"

Claire nodded. "Yes, I do, but I'm afraid that's confidential information. Why do you want to know?"

"Mostly, just curiosity," Charlotte answered. Charlotte waited several seconds in hopes that Claire would reveal the name of the guest anyway. When she didn't, she said, "So was she arrested — the maid, not the guest?"

Claire grinned. "I know what you meant." She shook her head. "No, the guest decided against pressing charges once she got her jewelry back."

"So what happened to the maid?"

Claire shrugged. "I had no choice but to fire her. Such a shame too. She really needed the job."

"Can you tell me *her* name?"

Claire sighed. "I'd rather not, Charlotte, what with you being in the business and all. Not that I think you would gossip about her or anything," she quickly added. "But I honestly don't think she stole anything. I've been in this business long enough to know that some guests can be vindictive — just downright mean."

"Vindictive? About what?"

Claire laughed. "Who knows? Maybe the girl forgot to leave extra coffee or maybe she didn't leave enough towels."

"Surely not," Charlotte whispered, appalled that someone could be so petty.

"You'd be surprised."

Surmising that Claire wasn't going to divulge the name of the maid, she decided to drop the subject for the moment. Too bad though, she thought. If she knew the name of the maid, then she could probably find out the name of the guest who had made the complaint.

Patrick approached the table again. “Claire, they need you at the front desk.”

Claire shook her head. “No rest for the weary,” she grumbled. “Okay, I’m on my way.” She stood. “Do me a favor though. Keep an eye on Charlotte for me.”

Patrick grinned. “Be glad to.”

Though Charlotte understood that Claire was just being nice, it irked her to be talked about in the third person, especially with her sitting right under their noses. Still, she held her tongue, and the more she thought about it, the more the idea of Patrick keeping an eye on her appealed to her.

She’d bet her bottom dollar that if anyone knew the name of the maid who was fired, Patrick would. Even if he didn’t know, he could probably find out. After all, bartenders overheard all kinds of things and talked to everyone.

A calculating smile pulled at her lips. She could always promise him that she’d introduce him to Judith.

Yeah, and Judith would murder you too.

With one last admonition that Charlotte was to go home and rest once the police talked to her, Claire hurried out of the lounge.

Once Claire disappeared through the doorway, Charlotte looked up at Patrick. "I've got a question for you," she told him.

At that moment, Patrick's gaze shifted to the doorway, and Charlotte followed his gaze to see several customers enter the lounge.

"Sorry," he said. "Maybe later."

"Sure — later." Her mind churning, Charlotte lowered her gaze to stare at her cup of coffee. First Lisa's murder and now, Ralph Jones's murder: one by strangulation and the other by gunshot. There had to be a connection between the two murders, but what?

She drummed her fingers against the tabletop. If she could figure out the common denominator between the two murders, she might figure out who the killer was.

Charlotte reached inside her apron pocket and took out her notepad and pen. Opening the small notepad to a clean page, she began writing names.

Tessa: The wife of Lisa's lover, and Ralph's daughter. Accused of murdering Lisa.

Belinda:

Charlotte swallowed hard, then wrote *Lisa and Belinda — so-called friends, and Lisa's affair with Belinda's father.* Then she added *Belinda is Ralph's granddaughter.*

Her pen stilled. Again she had to wonder if it was mere coincidence that Ralph had been killed in the same time frame that Belinda had called her. And what about Belinda's claim that someone had been in her room and had taken the file folder on Lisa? Could it all be a smokescreen to cover up the fact that she'd killed Ralph? But what earthly reason would she have to kill Ralph to begin with? After all, he was her grandfather.

With a shake of her head, Charlotte glanced back over her list. The next name she decided to add was *Mack.* Beside Mack's name she wrote: *Belinda claims that Lisa was blackmailing Mack. Both Ralph and Mack had been married to the same woman. Mack claims that Ralph was a no-good jailbird.*

Charlotte stared at the list, then decided to add another name.

Frank: Lisa's lover, and Ralph's son-in-law.

She tapped her pen against the pad, then wrote down Margaret's name as well.

Charlotte slid the pen back and forth between her fingers. Though there was a personal link of sorts between Margaret and Lisa, the personal link being that they both worked for Frank, as far as she knew, there wasn't one between Margaret and Ralph. She shook her head and added a question mark beside Margaret's name.

"We meet again."

Charlotte jumped at the sound of Gavin Brown's voice. When she jerked her head up, he was standing on the other side of her small table. How long had he been there? Even worse though, he was staring down at her notepad, and unless she was mistaken there was a definite gleam of interest in his eyes. Surely the man couldn't read upside down.

Chapter 15

"Only two days have passed this time," Gavin Brown drawled nastily. "That has to be some kind of record." He pulled out a chair and seated himself, then motioned towards her notepad. "What'cha got there?"

"Nothing." Charlotte slid her hand over the top page of the notepad and closed it. "Just business stuff."

Yeah, monkey business.

Ignoring the pesky voice in her head, she slipped the notepad and the pen back inside her apron pocket.

A sneer pulled at the detective's lips as he reached into his suit coat pocket and produced his own notepad and pen. He placed the notepad on the table in front of him, then crossed his arms on the table and leaned forward. "So, Charlotte, what's your story this time?"

Not liking the way he'd emphasized "this time," nevertheless, she was determined to keep her temper under control. As calmly and succinctly as she could, she went through her movements that morning, step by step, up until the time that she had called Claire, then left the room to wait for hotel security.

"So where were you between six and eight o'clock last night?"

There were only two reasons that she could think of why he would ask such a question. One, he was trying to make her a suspect, or two, he somehow already knew that she'd picked up Belinda at the hotel.

Charlotte held on to her temper by a thread. That he'd even think for one moment that she was a suspect was insult enough, but until she knew more about Belinda's so-called timing, there was no way she was giving Gavin Brown that information.

Taking the chance that he was simply on a fishing expedition, she forced a smile. "I was home having pizza with my niece and my neighbor." That much was true. It just wasn't the entire truth.

"Names please — your niece and your neighbor." His pen hovered over the notepad as he waited expectantly.

Gotcha, she thought with glee. Careful to keep her expression under control, she said,

"I only have one niece, and her name is Judith Monroe. She's a homicide detective too. And my neighbor's name is Louis Thibodeaux. Louis was Judith's partner before he retired."

Wanting badly to give him a Cheshire cat grin, she affected a confused expression instead. "But you already know about Judith, don't you? Remember? I told you about her being my niece that other time that you interviewed me when I was working for the Rossis. And surely you know Louis. He hasn't been retired that long."

The look on Gavin Brown's face reminded Charlotte of someone with a serious constipation problem.

"Yeah," he ground out. "I know them." For a moment more he glared at her. Then, with more force than necessary, he clicked his pen closed, snatched up the notebook, and stuffed both of them back inside his pocket. Shoving his chair back, he stood. "You can go now," he snapped, glaring down at her, his voice as cold as the look in his eyes. With that, he executed an about-face and stalked out of the lounge.

"Serves you right for being such a jerk," Charlotte muttered as he disappeared through the doorway. After a moment, she took a deep cleansing breath, and then she checked her watch. She still had an hour or so before meeting Judith for lunch. Should she stay or should she go home and then come back?

Charlotte stared at the lounge entrance door. With the additional murder, would Judith even have time for lunch? She sure didn't want to waste an hour sitting there just to find out that Judith couldn't meet her after all.

Only one way to make sure, she decided. Reaching into her pocket, she pulled out her cell phone and tapped in Judith's cell number.

Judith answered on the fourth ring. "Judith Monroe here."

"It's Aunt Charlotte, hon. I was wondering if we were still on for lunch."

"Lunch?" Judith paused, then said, "Oh, yeah, lunch. I'd completely forgotten. Sorry, Auntie, but I don't think I'm going to make it. You probably already know that there's been another murder at the Jazzy."

"Ah — yes, yes I do. Unfortunately, I was the one who found the body."

For several seconds there was complete silence, then, "That was you, Aunt Charley? You're the maid who found the body?"

"Afraid so."

"Why that son-of-a —"

"Judith!"

"Okay, okay. Sorry. But Gavin didn't bother telling me that my aunt was the one who had found that man."

"I told you he doesn't like me."

"More like he doesn't like me," Judith retorted. "Sour grapes and all. Anyway — right now I've got to run. We'll talk later."

Wondering what Judith meant by "sour grapes," Charlotte switched off her phone. She stood and had just slipped it inside her pocket when she saw Patrick headed her way.

"You leaving?"

When Charlotte nodded, he said, "What was it that you wanted to ask me earlier?"

Charlotte sat back down and indicated that Patrick should be seated as well.

With a quick glance toward the bar, Patrick sat down too.

Charlotte folded her arms on top of the table and leaned forward. "Patrick, I wanted to ask you if you happened to know the name of the maid who was fired for stealing?"

Patrick stiffened, and a guarded look came over his face. "Depends," he said.

"Depends on what?" Charlotte asked.

"Depends on why you want to know her name."

Since she didn't want to tell him the real reason, she said the first thing that popped into her head. "I thought I might have a job opportunity for her."

"Even though she was fired for stealing? Why would you do that?"

Oops, he had her there. Charlotte's mind raced. "From everything I've heard, she got a bum deal. Claire doesn't believe that the girl really stole anything, but she had no choice but to fire her anyway."

"Neither do I," Patrick said.

Though some of the wariness in his expression faded, Charlotte grew curious as to why he seemed so defensive about the fired maid.

"So, what kind of job opportunity are you talking about?"

Charlotte hesitated, then decided to sidestep his question for the moment. "Earlier you said that you really didn't know her."

Patrick shook his head. "I don't. I just hate to see anyone railroaded, especially someone who really needs the job. Did Claire tell you that the woman has a kid?"

"No she didn't."

"Yeah, she's a single mother. Little girl's about five, I think."

"That's too bad," Charlotte murmured. Since she had also been a single mother and knew how hard it could be trying to work and raise a child alone, her heart went out to the nameless woman.

"Listen, Patrick, I own a maid service. It's called Maid-For-a-Day. If you want to check it out, it's listed in the yellow pages. I'm only working here for a couple of weeks as a favor for an old friend of mine because they were short-handed," she explained. "Anyway, I employ several maids, but I'm always on the look-out for more."

Patrick tilted his head to one side, and after a moment, he nodded. "Her name is Julie — Julie Harper." He grabbed a napkin, took a pen out of his shirt pocket, and jotted down a phone number. "You can reach her at this number." He slid the napkin across the table to Charlotte.

Charlotte narrowed her eyes as she picked up the napkin. "You don't really know her, but you know that she has a little girl and you've got her phone number memorized?"

He shrugged then grinned. "Would you believe that I have a photographic memory?"

"Yeah, and I suppose you have some waterfront property in Arizona that you want to sell me too."

Patrick laughed, then his gaze shifted to the bar. "Duty calls. Gotta go."

Charlotte smiled. "Sounds like a pretty convenient excuse, if you ask me," she called out as he hurried toward the bar.

By the time Charlotte pulled into her driveway, she still hadn't decided what to do about Belinda.

"At least it's stopped raining," she murmured as she shoved the gear into PARK, climbed out of the van, and locked the door.

She glanced up at the sky. There were fewer dark clouds, and a sickly sun was trying to peek through those that were left. "Just in time to steam up the afternoon," she muttered.

All too soon, thoughts of the weather were replaced by thoughts of Belinda again.

Her feet dragging, Charlotte headed for the steps. What if Belinda calling her around the same time that Ralph had been murdered was just coincidence? But what if it wasn't? If it was though, then she'd have to be the one to break the news to Belinda that Ralph had been murdered.

By the time Charlotte had climbed the steps and unlocked her front door, she'd decided that there was no good answer to her dilemma. She'd just have to play it by ear and see what happened.

The first thing Charlotte noticed when she

opened the door was the silence. There was no TV on, no radio playing, and no sounds of movement in the house. Even Sweety Boy seemed unusually subdued.

With a frown, Charlotte placed her purse on the small table near the doorway, took off her apron, then stepped out of her shoes and into her moccasins. "Hello!" She called out. "Belinda?"

Other than the sound of Sweety Boy ruffling his feathers, there was no answer. Feeling a bit uneasy, Charlotte cautiously headed for the guestroom. At the doorway, as her gaze inspected each corner of the room, she noted that the bed was made and that Belinda's suitcase was still sitting next to the small dresser. So, where was Belinda?

With a puzzled frown, she walked to the bathroom and flipped on the light. Everything looked about the same as she'd left it.

After checking her bedroom and finding no sign of the girl there, she headed for the kitchen.

The moment she entered the kitchen she quickly scanned the room. There were no dirty dishes in the sink and nothing was out of place on the countertops. Even Belinda's coffee cup had been put away.

Then she saw it: a single piece of paper on the table. She walked to the table and picked up the paper.

Charlotte, it quit raining, so I decided to walk over to Magazine Street and look around. See you later.

Belinda.

Outdone with herself for being so paranoid, Charlotte sighed. "You're such a dummy," she grumbled. Then, after a moment she said, "What you need is food and a shrink, and not necessarily in that order."

But as she prepared herself some lunch, she couldn't stop thinking about Belinda. Considering the circumstances, with her mother in jail for murder and all, either the girl was a cold-blooded killer or she was a heartless, self-centered brat.

Or maybe she just needed a break from thinking about it all.

"Yeah, yeah," Charlotte muttered as she sliced her smoked turkey sandwich in half, then poured the chicken noodle soup that she'd warmed into a bowl. It wasn't her favorite meal, but it was quick and filling.

Over the years Charlotte had gotten into the habit of eating her meals either in front of the television or while reading. Today, with all that had happened weighing so heavily on her mind, neither choice appealed to her.

After settling at the table, she stared out

the back window. As she ate, thoughts of the morning's events swirled through her mind. Again she had to ask herself why anyone would want to murder Ralph Jones. The only candidates that she could think of were Mack and possibly Belinda. As far as she knew, they were the only ones who had had contact with him or even knew who he was . . . except for Tessa. But Tessa was in jail.

Out of the two, and she hated to admit it, Mack was the best possibility. He'd certainly been angry with Ralph for trying to horn back into Tessa and Belinda's lives. But for the life of her, Charlotte couldn't think of a single motive for Belinda killing him. After all, Ralph had been in prison when she'd been born, and according to what Mack had said, Ralph had never been a part of Belinda's life.

Charlotte loaded her dirty dishes into the dishwasher. As she latched the dishwasher door, her thoughts fast-forwarded to the conversations she'd had with Claire and Patrick about Julie Harper.

Why did the so-called theft keep nagging at her? What could it possibly have to do with the two murders?

Suddenly, out of nowhere, it came to her. "The earrings," she whispered

Julie had allegedly stolen jewelry, and one of Tessa's earrings was found near Lisa's body. Was there a connection between the two incidents?

Then she remembered what Claire had said. *I honestly don't think she stole anything.* Neither Claire nor Patrick thought that Julie Harper was a thief, and according to Claire, the guest got her jewelry back. But what if they were wrong?

Charlotte sighed. There was only one way to find out the truth, and that was to give Julie Harper a call. She could always use the excuse that Patrick had recommended Julie as a prospective employee. It wasn't exactly the truth, but it wasn't exactly a lie either. Surely once she began talking to the woman, she could figure out someway to bring up the subject of the jewelry.

Charlotte reached inside her pants pocket, pulled out the napkin, then stared at the number that Patrick had written on it. "No time like the present," she whispered. But as she turned to head for the living room, there was a loud knock at the front door.

Stuffing the napkin back inside her pants pocket, she hurried to the living room. "Who's there?" she called out when she reached the door.

"It's me, Belinda."

Charlotte unlocked the door and opened it.

Even though Belinda was dressed in a pair of shorts and a halter-top, her hair hung limp from the humidity and her face was flushed from the heat.

She smiled at Charlotte. "I saw that your van was in the driveway, so I didn't need the key after all," she explained as she came inside.

"You look hot," Charlotte said. "How about a glass of iced tea?"

"That sounds wonderful."

Charlotte headed for the kitchen, and Belinda trailed along behind her. "Aren't you home earlier than usual?" Belinda asked.

Charlotte simply said, "Yes," but for the moment, she chose not to elaborate on the reason why she was home early. "What did you think of Magazine Street?" she asked instead.

"I loved it. At least what I saw of it," Belinda added. "Some day I'd like to look around some more, but not today. It's just too hot. I thought the rain would cool things off, but it's like a sauna out there."

In the kitchen, Belinda sat down at the table, and Charlotte took two glasses out of the cabinet. "Have you eaten?" Charlotte asked as she opened the freezer door and filled the glasses with ice.

"Yes, ma'am. I found the neatest little café and had the best shrimp salad that I've ever tasted."

Charlotte closed the freezer door then opened the refrigerator, took out a pitcher of tea, and filled the two glasses.

"Here we go," she said, handing Belinda one of the glasses. "It's unsweetened, but if you want sugar or sweetner —"

"Unsweetened is fine." Belinda immediately took a long drink. "Hmm." She smacked her lips. "That hit the spot."

Charlotte nodded and sat down at the table across from the girl. Dreading what she had to tell Belinda, Charlotte sighed. "Belinda, there's a reason why I'm home earlier than usual. There's no nice way to say this, but there's been another murder at the hotel."

Belinda's eyes widened. "What!" She blinked several times. "Who?"

Charlotte reached out and took hold of Belinda's hand. "I'm sorry to have to tell you, but your grandfather was murdered."

"Granddaddy?" she cried. "No — not, Granddaddy!" Her lower lip trembled and tears sprang into her eyes.

Charlotte quickly shook her head and squeezed Belinda's hand. "No, no — not your granddaddy Mack, hon. The murdered man was Ralph Jones."

Belinda blinked back the tears. "Grandpa Ralph? But why would anyone want to murder him?" she cried.

Charlotte narrowed her eyes. Was it all an act? Belinda's reaction appeared to be genuine, but if there was one thing that Charlotte had learned in her lifetime, appearances could be deceiving.

"I don't know why," Charlotte finally answered. "I was hoping that you could tell me." She paused for a heartbeat, praying for the right words; then she said, "The police think it happened last night, around six or seven. His room was right down the hallway from yours, and you'd have had to go past it to get to the elevator. Since he was shot, I was hoping that maybe you saw or heard something."

For what seemed an eternity, Belinda stared at Charlotte. Then slowly, comprehension dawned in the girl's eyes, and her grief and despair metamorphosed into shock, outrage, and something akin to betrayal.

"You think *I* killed him?" she cried. "Why would you think such a thing?" Her eyes filled with tears, she visibly swallowed, then, after a moment, she sighed. "Of course you would think it," she whispered. "Who wouldn't, considering the way I carried on last night." She shook her head slowly. "I didn't though." Her eyes bored into Charlotte's. "I know it looks bad, but I swear to you, I didn't do it. Please believe me. You've got to believe me." She threw up her hands. "I don't even own a gun," she cried. "Never even held one or shot one."

At that moment Charlotte wasn't sure what she thought or believed. "Look, hon, it doesn't matter what I think. What matters is what the police will think if they find out about last night — about me picking you up and all."

"Oh, Charlotte, don't you see, it *does* matter what you think. It matters to me. I-I —" She shook her head. "I thought — I mean —" She shrugged. "It's just that with my mom in jail, and after the fight I had with Grandddaddy and what he said about my father — you were so nice to me and all . . ." Her voice trailed away and fresh tears filled her eyes. Crossing her arms on the tabletop, she bent over, her forehead resting on her wrist. "I have no one else," she sobbed.

Not an act, Charlotte decided. Feeling as if she'd just plucked the wings off a defenseless butterfly, she reached over and stroked the back of Belinda's head with her hand. "There, there," she soothed. "I know you're confused and hurting, hon. I also know that it seems like everything's a mess right now. But nothing stays the same, and things will get better."

"I don't see how," Belinda sobbed. "Not when I've made such a mess of things."

Charlotte's hand stilled, then she withdrew it. "What do you mean that you've made a mess of things?"

Belinda slowly raised her head, and wiped her cheeks with the back of her hand. "It's killing me — eating me up inside, and I don't know what to do about it."

"You don't know what to do about what, hon? I don't understand."

Belinda's face contorted with misery. "Just promise me that you won't hate me. Promise me."

"Of course I won't hate you," Charlotte retorted.

"You swear?"

Charlotte threw up her right hand. "Okay, I swear."

Belinda closed her eyes and bowed her head. "I did it," she whispered. "I-I choked Lisa."

CHAPTER 16

Stunned speechless, all Charlotte could do was stare at Belinda.

Belinda opened her eyes and jerked her head up. "But I didn't kill her," she cried. "I swear I didn't kill her. She was still breathing when I left. She was breathing and cursing a blue streak."

Thoroughly confused, Charlotte, said, "Whoa, back up a sec. Let me get this straight. You're telling me that you choked Lisa but you didn't kill her?"

When Belinda nodded, Charlotte's eyes narrowed suspiciously. "I think you'd better explain just exactly what that means."

Belinda took a deep breath. "You remember the dinner and all." When Charlotte nodded, Belinda continued, "And how my father and I got into an argument, and I got mad and left?"

Again Charlotte nodded.

"Well, Lisa came after me, and when she

found me I was sitting on the restaurant patio, mostly feeling sorry for myself. Then she started in on how I should treat my father better and how I had embarrassed him in front of everyone. When I tried to explain, she wouldn't listen — called me a spoiled brat. I told her that I didn't have to listen to her and to just leave me alone. I got up and walked off toward the azalea bushes, but she followed me, all the while calling me names and trying to start a fight."

Belinda shrugged. "I called her a few names back, and she slapped me." Belinda shuddered. "She had no right to do that — no right at all — so, I slapped her back. But that only made her madder, and she grabbed my hair and yanked so hard it —"

Belinda paused, her eyes begging Charlotte to believe her. "I swear, all I was trying to do was make her let go of my hair. I just wanted her to leave me alone. So I — I grabbed her around the neck and squeezed until she let go of my hair. Then I let go of her and she stumbled backwards and fell. When I left that time, she was sitting there on the ground glaring at me and calling me names, but she didn't follow . . ." Belinda's voice trailed away. "I didn't kill her," she whispered. "And neither did my mother."

Charlotte didn't speak for several minutes

as she tried to process everything Belinda had told her. Her gut feeling was that Belinda was telling the truth. And if Belinda was telling the truth, then that still left Christopher, Margaret, Mack, and possibly Frank as suspects.

"Please say that you believe me?" Belinda begged. "I thought about going to the police and telling them what happened — honestly, I did — especially after my mother was arrested. But I was afraid that no one would believe me." Suddenly she laughed, but it was a sound without humor. "Like an idiot, I thought that I could find out who really killed Lisa. But after what Granddaddy told me, I got all confused. And now, with grandpa Ralph dead too, and someone breaking into my hotel room, I don't know what to do. I'm scared, Charlotte. Really, really scared."

"I don't blame you for being scared," Charlotte murmured, but her mind was sorting through the suspects left. "Let me ask you something. What do you know about a man named Christopher?"

Belinda shrugged. "Not much except that Lisa used to date him before —" She rolled her eyes. "Before she started seeing my father."

"I guess what I'm trying to get at is, do

you think that Christopher could have killed Lisa?"

Belinda slowly shook her head. "I don't think so but I suppose anything's possible."

"Well, let me ask you something else. Was Lisa pregnant?"

"Pregnant? Lisa? Ha! No way. For one thing, my father is too smart to let something like that happen."

"Is it possible that she could have been pregnant by Christopher?"

"Not unless she slept with him in the past six months that she's been seeing my father." Belinda frowned. "Why would you think that?"

Not wanting to admit that she'd overheard the conversation between Lisa and Christopher, Charlotte shrugged. "Just trying to figure out motives. And speaking of motives, what about your grandpa Ralph? Did he know Lisa? Could he have murdered her?"

A shadow of sadness crossed Belinda's eyes and she shrugged. "I don't know. I don't think so, but up until I met him the other day, I didn't even realize that he was still alive. No one ever really said so — and I never really asked about him — but I guess I always assumed that he had died. All of my life, granddaddy Mack was the only grandfather I had. Oh, I knew he was my step-grandfather," she explained. "But — like I said — he's the only one I knew."

"When you met your grandpa Ralph for the first time, what did he say to you?"

Belinda shrugged. "Just stuff. He told me about being in prison and all, but he mostly talked about how he'd thought about me and my mom a lot and wished that things could have been different. He said that now that he was out of prison, all he wanted was to get to know us — make up for lost time."

Charlotte nodded absently. If that was all that Ralph talked about to Belinda, then why had Mack gotten so angry? Guess she'd have to make a point of asking Mack if, and when, she saw him again.

"May I have some more tea?" Belinda asked.

"Sure, hon." With intentions of refilling Belinda's glass, she shoved her chair back.

"I'll get it," Belinda said, motioning for her to stay seated. "And if you don't mind, I think I'd like to take a nap."

"I don't mind at all." Charlotte smiled. "That's probably a good idea. And by the way, I saw Mack this morning. He's been worried sick about you."

Belinda stopped in her tracks. "You didn't tell him where I am, did you?"

Charlotte shook her head. "No. What I

told him was that you were okay, and that you just needed some time."

"Yeah, I guess I should have let him know I was okay."

"Yes, you should have," Charlotte agreed. "And if he hasn't figured it out already, once he really thinks about it, he'll probably figure out that you're staying with me."

"I'll call him in a while." Belinda refilled her glass with tea and took it with her to the guestroom.

Charlotte dumped the rest of her tea into the sink. She'd just put the glass inside the dishwasher when the phone rang.

Walking quickly, she headed for the living room. At her desk, she glanced down at the caller I.D. The display read UNKNOWN CALLER. Not recognizing the number, she picked up the receiver. "Maid-for-a-Day, Charlotte speaking." She waited several seconds, but all she heard was muted noise that sounded suspiciously like traffic. "Hello?" She said again. After a moment, she sighed. "If this is Joyce, please say something."

"Charlotte, please don't hang up."

Joyce.

"Why would I hang up?" Charlotte asked her.

Instead of answering her question, Joyce

said, "Is Louis home?"

"I don't think so, but Joyce, he and Stephen have been frantic with worry about you. Where are you? Are you okay?"

"Liar."

Charlotte stiffened. "Excuse me?"

"You heard me," Joyce sneered, her tone full of contempt.

Charlotte felt her temper spike. "That's kind of like the pot calling the kettle black, don't you think?"

"I'll tell you what I think. Stephen might be worried, but Louis doesn't give a tinker's damn about me. All he wants is to put me away somewhere."

Trembling with fury, Charlotte saw red. "Now, you listen and listen good! Everyone — including Louis — has only tried to help you and support you, and how do you pay them back? You lied from the get-go. But not just any old lie. You told the grandfather of all lies. How could you have done that to your son — to your little granddaughter? You're sick, Joyce. You need to be in a detox program and you need to be in AA. And whether you believe it or not, all that Louis wants — all everyone wants — is for you to get well. And if you can't see that, then you're blind as a bat."

Charlotte was still trembling and breathing hard when she'd finished her tirade. It had been a long time since she'd truly lost her temper, but for once, she didn't feel the first iota of guilt. She'd said what needed to be said, and if Joyce didn't like it, she could go take a flying leap.

"Are you finished?" Joyce asked, her tone still belligerent.

"Yeah, I'm finished. Now, what do you want, Joyce? And why call me?"

"I want to get my stuff from Louis's place, but I don't want to go there if he's at home. You have a key, don't you?"

"Yes, I have a key."

"Then you could let me in."

Charlotte's immediate reaction was to refuse. Then she remembered what Louis had said.

If she calls again, try to get her to meet you somewhere, then call me.

"When?" Charlotte asked.

"I can be there in about twenty minutes."

"Okay, see you then."

Charlotte depressed the switch hook, then immediately dialed Louis's cell phone. When he answered, she said, "I heard from Joyce, and she's coming over in about twenty minutes. She wants to get her things."

"Her things? Ha! That's rich, but thanks,

Charlotte. I'm on my way. Should be there in about ten minutes, but just in case, keep her there as long as possible."

"I don't like this, Louis. Don't like it one bit."

"I know you don't, and I'm sorry you're being dragged into my problems. But it's for the best. She needs help."

With Louis's words still ringing in her ears, Charlotte hung up the receiver. Praying that Louis would get there in time, she searched in the top desk drawer for the spare key she kept for Louis's half of the double, but it wasn't there.

Drumming her fingers against the desktop, she frowned. It had been a while since she'd had to use it. Maybe it was in the kitchen junk drawer.

She headed for the kitchen, and after several minutes of digging, she finally found it. Vowing that somehow she would find the time to clean out drawers and cabinets, she slipped the key into her pants pocket.

Returning to the living room, she walked to the front window. "Hope he gets here before she does," she told Sweety Boy as she pulled back the curtain and peeked outside.

For an answer, the little bird ruffled his feathers, then sidled over to his cuttlebone.

"Yeah, well, what do you care, huh, boy?" Restless, she dropped the curtain and paced the length of the living room. "Just the way I wanted to spend my one afternoon off," she grumbled. Stopping by the coffee table, she picked up the TV remote and pressed the POWER button. For several minutes, she flipped through the channels, but finding nothing of interest, she turned the TV off, and once again returned to the window.

Just as she reached for the curtain, a loud knock at the door made her jump. Taking a deep breath, she said, "Yes, who's there?"

"It's Joyce," came the muffled reply.

Remembering what Louis had said about trying to keep Joyce there as long as possible, Charlotte said, "Just a minute." She slowly counted to ten then took her time unlocking the door and opening it.

Still dressed in stolen scrubs, Joyce stood there pale and dirty. Her hair was a greasy looking mess, and worse, she smelled of alcohol and filth.

"Why don't you come in for a minute," Charlotte told her. "If you're hungry I can fix you a sandwich."

Joyce shook her head. "No time. I don't want to be here if Louis comes home. Have you got the key?"

Charlotte nodded, but as she reached into

her pocket for the key, she gave herself a mental kick. If she'd been on the ball, she could have wasted some more time by pretending that she couldn't find it. Too late now.

When Joyce held out her hand for the key, Charlotte said, "I'll let you in."

When they crossed the porch, out of the corner of her eye Charlotte spotted a beat-up shopping cart near the steps. Wondering which store Joyce had stolen it from, she unlocked Louis's door.

Once inside Louis's half of the double, Joyce headed straight for the bedroom. When she realized that Charlotte was right behind her she stopped and whirled to face her. "You don't have to hang around now. You can go."

Charlotte gave her a no-nonsense, level look. "Yes — yes, I do have to hang around."

Joyce glared at her, but finally shrugged. "Suit yourself." Then she whirled back around and stomped into the bedroom.

Charlotte stopped at the doorway, and leaning against the doorframe, she watched as Joyce pulled the pillow cases off of the pillows on the bed, then made quick work of cleaning out two of the dresser drawers and stuffing the contents into one of the pillow cases.

Charlotte's hand tightened around the key. Where was Louis? And how in the devil was she going to keep Joyce there if he didn't show up right away?

Once Joyce had finished with the dresser, she turned to the closet. For several seconds she simply stared at the contents, then ignoring the hanging clothes, she bent down and gathered the shoes.

Joyce had just stuffed the last pair of shoes into the second pillow case when Charlotte heard the sound of the front door opening. *Louis. Finally.* Holding her breath, Charlotte watched Joyce closely, but Joyce continued rooting around in the closet and didn't give any indication that she'd heard anything.

Within seconds, Louis appeared at the doorway followed by two paramedics. Charlotte released her breath and stepped back to let him enter the room.

"Joyce, it's time to go," Louis told her, and at that moment, the paramedics stepped up to block the doorway.

Joyce jumped to her feet, and like a cornered animal searching for an escape, her eyes darted around the room. But there was nowhere to run, nowhere to hide. Still clinging to the pillowcase, she backed toward the closet. She glared at Charlotte with hate-filled eyes, and Charlotte felt the hairs on the back of her neck stand on end.

"You did this," Joyce whispered fiercely. "This is your fault." She turned her gaze to Louis, tears filling her eyes and spilling over down her cheeks. "Please, Louis, please don't do this," she begged. "I can't be locked up. I'll go crazy."

"You should have thought about that sooner," Louis told her. "And by the way, this is no one's fault but yours. And deep down inside you, you know it's for the best." He leveled a no-nonsense look at her. "There are two ways we can do this. We can do it the hard way or we can do it the easy way — your choice."

Chapter 17

Joyce was a drunk, but that didn't mean that she was a stupid drunk, Charlotte decided as she watched the paramedics escort her out to the ambulance. Once Joyce had realized that she had no choice, she'd gone with them without causing a ruckus.

"Is this legal?" Charlotte asked as she and Louis stood on the porch and watched the ambulance back out of the driveway.

"I have a friend in the Coroner's office," Louis replied. "They can hold her in protective custody for seventy-two hours."

"But I thought there had to be a hearing or something."

Louis shrugged. "Not necessarily."

Charlotte shuddered at the ease in which Louis seemed to be able to incarcerate Joyce against her will. But then she reminded herself that this was for Joyce's own good.

"Would you mind locking up?" Louis asked as he headed for the steps. "I need to follow the ambulance."

"No problem," she called out. By the time she'd locked his front door, Louis was in his car and backing out of the driveway. As she automatically slipped the key inside her pants pocket, her fingers brushed against the napkin with Julie Harper's phone number on it.

Charlotte pulled the napkin out of her pocket, and as she stared at the phone number that Patrick had written, thoughts of Joyce fled, and the events of the past few days at the hotel filled her mind again.

Why did the theft incident keep nagging at her? Most likely, it had nothing to do with Lisa's murder.

"Give it a rest," she murmured, and with a shake of her head and the napkin in hand, she walked across the porch to her front door.

When Charlotte stepped inside, Belinda was standing in the middle of the living room.

"What's going on?" she asked. "I saw an ambulance leave your driveway."

Charlotte closed the door behind her. Not really wanting to discuss all of the details about Joyce and Louis, she said, "It's a long story. Bottom line, my neighbor's wife is ill." Eager to change the subject, she summoned a smile. "Did you get a nap?"

Belinda shook her head. "Not really. I couldn't sleep for thinking about everything."

"Yeah, I know what you mean. I would love to have taken a nap myself." Charlotte walked over to her desk and placed the napkin by the phone as a reminder to call Julie Harper.

Belinda stepped to the desk. "If it's okay with you, I think I'll call Granddaddy now."

Charlotte nodded. "Of course it's okay. I think that's a good idea." Maybe, if Belinda made peace with Mack, then he'd see to her future accommodations. "I also think it would be a good idea if you gave your father a call too."

"Yes, ma'am."

Not wanting to eavesdrop on Belinda's conversation, Charlotte went into the kitchen. While she was there, she took a package of chicken breasts out of the freezer to thaw for supper. Then she made a pot of coffee.

Charlotte was seated at the kitchen table and sipping on a cup of freshly brewed coffee when Belinda entered the room. "Did you reach him?" she asked.

"Yes, ma'am. He's going to pick me up in a little while and take me to dinner. He said for me to invite you to come with us."

Charlotte hesitated. In her mind's eye she could still see Mack yelling at Claire, still hear the belligerence in his tone when she'd dragged him away from Claire and tried to calm him down. She shook her head. "I appreciate the invitation, but I'm a bit tired. I think I'll just stay home this evening."

Belinda nodded, then wrinkled her nose. "I guess I'd better take a shower and get cleaned up."

"Before you go, did you call your father?"

"I tried but only got his answering service. I did leave him a message though, just to let him know that I'm okay. I told him I was staying with a friend."

"Good," Charlotte said.

Managing a lopsided smile, Belinda headed for the doorway and paused. "Ah, Charlotte?" She turned to face Charlotte, her expression tight with strain. "Is it okay with you — I mean, would you mind if I had Granddaddy bring me back here after dinner? You know — to stay another night or so?"

One look at Belinda's face, and Charlotte didn't have the heart to refuse her. So much for Mack finding other accommodations for her.

"It's okay," Charlotte told her, but even as she agreed she couldn't help wondering how she'd ended up with what was turning out to be a long-term houseguest — a houseguest who was, for all purposes, a stranger.

Because you're a pushover and a wimp.

Charlotte winced, and telling her inner voice to just shut up, she finished her coffee.

An hour later when Charlotte opened the door to Mack he seemed a bit standoffish and didn't have a whole lot to say. Wondering if he was still miffed about their run-in that morning at the Jazzy, she said, "I think Belinda is almost ready. Want to come in for a minute?"

Mack shrugged. "I guess — for a minute," was his lackluster reply. He stepped inside and Charlotte closed the door. "I made early reservations for us at Commander's," he said. "I figured after everything that's happened, what with Ralph's death and all, that she could use a little R & R at a really nice place." He paused for a moment and conflicting emotions played across his face. "Like I told Belinda earlier, you're welcome to join us."

Since Commander's Palace was absolutely Charlotte's most favorite restaurant in the city, and since she suspected that this was Mack's way of apologizing, she was sorely tempted to accept the invitation. Then she reminded herself that she really needed to rest up before going back to work at the hotel tomorrow. And she needed some alone time as well. Besides, she still hadn't made up her mind whether further involvement with Mack was such a good idea. "I appreciate the invite, but if it's okay, I'll take a rain check," Charlotte told him.

"You know it's okay," he responded.

There was no way she could misinterpret the unspoken invitation in his eyes. Eager to change the subject, Charlotte gave him a quick, noncommittal smile. "By the way, did you get in touch with my nephew about representing Tessa?"

"Sure did. Thanks again for recommending him."

At the sound of footsteps, Charlotte and Mack turned, and Belinda entered the room.

"Hey, baby girl," Mack call out. "You look great!" When he held out his arms, Belinda gave him a shy smile, then hurried over and stepped into his embrace for a hug. Once he released her, he said, "Is that a new dress?"

"Yes, sir. I got it in the French Quarter the other day."

The backless dress looked really good on the girl, Charlotte decided. Though it wasn't exactly a style or a color that she would have picked out for herself, the mint green sundress suited Belinda.

"You ready for a night out on the town?" Mack asked.

Belinda grinned. "More than ready."

Once Mack and Belinda had left, Charlotte closed the door behind them. As she threw the deadbolt, her phone rang.

Charlotte stepped over to her desk, and squinting, she stared at the caller I.D., then, with a smile, she immediately picked up the receiver. "Hey, hon."

"Hey, yourself, Mom. Haven't heard from you in a few days, so decided I'd better check up on you. What's going on?"

No way could she tell Hank what was really going on. He'd have a hissy fit. "Just work and more work," she quipped. "So how's that future granddaughter of mine coming along?"

"Your future granddaughter is doing just fine. It's your daughter-in-law that worries me."

"What's wrong with Carol?"

"She's like you — a workaholic who won't slow down. I want to hire someone to come in and clean, but she won't hear of it."

Charlotte grinned. "I know of a good maid service that I highly recommend."

"Mother!"

Charlotte laughed. "Sorry, couldn't help it."

"Speaking of your maid service, I thought you were cutting back so that you'd have more time once the baby comes."

"I am . . . after this job."

"You know I'm going to hold you to it."

Charlotte sighed and wondered if they would ever have a conversation without him nagging her about retiring. "Yes, I know. And like I said, I intend to cut back right after this job."

Tell him about Mack.

"Before I forget, I wanted to tell you that I ran into one of your father's old friends. His name is Mack Sutton, and he and your father were roommates at Tulane, before they both went off to Vietnam. He'd really like to meet you — that is, if it's okay with you."

"No kidding?"

The lilt of excitement in his voice made Charlotte smile. "No kidding," she assured him. "So, what do you think?"

"I think that would be great. How long will he be in town?"

"Several days, I think."

"Good, then let me check my schedule and get back to you with a day and time."

"Okay, honey. Talk to you later then. And give Carol a hug for me."

As Charlotte hung up the receiver, she stared at Julie Harper's phone number on the napkin lying beside the phone, but her thoughts spun back in time to when Hank was just a little boy.

"Where's *my* daddy?" he'd asked her after his first day at kindergarten. "All the other kids have daddies."

"Your daddy is in heaven, sweetheart," she'd told him. "He was a brave soldier and a hero."

"Can we go see him in heaven, Mommy?" he'd asked.

"One of these days, honey. One of these days we'll all be together again," she'd told him. "But not for a long, long time."

Swallowing the ache in her throat, Charlotte glanced up at the cuckoo clock on the wall behind the sofa. Time to see about dinner. Then she glanced back down at the napkin. With Belinda gone, now would be the ideal time to place that phone call.

Before she could change her mind and hoping that she wouldn't be interrupted, she picked up the receiver and tapped out the number.

On the third ring, a breathy feminine voice answered, "Hello."

"Hi, is this Julie Harper?"

"Who wants to know?"

"My name is Charlotte LaRue, and I own Maid-for-a-Day. Patrick, the bartender at the Jazzy hotel gave me this phone number. I'd like to talk to Julie about a job."

"Ah — yes, ma'am — I mean, I'm Julie, and I'd be real interested."

Not wanting to give the woman false hope, Charlotte explained. "It wouldn't be full-time to begin with," she said. "Just part-time for now. But I plan to really cut back my hours in the next couple of months, and part-time could very well turn into full-time."

For several moments, Julie didn't respond, then, in a thick, unsteady voice she said, "Did — did Patrick tell you about my last job?"

"The one at the Jazzy?"

"Yes, ma'am."

"Yes, he told me," Charlotte replied. "But he also told me that he thinks you got railroaded. And Claire, the manager, essentially told me the same thing. But being the manager and all, she said that she had no choice but to let you go."

"I — I know she had no choice, and I know that you have no reason to believe me, but I swear I didn't steal that woman's jewelry. I've never stolen anything in my whole life."

"Maybe if I understood exactly what happened . . ." Charlotte purposely left the sentence open in hopes that Julie would elaborate.

"All I did was try on a pair of her earrings. I didn't intend on taking them. They were just so beautiful though, and —" Her voice broke. "I shouldn't have done it — I know that now. I just wanted to see how they would look on me. Anyway, just my luck, she walked in and caught me, and well, you know the rest."

Remembering her own fascination with Tessa's lone earring, Charlotte said, "If it helps, I know exactly how you felt. Believe it or not, just recently I came across a beautiful earring while cleaning. If the woman who owned it hadn't been standing right there in the same room, I would have been tempted to do the same thing." Suddenly, inspiration struck. "Hey, wouldn't it be a hoot if your lady's earrings and my lady's earrings were the same?"

Encouraged by the soft giggle Charlotte heard over the phone line, she said, "My earring belonged to a woman named Tessa."

There was silence for a minute, then Julie said, "No — that name doesn't sound right.

I'm pretty sure that wasn't her name."

Disappointed, Charlotte tried another tack. "So what did your earrings look like?"

As Charlotte listened to Julie describe the pair of earrings, she could hardly believe her ears. Julie's description sound suspiciously like Tessa's earring, right down to Julie relating how the shape of them reminded her of Egyptian pyramids. Coincidence? Now what were the odds that there would be two sets of earrings exactly the same, especially since Tessa's more than likely came from Shreveport.

"They do sound beautiful," Charlotte murmured absently.

"Oh, they were," Julie responded.

Suddenly Charlotte's stomach knotted with frustration. Even if the earrings were the same, now that she knew Julie hadn't actually stolen anything, knowing that someone else had a duplicate pair still wouldn't help prove Tessa's innocence. It didn't change the fact that one of Tessa's earrings was missing and was found near Lisa.

"Ah, Charlotte?"

"Yes," she answered.

"About that job offer — it's not that I don't appreciate the offer — I do — but I really need a full-time job."

"I understand," Charlotte told her. "I'm just sorry I can't offer full-time right now. But listen, Julie, if you change your mind about working part-time, don't hesitate to call me. And if I hear of something full-time, I'll let you know."

"Thanks, Charlotte. And when you see Patrick again, tell him thanks too for me."

"I will. Bye now, and take care."

Even after Charlotte hung up the receiver, she stood by the desk, her mind still racing with thoughts about the earrings. If only there was some way she could find out who owned the other pair of earrings . . .

And what good would that do?

"Oh, for pity's sake," she exclaimed, aggravated that she couldn't stop thinking about the stupid earrings. "Just give it a rest, why don't you?"

With a shake of her head, she headed for the kitchen. At the kitchen sink, she stared at the package of chicken that she'd set out to thaw earlier. With Belinda gone, there was no use in cooking all four of the breasts. Opening the package, she took one out, then dropped the remaining pieces into a small storage bag, zipped it closed, and placed the bag back inside the refrigerator.

After sprinkling the breast with Tony Chachere's seasoning, she placed it in a broiling pan and put in the oven. Wrapping a sweet potato in wax paper, she stuck it inside of the microwave to cook. Then, she opened a small can of English peas and heated them on top of the stove. Once her food was ready, and sorely needing a mindless distraction, she decided to eat in front of the television.

Settling on the sofa, she picked up the remote and flipped through the channels. Finally choosing the channel that aired *CSI* reruns, she set the remote on the coffee table and picked up her fork. Just as she put a forkful of peas in her mouth, the scene on the television screen switched to an autopsy being performed on a victim. Suddenly, it seemed as if the peas in her mouth had doubled in size.

Wrong show to watch while eating, she thought, swallowing the peas with a gulp. Then the scene switched again to the crime scene where one of the characters was busy lifting a fingerprint from a small medicine bottle.

Wondering if it was possible to get a fingerprint off the earring found near Lisa, Charlotte frowned as she chewed a bite of chicken. Maybe not a complete fingerprint, but possibly a partial. She'd have to remember to ask Judith the next time they talked.

Charlotte had finished her dinner and was stacking her dirty dishes into the dishwasher when she heard a knock at her front door. Surely Belinda wasn't back from dinner already.

Charlotte rinsed her hands and quickly dried them with a paper towel before heading for the living room. After peeking out of the front window, she opened the door.

"Hi, Auntie," Judith said. "I need to talk to you about the murders at the Jazzy."

With a nod, Charlotte stepped back to let Judith inside, and then she closed the door. "You look tired, hon," she said, motioning toward the sofa. "Have you eaten dinner yet?"

"Yes, ma'am." Judith walked over to the sofa and sat down. "I grabbed a sandwich earlier."

"How about something to drink? Tea? Coffee?"

When Judith shook her head, Charlotte sat on the other end of the sofa and turned to face her niece. "Any news yet about Ralph Jones?"

"Nothing that you don't already know," Judith answered. "And speaking of what you already know, I need you to tell me everything that you know about this family." Judith threw up a hand, palm out. "And don't bother denying that you know anything about them. A little bird told me about your relationship with Mack Sutton, and I also know for a fact that Tessa Morgan's daughter Belinda is staying with you."

Figuring that Judith had probably talked to Louis, Charlotte lowered her gaze to stare at the sofa cushion. "Yes, I do know Mack, and yes, Belinda is staying with me."

"And?"

Charlotte shrugged. "And I don't think Tessa Morgan murdered that girl Lisa."

"Why don't you think she did it?"

Charlotte raised her gaze and stared at Judith. "Several reasons."

"Give me one."

"Lisa was Tessa's illegitimate daughter."

The fact that Judith didn't seem the least bit surprised about Lisa being Tessa's daughter told Charlotte that her niece already knew. Probably from questioning Tessa, Charlotte decided.

"Okay, what else?"

"The earring that was found near Lisa, the one that Frank Morgan claimed belonged to Tessa. Tessa complained about it being missing *before* Lisa was killed."

Judith sighed. "For one, we already know about Lisa being Tessa's illegitimate daughter, which — I might point out — could be even more motive to get rid of her. For two, Tessa's fingerprints were found on the earring, Auntie."

Charlotte shook her head. "I disagree. After giving her baby up for adoption — the ultimate sacrifice — there's no way a mother would murder her own daughter."

"I know that's what you think, Aunt Charley, but in the real world — the world I deal with — there are mothers who murder their children, and especially if that child was bitter and vindictive and caused a threat to the mother's family."

"So, you're saying that Lisa knew Tessa was her mother all along? And that she set out on purpose to get even with Tessa for giving her away at birth?"

Judith nodded. "Yes, and Tessa, realizing what was happening, decided to remedy the situation once and for all. But —"

Judith crossed and uncrossed her legs. Charlotte could always tell when Judith was nervous. Any time that her niece was bothered about something or uncertain, she resorted to what Charlotte called the nervous fidgets.

"But," Judith repeated, "That's Gavin Brown's theory. If it's any consolation, I'm not totally convinced that Tessa Morgan is our murderer. The autopsy showed that the victim was choked to death, but the bruising around her neck indicates that someone choked her with their hands — someone with large, strong hands — not the scarf as we first believed. It's possible that that same someone tried to make it appear as if the victim had been choked with the scarf after she was already dead, someone who knew that the dye would rub off onto the victim's neck."

Charlotte felt her stomach tighten. Belinda had confessed to choking Lisa but had claimed that Lisa was alive when she left her. Had she lied?

"There's also the fact," Judith continued, "that, like you said, Tessa Morgan claims that she discovered one of her earrings missing before Lisa was murdered. From our interviews there were any number of people in and out of her room who could have taken the earring for the express purpose of setting her up to take the blame for the murder."

Remembering her conversation with Mack and his conspiracy theory, Charlotte suppressed a shudder.

"Then there's Ralph Jones's murder," Judith pointed out. "Somehow he's connected to it all. And that brings me to the reason that I need you to tell me everything you know about these people."

. . . someone with large, strong hands . . . Then there's Ralph Jones's murder. Somehow he's connected to it all.

Her niece's words were hammering in her head, and the longer Judith talked, the more uneasy Charlotte had become. While Belinda was still a possibility, Mack had admitted having a run-in with Ralph, and Belinda had confessed that Lisa was indeed blackmailing Mack.

A heavy feeling settled in Charlotte's stomach. No matter how badly she wanted to believe otherwise, unfortunately, her old friend Mack Sutton fit the bill for both murders.

Chapter 18

"Aunt Charley? Earth to Aunt Charley?" Charlotte jumped when Judith touched her arm.

"Where were you just now, Auntie? You zoned out on me."

"Sorry," Charlotte replied. "Just thinking. I seem to do that a lot lately."

"Care to share those thoughts?"

Should she tell Judith what she'd been thinking, or should she keep her mouth shut? She didn't want to believe that her friend was capable of not only committing one murder, but two. And she really didn't want to be the one to point an accusing finger at him. On the other hand, if Mack was guilty of both murders, then what choice did she have? No one should get away with murder.

Then an idea began to form. There was more than one way to get around a brick wall. She could simply tell Judith everything she knew about Mack and his family and let Judith draw her own conclusions.

After a moment, Charlotte nodded. "Okay." When she began talking about the first day that she worked at the Jazzy and her run-in with Tessa, Judith pulled a notebook and pen from her purse and began jotting down notes.

When Charlotte mentioned the argument that she'd overheard between Lisa and Christopher, Judith shook her head. "The vic wasn't pregnant. My guess — she was using that as an excuse to force Frank Morgan to marry her."

The ploy was as old as time, and Charlotte felt like a ninny for not thinking of it herself. She wondered if anyone had bothered to share that bit of news with Christopher. Then again, if Christopher had somehow found out beforehand, he could have been so enraged . . . *Dead end.* Judith thought that Lisa and Ralph's murders were connected, and as far as she knew, Christopher knew nothing about Ralph.

Taking a deep breath, Charlotte went on to explain about running into Mack. Then, she told Judith about her dinner date with Mack, including the argument between Belinda and her father, and Lisa volunteering to go after Belinda.

"I also happened to be looking out the window and saw that man Christopher follow Lisa," she added. "I figured he must have been waiting for her."

Judith nodded. "Yeah, we have a witness that saw the two of them arguing back at the hotel. But that same witness saw Christopher head for the bar after the argument, and the bartender said that Christopher drank himself into a stupor. Had to call security to take him to his room."

So much for Christopher being a suspect. "There's something else you need to know," Charlotte continued. "Ralph Jones was at the restaurant that night too." As Charlotte began explaining what Mack had said about Ralph, there was a loud knock at the front door. As if on cue, Judith's phone rang.

"You get the door," Judith told her, "and I'll take this call."

Though Charlotte was fairly certain that it was only Belinda at the door, she peeked out of the front window to make sure. Yep, Belinda. Charlotte opened the front door. "How was your dinner?" she asked as she stepped aside to let the girl in.

But Belinda's attention was riveted on Judith, still talking on her cell phone.

"Isn't she one of the homicide detectives?" Belinda demanded, in a shrill voice.

"Yes, she's —"

Belinda's eyes darted nervously from Judith to Charlotte, and she stepped back from the doorway. "What's *she* doing here?"

Charlotte reached out, took a firm hold of Belinda's arm, and pulled her inside. "Come inside," she told her. "You're letting mosquitoes in." Once Belinda was inside, Charlotte firmly shut the door, then faced the girl with a stern look. "*She* is my niece. Remember, I told you that I had a niece who was a detective."

"But what's she doing here?" Belinda asked again, her voice low, her eyes glued to Judith.

"She came by to ask me some questions about the murders."

"You didn't tell her about — you know, about —"

At that moment Judith ended her call, stood, and approached Charlotte and Belinda. With a nod for Belinda, she turned to Charlotte. "Got to run, Aunt Charley. We'll have to finish our talk later." She gave Charlotte a quick hug, then left.

Once Charlotte had closed the door and locked it, she faced Belinda.

"What did you tell her?" Belinda demanded, her voice edgy, her tone suspicious.

"Nothing about you, if that's what you're asking," Charlotte responded, not liking the girl's tone.

Belinda seemed to visibly relax, then she tensed again and her lower lip quivered. "Will your niece be coming back tonight?"

"She said she would see me later. That could mean tonight or —" Charlotte shrugged. "Or tomorrow. Why?"

"I think I need to talk to her about — you know — about what happened between me and Lisa."

Charlotte motioned toward the sofa. "Let's sit down." Once they were seated, Charlotte took both of Belinda's hands into her own. "Why the change of mind?" she asked.

For long seconds, Belinda didn't respond. When she finally did answer, her face was tight with strain. "Ever since I found out that Lisa was killed, I've been scared and jumpy. I didn't kill her, but the police might think I did." Tears welled within her eyes. "I — I hate feeling that way. And I hate that my mother is in jail. I thought if I just told the truth about the fight that I had with Lisa, then maybe these feelings would go away."

Charlotte nodded and squeezed Belinda's hands. " 'The truth shall set you free,' " she murmured as the last of her suspicions about Belinda melted away. Seeing the confused look on Belinda's face, she explained, "It's a Bible verse. John 8:32. It has a deeper meaning, but it can also mean exactly what you said about the bad feelings going away if you tell the truth." Charlotte paused a moment to let her words sink in, then she squeezed Belinda's hands again and released them. "I've been thinking about Lisa's murder," she said. "And about your Grandpa Ralph's murder. You know that they found one of your mother's earrings near Lisa."

Belinda blinked back the tears and nodded. "Yes, but that earring had been missing since we checked in."

"I know that's what your mother said, but do you remember Mack's theory about why the earring was found near Lisa?"

Again, Belinda nodded. "He thinks my father planted it to make my mother look guilty."

"Just so you know, my niece thinks there's a possibility that he's right — not necessarily about your father though. But what she did say was that there are several people who had access to your mother's room, and if it makes you feel any better, I don't think that your father was one of them."

Belinda's eyes brightened. "You're right. My father never came to our room."

"Your mother said that the earrings had been an anniversary gift from your father. Do you happen to know where he bought them?"

"No, not really," Belinda answered. "If I had to guess, I'd say Keenan's Jewelry Store though. But why do you want to know that?"

"Honestly, I don't know why. For now, let's just say I'm curious. So, is this Keenan's Jewelry Store in Shreveport?"

"Yes, it's kind of a specialty store. The man who owns the store — Keenan Roberts — designs most of the jewelry himself."

Charlotte could hardly believe that it was already Wed nesday as she entered the Jazzy Hotel the next morning.

Time flies when you're having fun.

She grimaced as the old adage came to mind. While it was true that the days had flown by, two murders in less than a week certainly weren't her idea of fun.

Charlotte approached the registration desk where Claire was talking to one of the guests. No, not a guest, she decided, as she overheard the man grilling Claire. More than likely, he was a reporter.

"Come on," he drawled. "Surely the police told you something about this Ralph Jones guy. At least tell me who found the body."

Claire slid her gaze to Charlotte then back to the reporter. "I told you, no comment," she responded in a steely tone. "And no comment means just that — no comment. Now, if you'll excuse me, I have work to do."

Though the man did finally turn and walk away, Charlotte noticed that instead of leaving, he headed for the restaurant. Probably to grill the poor waitresses, she decided, as she stepped up to the desk.

Claire let loose a frustrated growl as her gaze followed the man. "I swear, those people are like flies. The more you swat at them, the more they aggravate you."

Remembering her own past experience with nosy reporters, Charlotte nodded. "Good analogy."

Claire reached under the desk, pulled out a folder, and handed Charlotte her room assignments for the day. "Most of the Red Scarf group have checked out," she said, "and unfortunately, that writer's group we were expecting for Friday has cancelled. Bad news travels fast, and with two murders within three days . . ." Her expression grew tight with strain. "Not good," she murmured. "Not a good sign at all. If this keeps up, we'll both be out of a job."

"Business will pick up again," Charlotte told her. "Just give it time."

"Yeah, well, tell that to the owner," Claire retorted. Then she rolled her eyes. "Sorry, Charlotte. I don't mean to take out my frustrations on you."

Charlotte gave Claire a sympathetic smile. "No problem." She glanced down at her room assignments and did a quick mental calculation. If she hurried, she might get finished by lunchtime. If not by lunchtime, then shortly thereafter. "Guess I'd better get busy," she said.

At the supply closet, she gathered the supplies she needed and loaded the cleaning cart, but her thoughts were on the conversation she'd had with Julie Harper and the theft accusation against her. What was it about those earrings that kept nagging at her? According to Judith, the earring found at the murder scene clearly belonged to Tessa. Even so, she couldn't shake the feeling that it was somehow important.

By the time Charlotte had finished her first assigned room, she'd made up her mind that the only way to satisfy her strange obsession with the earrings was to find out as much about them as possible.

Once she let herself into the second room, she took out her cell phone, a pen, and her mini-notebook, and called Directory Assistance.

"Shreveport, Louisiana," she told the operator. "For Keenan's Jewelry Store." Once she'd jotted down the phone number, she disconnected from Directory Assistance, and then dialed the number.

"Keenan's Jewelry," a feminine voice answered.

"Hi, my name is Charlotte LaRue, and I was wondering if I might speak to Mr. Roberts about a pair of earrings."

"Mr. Roberts isn't in at the moment, ma'am. Can someone else help you?"

"No, I don't think so," Charlotte told her. "Would you ask him to give me a call when he comes in?"

"Sure. Just give me a number where he can reach you."

Once Charlotte had given the woman her cell phone number, she headed for the bathroom and began cleaning.

When Charlotte approached the third assigned room on her list and noted the absence of the DO NOT DISTURB sign on the doorknob, she went through her regular routine of knocking and announcing herself. When no one answered, she used her master key and unlocked the door.

Leaving the door ajar, she stepped inside the room and glanced around, assessing what needed to be done. Except for the unmade bed, a stack of files and briefcase on top of the desk, and the two suitcases near the door, the room had been stripped of the guest's personal things. She slid the closet door open, but found it empty. Then her eye spotted an envelope on the desk with the word HOUSEKEEPING written on the front. Enclosed were a five-dollar bill and a card key to the hotel room.

With a shrug, she folded the envelope and slid it into her pants pocket, then headed for the bathroom and peeked inside. There were no personal items on the sink countertop and only a small pile of washcloths and towels on the floor near the bathtub. Whoever was occupying the room was, more than likely, checking out.

In the bedroom, Charlotte stripped the bed. Bundling up the dirty linens, she took them out to the supply cart where she stuffed them into the huge laundry bag attached to the cart.

From the cart she gathered a stack of clean sheets and pillowcases, and headed back inside the room. After she'd made up the bed, she dusted, careful to put the briefcase and files back exactly like she'd found them.

Back out in the hallway, once she'd selected the bathroom cleaning products and the large trash bag that she'd need from the cart, she headed for the bathroom. Pulling on a pair of disposable gloves, she started with the bathtub. Then, in record time, she cleaned the toilet, wiped down the mirror, and cleaned the sink and the countertop.

Making another trip to the cart, she put away the cleaning products, then took sample bottles of shampoo, crème rinse, body lotion, and a couple of small bars of soap back to the bathroom. After setting out the beauty products, she bent down and picked up the small trashcan. With a frown, she stared at the contents. There was only a folded-up white paper sack and a handful of torn scraps of paper.

No use wasting another trash bag, she decided, especially since this one wasn't really dirty. She took the sack out first, but frowned when she saw the bits of purple in the fold. Why did that sack look familiar? she wondered. And unless she was mistaken, there was something inside it.

With a shrug, she stuffed it into the larger trash bag that she'd brought with her, then turned back to the trashcan. As she picked out the pieces of paper, it suddenly dawned on her just exactly what the torn scraps were. Someone had ripped up a check.

Charlotte had always loved puzzles as a child, but it had been a long time since she'd put one together. Growing more curious about the tiny scraps of paper, she placed the pieces on the countertop and set the trashcan on the floor.

With a grin, she slid the torn pieces of paper around until they fit together. Just as she'd suspected, they were part of a torn-up check. She leaned closer and squinted to see the writing more clearly.

Suddenly the handwriting came into focus and when Charlotte saw who the check was made out to, she gasped. Her heart pounding like a jackhammer, her gaze quickly slid across to the amount of the check. Fifty thousand dollars! Then her gaze slid down to the signature of the person who wrote the check.

"Oh, dear Lord in heaven," she whispered.

Chapter 19

Still stunned by what she'd seen and her mind racing, Charlotte reached inside her pocket and pulled out the list of her assigned rooms. She was in the third room on her list. "Room 205," she murmured, as she shoved the list back into her pocket. Heading for the phone on the bedside table, she kept repeating "205." She picked up the receiver and tapped out the number to the front desk.

Recognizing Claire's voice when the call was answered, she said, "Claire, this is Charlotte. Could you please tell me the name of the guest in room 205?"

"You didn't find another dead body, did you?"

"No, no, nothing like that, thank the Lord."

"Whew! That's a relief. Hold on a sec," Claire told her. "Let me pull up that account." A moment later, she said, "A Ms.

Margaret Green has that room, but she stopped by earlier and said that she'd be checking out today. Said something about a lunch meeting and that she might be a few minutes later than the one o'clock check-out time."

Just as she'd suspected. This was Margaret's room. Charlotte had never been told what Margaret's last name was, and though she was almost positive that Margaret Green was the same Margaret who worked for Frank Morgan, the very same Margaret who was supposedly Tessa's friend, she wanted to be absolutely certain. "Does she happen to be the same Margaret Green who had the room Friday?"

"Yes, one and the same. Why? Is there a problem?"

Instead of admitting that there might be a huge problem if she was right about Margaret, she said, "No problem." No use in alarming Claire until she knew for sure that Margaret was involved. Searching for a plausible excuse, she finally said, "She left a nice tip and I thought I'd leave her a thank-you note."

As Charlotte hung up the phone, she glanced at the clock on the bedside table. It was only eleven. She still had plenty of time, but the one thing that she didn't want was to be caught in the room when Margaret returned.

Deep in thought, Charlotte walked slowly back to the bathroom. At least now she knew for sure why the room number seemed familiar. She stared at the pieced-together check. But where on earth would Margaret, a mere secretary, have gotten that much money? And why had she given it to Ralph Jones?

Charlotte was still staring at the signature on the check and trying to decide what to do with it when the sudden sound of her cell phone ringing made her jump. Taking a deep, calming breath and telling herself that she shouldn't rush to conclusions, she pulled out her cell phone. "Maid-for-a-Day, Charlotte LaRue speaking."

"Ms. LaRue, this is Keenan Roberts at Keenan's Jewelry. I believe you called earlier about some earrings?"

"Yes — yes, I did. I met a woman who was wearing a gorgeous pair of earrings, and I was told that they came from your store." Charlotte closed her eyes, and picturing how the earrings had looked, she described them. "I'd love to have a pair like them. I was wondering what the chances were that you had made more than one pair."

"Most of my jewelry is one-of-a-kind," the

man responded. "But if you know the woman's name, I can check my records to make sure."

"Wonderful," Charlotte gushed. "Her name is Tessa Morgan."

"Hold just a minute, ma'am."

A click sounded, and what Charlotte called elevator music played in her ear. It was her least favorite type of music, but thankfully, after a moment, the phone clicked again, and the music stopped. "Ms. LaRue, Keenan Roberts again."

"Yes," Charlotte answered eagerly.

"According to my records, I only made two pairs of that particular design: one pair for a Ms. Morgan, and the other pair for a Ms. Green."

"Ms. Green?" Charlotte repeated. "Ms. Margaret Green?" Her gaze dropped to Margaret's signature on the torn check. "Are you sure — I mean are you sure that you don't have a third pair?"

"Yes, I'm sure. I seem to remember that Ms. Green was the one who actually placed the order and picked them up. And no, there isn't a third pair. Sorry. I could try to duplicate a pair for you though."

Charlotte swallowed hard. "No, that's okay, but would you mind telling me when Ms. Green picked up the earrings?"

"It was about eight months ago, but why do you want to know?"

"Just curious. Thanks, thanks a lot." Charlotte quickly pressed the disconnect button. As she slid the cell phone into her pocket, she tried to make sense out of what she'd just learned.

Judith had said that she thought Lisa and Ralph's murders were somehow connected. If this check was what she suspected it was — a pay-off — then it could be the proof Judith was looking for. Unless she was wrong, Ralph, a large man, the type who would have big, strong hands, had been hired by Margaret to murder Lisa. What other reason could Margaret have had to give an ex-con, fresh out of prison, that much money? And after killing Lisa, then he'd set it up to look like Tessa had done it.

Charlotte frowned then slowly shook her head. That couldn't be right, especially after what Belinda had told her.

He said that now that he was out of prison, all he wanted was to get to know us — make up for lost time.

In spite of Judith's so-called real world where mothers and fathers murdered their own children, Charlotte didn't believe that Ralph would tell Belinda that, then turn around and knowingly set up Tessa, his own daughter, to take the blame for a murder. And if that was true, then the scarf and earring had to have been planted at the scene of the crime after Ralph had murdered Lisa, planted by someone who had plenty of opportunities to take them out of Tessa's room . . . someone like Margaret.

Charlotte turned to stare at the trash bag on the floor.

I was able to pick up that package for you before I left. But I'll need the ones you have for the exchange.

"That's it," Charlotte murmured, remembering the phone conversation she'd overheard between Margaret and Tessa. That's where she'd seen that sack.

Charlotte bent down and picked up the trash bag, opened it, and pulled out the white sack. When she unfolded it, she nodded. Yep, the same purple triangles and tulip, the same store. Opening the sack, one by one, she pulled out several red scarves, each with a tiny TM embroidered in the corner.

More proof, she thought as she stuffed the scarves back into the sack. But even with the additional proof, something still nagged her about the whole thing. Tessa was Ralph's daughter, which also meant that . . .

"Oh, no," she whispered. It also meant

that Lisa was Ralph's granddaughter. He'd murdered his own granddaughter?

Not knowingly, Charlotte finally decided. Not even Mack had known that Lisa was Tessa's illegitimate daughter. So, it stood to reason that Ralph, who'd had no contact with Tessa for years and years, had no way of knowing about her illegitimate daughter.

But Margaret knew.

Charlotte slowly shook her head. Margaret might have known, but she wouldn't have told Ralph, especially if she'd hired him to kill Lisa.

Charlotte placed the sack on the counter next to the check. As she thought back to the dinner party on Saturday night, she drummed her fingers against the counter-top.

Belinda had left first, and then Lisa. Not long after Lisa left, Frank had told Margaret to go find them. Then, as she and Mack were leaving, Mack had spotted Ralph.

Charlotte nodded as it all began to fall into place. Lisa had caught up with Belinda, and they'd argued. Belinda had said that she left Lisa sitting on the ground. Ralph could have been waiting in the wings, seen his opportunity, then stepped in and killed her. Once Lisa was dead, it would have been easy enough for Margaret to plant the scarf and earrings.

"Poor Ralph," Charlotte whispered, her gaze returning to the check. She could almost feel sorry for him. Charlotte could only imagine what kind of lies Margaret had fed him. He had probably thought that he was doing Tessa and Belinda a favor by getting rid of Lisa. And to an ex-con who wanted to make up lost time with his family, the money would have been hard to turn down.

"But why — why did Margaret kill Ralph?" she muttered.

Frustrated, Charlotte paced the length of the bathroom and concentrated on her moves the previous day when she'd found Ralph dead.

She remembered having to use her master key to let herself in, so that meant that the door to Ralph's room had been locked. And that meant that Ralph knew his killer and had opened the door and let the person come inside.

"But why did Margaret kill him?" she muttered again.

Trying to put herself in Ralph's shoes, she began playing the what-if game.

Tessa had been arrested on Monday and according to the police, Ralph had been murdered Monday evening. What if once

Ralph learned that Tessa had been arrested for the murder, rather than let his daughter take the blame, he'd decided to confess to the murder himself? And if he confessed to the murder, there was a good chance that he would implicate Margaret as the one who had hired him to make the hit in the first place. Charlotte figured that Margaret had somehow found out . . . or maybe she'd known all along what Ralph would do, which meant that she had also planned all along to eliminate him.

Charlotte stopped pacing and stared at the check again. The more she thought about it, the more she became convinced she was right. And she should have guessed, especially after . . .

Remembering the circumstances surrounding a former client's murder, her chest suddenly grew heavy. Though the method of murder was different, she strongly suspected that the motive was the same. Lusting after a married man wasn't anything new.

All those years of being at Frank's beck and call, of being his so-called "right-hand-man," was it any wonder that Margaret had fallen for him? The fact that she had ordered herself a duplicate pair of earrings proved that she had been obsessed with him, especially since the earrings were meant to be an anniversary gift from Frank to Tessa. By setting up Tessa to take the blame for Lisa's death, Margaret could get rid of all her competition, leaving the field wide open for her to step in and comfort the bereaved Frank. She'd probably figured that with both Lisa and Tessa out of the way, Frank would finally turn to her.

Charlotte sighed. There was just one problem with the whole scenario. With Ralph dead, proving that Margaret had hired him would be almost impossible . . . except for the torn-up check and the polyester scarves. But would the check and scarves be proof enough?

What she needed was more proof . . .

What you need is to tell Judith about this.

"Okay, okay," she muttered. "I will." She glanced at her watch. Time was ticking away. "What I need first is to hurry up and get out of this room." Then, in her mind's eye, she saw the suitcases standing beside the door.

Ralph had been shot. If she opened those suitcases, would she find a gun? She turned and stared into the bedroom at the suitcases.

Don't you dare.

The temptation was strong, but with a grimace, Charlotte sighed. Maybe this time she should listen to the irritating voice inside her head.

Then, her gaze strayed to the folders and briefcase on the desk. Before she could change her mind, she hurried over to the desk and thumbed through the files. When she got to the bottom file in the stack, she swallowed hard. It was the file on Lisa, the same one that Margaret had given to Tessa, and the same one that Belinda had said was missing from Tessa's room.

But how did Margaret get inside Tessa's room? And there was still the problem of the burned security tape in Tessa's wastebasket.

Charlotte pulled out her cell phone and called her house. "Answer the phone, Belinda," she whispered. "Answer the phone."

Instead, she got the answering machine. When it finally beeped, she said, "Belinda, this is Charlotte. If you're there, pick up the phone." A moment passed, and then she heard a click.

"I'm here, Charlotte," Belinda said.

"Listen, after your mother was arrested, did you give Margaret a key to your room or did she drop in to check on you or anything?"

"No, ma'am, but my mother could have given her one. They're good friends, you know. But why?"

"I don't have time to explain now — I've got to go — but I'll explain later." Charlotte quickly disconnected the call. If Tessa had given Margaret a key, that would explain a lot and would be even more proof. Margaret could have waited until Tessa and Belinda had gone, let herself into the room, and set it up to look like Tessa had burned the security tape.

The key in the envelope. Charlotte pulled the envelope out of her pocket, then slid the key out and stared at it. If it was the key to Margaret's room, then how did she plan on getting back inside to pick up her luggage?

Charlotte slipped the key back into the envelope and slid the envelope into her pocket. One way to test her suspicions was to try the key in the door . . . on her way out. But for now, she needed to grab the check and sack, and get out of that room, just in case Margaret returned early for her suitcases.

Back in the bathroom, she reached out to begin gathering the pieces of the check, and out of nowhere, a strange feeling came over her. The hairs on the back of her neck suddenly stood on end.

"Hello. Anybody in here?"

Charlotte froze. *Margaret.*

Charlotte whirled around to see Margaret standing just outside the bathroom doorway.

Margaret smiled. “We meet again.” Then she laughed. “You look like you’ve just seen a ghost. Sorry. I didn’t mean to startle you.”

Sudden spasms of alarm swept through Charlotte. The sack and the pieces of the check were still laying in plain view. All she had to do at this point was to hope that her body blocked Margaret’s view.

Act natural, Charlotte. Just act natural. Charlotte cleared her throat, and hoping her voice wouldn’t betray her, she said, “No problem.”

Margaret nodded. “I wondered if I’d see you before I left. Frank told me that Belinda has been staying with you.”

“Just a couple of nights,” Charlotte replied, her heart hammering in her chest. Forcing a smile and trying to remain calm, she said, “I’m almost finished in here.” Somehow, some way, she had to get that check and the sack and get out. But how without alerting Margaret?

Charlotte swallowed hard. If only there was some way to divert Margaret’s attention. All she needed were a few seconds to scoop up the check and the trash bag.

Giving Margaret a quick smile, she said, “As soon as I give the bathroom one last inspection and pick up the trash bag, I'll be out of your way. And if you're planning on leaving by check-out time, you might want to go ahead and call for some help with your luggage."

Margaret nodded. "Good idea."

The second Margaret turned her back and headed for the phone, Charlotte whirled around to scoop up the check pieces. In her haste, a couple pieces fluttered to the floor. She glanced up, just to make sure that Margaret's back was still turned, and her breath caught in her lungs.

The mirror. She'd forgotten about the mirror. It was the full length of the counter and reflected everything . . . everything, including Margaret staring at her.

Charlotte's mouth went dry. From the calculating look on Margaret's face and the way her eyes narrowed suspiciously, Charlotte knew that Margaret had seen what she was doing, and knew that she was in big trouble.

Margaret slammed down the phone receiver and stalked toward the bathroom. "What's going on here?" she demanded.

Out of the corner of her eye, Charlotte spied the check pieces on the floor. Holding Margaret's gaze and figuring that the only choice she had was to try and bluff her way out, she stepped on the errant pieces. "Nothing — it's just that I-I —" *You what?*

With a knowing, calculating look, Margaret pointed to Charlotte's foot. "Been digging in the trash, have you?"

Then, mumbling something about not being able to trust the maids in "this" hotel, Margaret pivoted and went back into the bedroom.

She knew. Charlotte broke out in a cold sweat. But if she knew, why had she walked away? Though Margaret's reaction confused Charlotte, the second that Margaret was out of sight Charlotte bent down, and with trembling fingers, she snatched up the check pieces on the floor. Then, keeping one eye on the mirror, she carefully slipped them inside her pants pocket. She'd just stuffed the sack into the trash bag when Margaret's reflection reappeared in the mirror.

Charlotte's mouth went dry. Margaret stood in the doorway, and from the calculating look on her face and the way her eyes narrowed suspiciously, Charlotte knew that she was in big trouble.

"What's that you're trying to hide?" Margaret demanded.

Charlotte figured that the only choice she had was to try and bluff her way out. "Nothing — it's just that I-I —" *You what?* "I put out the wrong towels. I've been replacing the stained ones, and I just realized that I forgot to get this one."

Margaret pointed to a piece of the check that had fallen on the floor when Charlotte dropped the towel. "Looks like you forgot something else as well," she drawled. Then, mumbling something about not being able to trust the maids in "this" hotel, Margaret pivoted and went back into the bedroom.

Momentarily confused by Margaret's reaction, Charlotte decided that the best thing she could do was grab the stuff and run. The second Margaret was out of sight Charlotte bent down and snatched up the piece on the floor. Then, keeping one eye on the mirror, she carefully lifted the towel and quickly gathered the other pieces and slipped them inside her pocket. She'd just stuffed the sack into the trash bag when Margaret's reflection reappeared in the mirror.

One look and Charlotte felt her knees grow weak with fear. In Margaret's hand was a small revolver, and it was pointed at her.

"I knew I should have burned that stuff," Margaret said.

Charlotte swallowed the fear. "Like you burned the security tape," she retorted.

Margaret narrowed her eyes. "Too bad you had to be so nosy," she sneered. "And to think, I was beginning to like you." She held out her free hand. "Give them to me," she demanded. "Every last piece. And hand me that trash bag."

Gathering every ounce of courage she could dredge up, Charlotte dropped the trash bag and glared defiantly at Margaret. Then she noticed something. Both of Margaret's hands were trembling — not badly, but trembling all the same. And Margaret's face was almost as pale as the white walls of the room, all signs of extreme stress. But why would a calculating, cold-blooded killer's hands be trembling?

They wouldn't.

Charlotte's brain raced. Then, suddenly, like the symbols in a winning slot machine, all the clues clicked into place.

Margaret wasn't the killer.

If she had been, she would have shot first and worried about the cover-up later. Margaret was only a pawn. Just as Mack had suspected from the beginning, Frank had orchestrated the whole thing.

Narrowing her eyes and praying that she was right, Charlotte crossed her arms against her breasts. "And if I don't give them to you?" she challenged.

Margaret's hand holding the gun wavered. "If-if you don't, I-I'll shoot you, and then I'll take them."

With a bravado she didn't feel, Charlotte laughed. "If you shoot me in here, the police will know you did it."

Margaret blinked nervously. "I don't intend on shooting you in here." She waved the gun again, signaling for Charlotte to come out, and she backed away from the door. "If-if I remember right, you have a master key to all of the rooms. I'll even let you pick which room. Now, come out of there!"

Nope, not the killer, Charlotte decided. No self-respecting killer would take such a risk. Charlotte figured that she had one chance, and one chance only, to get out of this alive . . . and one chance to make sure the real killer was caught.

"I said come out," Margaret snapped.

Charlotte held up her hands, palms out. "Okay, okay, I'm coming, but you don't have to do this, you know. The police are going to find out about your part in all of this. If you told them your story, your side of it —"

"Shut up! Just shut up!"

That Margaret was even more rattled was good, Charlotte figured, lots better than calm and calculating. The more flustered Margaret grew, the more likely she was to make a mistake. With a quick prayer for courage, Charlotte stepped forward. At the same time that she stepped, she grabbed the edge of the bathroom door, slammed it, locked it, and then dropped to the floor.

Gasping for breath and every nerve tensed, Charlotte waited for Margaret's reaction. No gun shots, not yet. But just in case Margaret decided to start shooting up the door, Charlotte quickly crawled away from it toward the bathtub.

The doorknob rattled, and then Margaret banged on the door. "Open this door!" She banged on it again. "Open it now!" she shouted.

Charlotte eyed the bathtub as she pulled out her cell phone. She pulled herself up to the side of the tub, slipped over it, and hunkered down. Hopefully, the tub would provide some protection from a stray bullet if Margaret began shooting. With trembling fingers, Charlotte tapped out Judith's phone number.

Judith answered on the third ring as Margaret pounded on the door again. "Come out of there, I told you!" Margaret yelled.

Careful to keep her voice low, Charlotte

said, "Judith — Aunt Charley. I've locked myself in the bathroom of room 205 at the Jazzy."

"Why —"

"Because Margaret Green has a gun," Charlotte interrupted. "And she's threatening to kill me."

"Hang tight, Auntie!"

Charlotte could hear Judith already moving.

"I'm on my way. Stay on the line."

"I will, but listen — I'm almost positive that Frank Morgan used Margaret Green to hire Ralph Jones to kill Lisa and set it up to look like Tessa Morgan killed her. Then Frank killed Ralph to cover up."

"Got'cha." Judith was out of breath, running. "I'm coming."

The pounding on the door suddenly stopped, and Charlotte grew even more uneasy. "Please hurry, Judith," she whispered.

Turning her head to the side and barely breathing, Charlotte strained to hear any sound from the other side of the door. Then, ever so faintly, she heard the murmur of a female voice. Had to be Margaret, she figured, probably calling Frank for reinforcement.

As the minutes dragged by and Charlotte

listened for any sign that help had finally arrived, she felt as if every nerve in her body was stretched to the breaking point.

CHAPTER 20

Charlotte stiffened when she heard the murmur of voices coming from the other room. When the light rap sounded on the door, she almost jumped out of her skin.

"Ms. LaRue? Frank Morgan here," he called out. "There's been a terrible misunderstanding." His voice oozed with false sincerity. "Margaret thought you were stealing from her, like that other maid, and she overreacted. She's really sorry."

Yeah, right, Charlotte thought. Did he really think she was that naive? At least now she knew for sure that Margaret was the one who had accused Julie Harper of stealing.

"You can come out now," Frank coaxed.

"Where are you, Judith?" Charlotte whispered into her cell phone. "Frank Morgan is at the door."

"Almost there, Auntie," Judith answered. "Stall."

Frank rapped sharply on the door. "Did you hear me, Ms. LaRue?"

She needed to buy time, and the only way to do that was to keep him talking. Charlotte cleared her throat. "I can hear you just fine," she told him.

"If you don't come out, I'll be forced to break down the door."

"That won't be necessary," she called out. "Just give me a minute." Now, how to stall? She quickly scanned the small bathroom until her gaze stopped at the toilet. No way was she going to get out of the bathtub, but if she stretched . . .

Charlotte leaned over the edge of the tub, and stretched. When the tips of her fingers made contact with the trip handle of the toilet, she flushed it. She waited until the bowl emptied and filled with water, and then she flushed it again.

"Open the door!" Frank demanded. "Open it now!"

Charlotte cringed. Uh-oh, no more Mr. Nice Guy.

A moment passed, then she heard him say, "Margaret, hand me one of those pillows to muffle the sound. I'm going to shoot the lock off."

"Oh, no," Charlotte whispered. Could he really do that? She'd seen it done in the movies, but — with a shiver of panic, Charlotte hunkered back down in the tub. Was this the end? Dear Lord, she hoped not. Squeezing her eyes closed, she tensed, waiting for the gun to go off, and in her mind's eye, she pictured a tiny baby, one who looked just like Hank had looked. She felt a sob building in her throat. "Please, Lord," she whispered, "just let me live long enough to see my grandbaby."

The sudden sound of a loud crash made Charlotte jump. But when she opened her eyes and peeped over the side of the tub, the bathroom door was still standing.

Then, she heard, "Police! Drop the gun! Drop it, I said!"

Recognizing the voice, Charlotte went limp. Even if the words had come out of Gavin Brown's mouth, they were the sweetest words she'd ever heard. "Now get down on the floor, face down, hands behind your head. You too, lady!"

Within reason, Charlotte knew that everything was okay, under control, but when she tried to push up out of the tub, every muscle in her body felt like mush.

A light rap sounded at the bathroom door. "Aunt Charley? You okay in there?"

"Yes," she blurted out. "I'm okay."

"You can come out now."

Taking a deep breath, and willing her body to move, Charlotte grabbed the side of the tub and pulled herself up. "I'm coming," she called out. Using the side of the tub for leverage, she finally got to her feet. Grabbing the towel bar for balance, she stepped over the edge.

By the time Charlotte unlocked the door and opened it, Frank and Margaret were handcuffed and being escorted out of the room by several uniformed policemen.

"What am I going to do with you?" Judith asked, as she wrapped her arms around Charlotte and gave her a brief hug.

"Let me go home?"

Judith released her and gave her a stern look. "You know the drill."

Charlotte nodded. "Afraid so."

Judith slid her arm around Charlotte's waist and nudged her toward the door. "How are you feeling?"

"Okay — just a little weak in the knees."

"Your blood sugar is probably low — stress. Let's get you down to the lounge and get you a bite to eat. We can interview you there."

In the lounge, Patrick the bartender was on duty. Charlotte was even able to work up a smile at how, once he spotted Judith, he tripped all over himself, trying to be helpful.

"Bring my aunt a glass of orange juice," Judith told him after they were seated at a corner table.

"No juice right now, hon. I don't think my stomach could take the acid." She glanced up at Patrick. "Make that a small Coke, please."

"Anything else?" Patrick asked her.

Judith turned to Charlotte, "What do you feel like eating, Auntie?"

"A bowl of chicken and Andouille gumbo, I think."

Judith nodded and turned back to Patrick. "Bring two bowls — no, better make that three. Another detective will be joining us shortly. And I'd like a Coke as well."

Patrick nodded and winked at Judith. "Won't take but a minute."

Once Patrick was out of earshot, Charlotte said, "You do know that he's very interested in you."

Judith rolled her eyes. "Right now I'm more interested in what happened upstairs and why it happened."

With a sigh Charlotte nodded. "Okay. Did you know that Margaret Green has a pair of earrings just like the one found near Lisa?"

"No, I didn't, but I'm sure you're going to tell me all about it."

"Don't be rude, Judith. And yes, I do intend to tell you. The earring business got me to thinking. But these —" She reached inside her pocket and pulled out several pieces of the check. "This will explain it better." Once she'd fished out all of the pieces and had laid them on the tabletop, she also pulled out the envelope with the extra key. Setting the envelope aside, she began sliding around the pieces of the check. "I found these in the trashcan in Margaret Green's bathroom." After Charlotte had finished putting them together, she crooked her forefinger for Judith to look.

Judith leaned forward and stared at the check.

"At first I thought that Margaret had set everything up, but —"

"Wait —" Judith held up her hand. "Wait until Gavin gets here." She straightened. Reaching inside her jacket pocket, she pulled out a disposable glove. Then she pulled out a small clear plastic bag. Once she'd slipped the glove on she carefully picked up the pieces of the check and placed them inside the bag.

Patrick approached the table with their drinks. "The gumbo is on its way," he said, placing the Cokes on small coasters. "And I took the liberty of ordering a basket of

French bread to go along with it."

Judith totally ignored him, so Charlotte said, "Thank you, Patrick. That was very thoughtful of you."

Only minutes after Patrick walked away, Gavin Brown entered the lounge. Once he was seated, Judith told him about the check that Charlotte had found. Then, she turned to Charlotte and said, "Okay, now explain, Auntie."

"First, there's a room key in this envelope. I found it, along with a tip on the desk in Margaret's room, and I believe if you check it out, you'll find that it fits the lock to Tessa Morgan's room." Then, beginning with the dinner party she'd attended with Mack, Charlotte went through everything that had happened, including what Mack had told her about Ralph, her talk with Mack right after Tessa was arrested, and Belinda's frantic phone call and confession about choking Lisa. Charlotte also explained about the earrings and about the white sack with the scarves inside, and how, once she'd found the check, everything fell into place.

When Patrick approached the table with their food, Charlotte waited until he left before she continued. When he was almost back to the bar, she said, "Like I started telling Judith earlier, at first I was sure that

Margaret had hired Ralph, but when I saw her hands trembling — well, I was right, but I was wrong. I figure that in the beginning Frank was just using Lisa as a way to force Tessa to divorce him, but when Lisa claimed to be pregnant, that made her a liability as well. I also figured that Frank knew all along how Margaret felt about him, and he used her feelings for him to convince her to help him rid himself of both Tessa and Lisa. Once Margaret told him about the detective report on Lisa and about Ralph, he had the perfect setup."

Gavin stared at her for several moments. Then, he turned to Judith. "Does she do this very often?"

Judith's lips tightened with disapproval. "Get used to it. Louis and I have talked till we're blue in the face, but —" She shrugged. "What can I say? My aunt tends to be a bit nosy as well as stubborn about certain things."

Charlotte wasn't sure if her feelings were hurt, if she was just plain furious, or simply being overly sensitive because of everything she'd been through. Probably all three, she decided as she glared first at her niece then at Gavin. Whatever the reason, she wasn't in the mood to be the object of her niece and Gavin Brown's ridicule. "I'd like to go home now."

"Come on, Auntie, don't be like that. Eat your lunch, then you can go home."

Charlotte picked up her bowl of gumbo and stood. Glaring down at her niece, she said, "I'm tired and I'm going home." Without waiting for a response, the turned and headed for the door.

"See? Stubborn," she heard Judith tell Gavin, but she ignored them both.

On her way out of the hotel, Charlotte stopped at the door to the restaurant and asked for a to-go container for the gumbo. Then, she went to find Claire to let her know that she was leaving.

After talking to Claire, she headed for the front entrance to the hotel.

"Charlotte! Hey, Charlotte!"

At the sound of Mack's voice, her steps slowed. When Mack caught up with her, he said, "I heard what happened. Are you okay?"

Charlotte stopped, but stared straight ahead. "Yes, I'm just fine," she retorted.

Mack stepped in front of her and leaned down until they were face to face. "You don't sound 'just fine.' You look like you could chew nails. What's going on?"

Charlotte sighed. "Nothing important. Just a family thing."

"If you say so." He straightened and stepped back. "I'm glad I caught you though. I've still got to tell Belinda what's happened."

Belinda. Charlotte bowed her head and closed her eyes for a moment. With everything that had happened, she'd completely forgotten about Belinda. She opened her eyes and looked up at Mack. "That poor girl. First her mother and now her father."

Mack nodded. "Yeah, it's been a tough week." He paused a moment, then said, "She really likes you, you know, and I was hoping that I could persuade you to help me tell her about what's happened. Especially since I've already alienated her once with my suspicions about her father," he added. "After Tessa gets released from jail, things will be better, but until then, I'm all she's got."

Later that evening, just before dark, Charlotte fixed herself a glass of iced tea, and took it out onto the front porch. Just as she settled on the swing, Louis drove into his driveway.

She hadn't seen nor heard from him since he'd gone to check on Joyce after the EMT's had taken her away, and she'd wondered if he was doing any better now that Joyce was in detox.

He looked tired, she thought as she watched him slowly climb out of his car and head for the porch. But then, who wasn't tired?

"Hey, Charlotte," he said as he climbed the steps.

"Hey, yourself," she answered and smiled. "How's Joyce?"

Louis shrugged, and instead of answering her, he suddenly leaned down and kissed her on the forehead. Charlotte froze. As far as kisses went, it was brief and not in the least bit sexual. "What was that for?" she blurted out when he straightened.

Just the hint of a sad smile pulled at his lips. "It was just to say thank you. I can't remember if I said so, but I appreciate everything you've done for me the last few days. You're a good woman, Charlotte LaRue."

Charlotte's breath caught in her throat as she stared up into his dark eyes, and the only thing she could think to say was, "You look tired."

Louis nodded. "I am, but there's no rest for the weary. I've got to get to the airport but decided to swing back by on my way to let you know I'll be gone for a while."

"Where to this time?"

"California — Hollywood. One of our former clients has a stalker." He glanced at his watch. "Guess I'd better get going."

For the briefest of moments, Charlotte thought he was going to kiss her again. He looked like he wanted to kiss her. Instead, he brushed his forefinger along her cheek.

"You take care now," he said gruffly. "And I'll see you when I get back." Then, he turned and headed for his car.

As Charlotte watched him back out of the driveway, in the distance, a lawn mower roared to life. Across the street, her neighbor's Doberman barked as he chased a squirrel. For a while Charlotte swung back and forth and watched the antics of the big dog, her thoughts on Louis and their strange relationship. Then they drifted back to Mack and Belinda.

Understandably, Belinda had been upset about her father's arrest, but the news that her mother would be released had helped soften the blow. Then Tessa had called.

After talking to Belinda and reassuring her the she would soon be released, she persuaded Belinda to move back to the hotel and wait for her. Then, she'd asked to speak to Charlotte.

"I don't know how I'll ever thank you," she'd said. "It's still hard for me to believe that a perfect stranger believed in my innocence when all of my so-called friends left me high and dry. And, speaking of my so-called friends, one of the first things I intend to do when I get out is burn every red scarf I own."

Charlotte took a sip of tea and sighed. Tessa was on the right track now, and Charlotte prayed that Tessa's new budding relationship with Belinda would be the one positive thing to come out of the whole mess.

Charlotte sighed again. Hopefully, things could get back to normal now. "Whatever that is," she murmured. It was the same thing she and everyone else in New Orleans had kept telling themselves ever since Katrina had hit.

Unexpectedly, her gaze clouded with tears, and she was suddenly assailed by the weight of the day's events. Today wasn't the first time that she'd faced death, but she prayed that it would be the last time, at least until the good Lord chose to take her home permanently. After all, she had a little granddaughter on the way. Just a few more weeks . . .

Charlotte blinked back the tears. Just the thought of being able to hold her grandbaby in her arms made her smile, and out of nowhere, an idea popped into her head.

Why hadn't she thought of it before? Working for Carol and Hank would be the perfect job for Julie Harper. Hank wanted Carol to have a maid. Once Carol knew the circumstances surrounding poor Julie, Charlotte was sure that she would be able to persuade Carol to hire her, especially if Carol thought that by doing so, she'd be helping out someone less fortunate than herself.

A soft breeze kicked up, and the last rays of the sun disappeared. Feeling much better, Charlotte smiled and rose from the swing. Time to make supper.

A Cleaning Tip from Charlotte

Dryers are a wonderful invention, and in Charlotte's opinion, so are cotton knit clothes. But the two don't necessarily go together. Just take a look at the layer of lint on your dryer filter after drying your clothes. Truth is, dryers dry the very life out of those comfortable knits. One way to avoid this is to dry the cotton knits in the dryer just long enough to warm them up. The initial heat allows the wrinkles to relax. Ten minutes should do it. Then hang the clothes on hangers to finish drying. Your clothes will last longer.

SHRIMP PO-BOY

Charlotte absolutely loves shrimp po-boys. According to several sources, these New Orleans sandwiches have been around since the late 1800s.

What defines the po-boy from other sandwiches is the bread. Fresh French bread with a crispy crust on the outside and a soft interior is a must.

Ingredients:

1 4″ to 6″ loaf of fresh French bread (You must cut a longer loaf in half)
Butter to taste
Mayonnaise to taste
Fried Shrimp
Lettuce
Sliced Onion
Sliced Dill Pickle
Sliced Tomato

Slice the French bread in half lengthways,

slather butter or mayonnaise on the inside of each half, and fill it with fried shrimp. Now, do you want it plain or "dressed?" If you want it "dressed" add shredded lettuce, onions, pickles, and tomatoes.

CHICKEN AND ANDOUILLE GUMBO

Charlotte often cooks Chicken and Andouille Gumbo for her family.

1/3 cup oil
1/3 cup flour
2 cups chopped onion
1 cup chopped celery
1/2 cup chopped bell pepper
1/2 cup chopped green onion
1 raw chicken (cut in serving pieces)
1 lb. Andouille sliced (you may substitute hot smoked sausage)
1/2 tsp. garlic powder
1 tbs. salt
1/2 tsp. black pepper
1/2 tsp. cayenne pepper
1 1/2 quarts hot water
Filé (optional)

In large pot, heat oil and stir in flour, stirring constantly till creamy and the color of dark caramel. (Hint: this step can be done in a microwave, but stir every 20 seconds; then, transfer to pot.) Add onion, celery, bell pepper, and green onions. Cook on medium heat until vegetables are tender (about 5 minutes). Add remaining ingredients and simmer about 1 1/2 hours. Serve over cooked rice. Sprinkle with filé. Serves 6–8.

ABOUT THE AUTHOR

Barbara Colley is an award-winning author whose books have been published in sixteen foreign languages. A native of Lousiana, she lives with her family in a suburb of New Orleans. Besides writing and sharing her stories, she loves strolling though the historic New Orleans French Quarter and Garden District, which inspired the setting for her Charlotte LaRue mystery series. Readers can write to Barbara at P.O. Box 290, Boutte, LA, 70039, or visit her Web site at www.barbaracolley.com.

The employees of Thorndike Press hope you have enjoyed this Large Print book. All our Thorndike and Wheeler Large Print titles are designed for easy reading, and all our books are made to last. Other Thorndike Press Large Print books are available at your library, through selected bookstores, or directly from us.

For information about titles, please call:

(800) 223-1244

or visit our Web site at:

www.gale.com/thorndike
www.gale.com/wheeler

To share your comments, please write:

Publisher
Thorndike Press
295 Kennedy Memorial Drive
Waterville, ME 04901